# NIGHTMARE RITUAL

A small girl, tied hand and foot, her dress torn from hem to neck exposing the child's nakedness, lay on the platform.

Nita stopped dancing and stared at the bizarre sight. The girl looked from side to side, her eyes wide with fright, large tears running down either side of her face. Nita felt her own eyes welling with tears, then she swallowed a scream. She suddenly realized who the girl was. *It was she.* It was Nita lying on the table. No, it wasn't a table. It was more like . . . like an altar.

# JOHN TIGGES

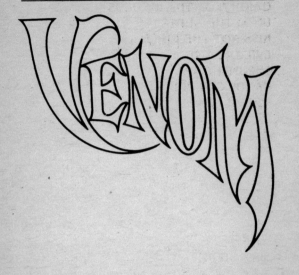

**VENOM**

LEISURE BOOKS    NEW YORK CITY

For Tracey;
Without whose help I never could have written
VENOM!

A LEISURE BOOK

Published by

Dorchester Publishing Co., Inc.
6 East 39th Street
New York, NY 10016

Printed in the United States of America

Be not afraid of the serpent . . .
he is a god and your brother.

It is said that each one of us
bears qualities that are serpentine in nature . . .

Indian Proverbs

# PROLOGUE

India - 22 years ago.

The man had paced about the hotel lobby for hours, following the same route—past the main desk, toward the front entrance, near the elevator doors, around the information desk and back to the entrance of the tobacco shop. Periodically checking his watch, he would mop his brow, shaking his head before peering at the man behind the desk. On occasion he would open his mouth as if to address the clerk but, thinking better of it, would turn away to retrace his path once more. Deserted at 2:00 o'clock in the morning, the lobby seemed smaller than during the day when it was filled with busy people hurrying to and from their rooms and guests checking in and out.

Turning on his heel, the man rushed to the desk when the phone jangled shrilly in the quiet of the lobby. His face reflecting an inner anguish, which might be relieved with the correct and proper words from the clerk, the man gripped the edge of the counter. His face twisted animatedly while the clerk spoke in his native dialect, confirming some distant traveler's hotel accomodations. Dejected, the guest turned away but stopped, spinning about to face the man behind the counter when he hung up the receiver.

"Are you certain you haven't heard?" His voice cracked from fatigue, his breath coming in shallow puffs.

The clerk patiently shook his head. "I am positive, Reverend Sahib. There have been no telephone calls other than the one I just received. It was not for you."

The Indian's singsong way of speaking English grated on the man. Not once in his four years in India had anyone's speech bothered him. Now, it seemed to mock him and his predicament. All he wanted was to get out of this country and back to his own. What had happened had been awful, devastating.

He turned away to walk his circuitous route of the hotel lobby once more. After three completed turns, he froze when the elevator motor whined through the desolate lobby. Someone was coming. Who? Who would be up and about at this hour? Surely it couldn't be . . . ? He stood, poised as if waiting for a signal to flee. But from what? From whom? Did he and his family have anyone to fear in Calcutta? For that matter, did they have any enemies in all of

India? There were those who had sought to hurt them in Jawrine but he felt certain that the episode had not been meant personally. Still, the aftereffects had been tragic. Now, he and his family were fleeing back home to the United States. Did that mean he had failed? He had to make a decision between God and his daughter. For practical reasons, his daughter had won, yet, a feeling of failure hammered at him.

He watched as the elevator opened to reveal the figure of his wife framed in the doorway. He rushed to her as she stepped into the lobby.

"What are you doing here? Where is she?"

"I had to get out of that room. She's sleeping."

"Soundly?"

His wife nodded. "Have you heard anything yet?"

"No. It seems to take forever when one is in a hurry. Our reservations will come through, the only unknown element being when. You are certain she is sound asleep?"

"Yes, my dear, she is exhausted from the train ride to Calcutta. She will sleep well."

He turned away. "Do you think it wise to leave her like that? The nightmares might strike again."

His wife shrugged. "She's sleeping so soundly. The dreams seem to come when she is restless and not completely relaxed. There have been times when that isn't true but for the most part . . ." Her voice trailed off.

He smiled, reaching out to touch her hand. "I suppose it is all right. We won't be able to be with her every minute of her life, will we?"

"Do you think she really will be all right, my dear?" She looked intently at her husband, choosing to ignore his question and waiting for him to speak.

"You've asked me that hundreds of times. I don't know. All I can do is hope and pray to God Almighty that she will be fine. Perhaps when we get back to the States, we can consult a doctor. I'm sure a psychiatrist or psychologist could answer all of our questions, as well as relieve our anxieties."

She took his hand in hers. "Was it our fault? Somehow I feel that we're to—"

"No! No, it wasn't our fault. We had nothing to do with it. The circumstances just happened to be right that our daughter . . ." He stopped, choking back a sob. After a moment, he continued. "It just happened to be our daughter who was in the wrong place at the wrong time. Had she not wanted to go to the bathroom, nothing would have happened. No, it was not our fault."

"But I let her go. I gave her permission to go. I should have gone with her."

"But you never had before. We've always tried to teach our child to be self-reliant and self-sufficient. It would have been contrary to our own tenets for you to have accompanied her to the bathroom. The whole thing was normal. You had no way of knowing anything out of the ordinary would happen."

The woman fought to control her tears. "But I should have gone with her."

"Really, my dear, listen to me. Please. You had no way of knowing that anything would happen."

She looked at her husband with trust filling her eyes. "You're sure they did nothing?"

He shrugged. "Not that I know about. I think the constable and I arrived just in the nick of time. Yes, I'm sure of it. They hadn't really started their—"

"But what if you're wrong? What if you arrived too late? What if they really did do something to our daughter?"

"I . . . I'm not wrong. I'm just not. That's all."

"If something *did* happen, if something *was* done to her, if she *was* harmed in any way . . . I'll never forgive myself." She stopped, directing her full attention at her husband. "Or you."

"That's hardly fair or rational, my dear. Neither of us had anything to do with it."

She stamped her foot, clenching her fists. "We were negligent!"

The man looked around to see if anyone had heard his wife, gratefully recalling that the lobby was all but deserted.

"Reverend?" The clerk called from behind the desk.

"Yes?" The man and woman hurried to confront him.

"You were so busy talking, you apparently did not hear the phone ring. Your reservations are confirmed. You and your wife and daughter will leave Calcutta at eight a.m. this morning."

He handed the man a slip of paper. "Here is your reservation number. Simply give it to the ticket attendant and he will have your tickets all prepared. Are there any questions? Can I be of further help?"

"No. No thank you. You've been most kind."

Turning from the desk, he took his wife's arm, guiding her toward the elevator. "You'll see, my dear. Once we reach home, everything will be quite all right. You'll see."

Clutching her husband's hand to her side, she nodded. "I hope you're right. I sincerely hope you are right."

The elevator doors closed and they rode silently to their floor.

# PART I

## THE AWAKENING

# 1

"Careful of that box, Cricket," Dave yelled at his partner. "Don't drop it, for Chrissake!"

"What the hell's inside that's so valuable?" Cricket carefully placed the crate on the tailgate of the delivery truck.

"You got me, but it's going to the University . . ." He paused, turning his head to read the address label. ". . . to the University Science building. Who knows? Maybe there's something really valuable in it. I don't want to have to pay for anything I can't eat, drink or fuck."

"Right!" Cricket eased the container back into the dark confines of the van. "How many are there?"

"Three. Come on, we'll get the other two and be on our way. It's going on one thirty. It'll damn near be two by the time we get out there and get this stuff delivered."

The two men hurried away from the truck to get the other two wooden crates. When they found them, each picked one up and started back toward the van at the shipping company loading dock.

"What the hell's in here? It sounds like a dog growling." Dave bent down, placing an ear to the box he carried.

"I don't hear nothing out of mine," Cricket said, shaking the box.

When they reached the truck both men gingerly lowered the cases they carried to the tailgate. Cricket jumped in the van, pulling the boxes to the front of the truck. "Hey, I can hear it now. Sounds more like something leaking."

"Well, let's hustle our asses and get out there. If it's gas or something, let it blow them up and not us."

Cricket closed the doors of the van, ran around to the passenger's side and got in as Dave gunned the motor.


The *thwonk* of the ball against the far hand-ball court wall, resounded loudly and Nita Galforth dove headfirst to return it but missed by a fraction of an inch, fouling and losing the point. Scrambling to her feet, she blushed, her oval face twisting in an angry mask.

"Damn!" She mumbled the one word under her breath, retrieving the ball at the same time.

"My God, can't you let up for one minute. That's the first return you've missed this game. What do you want to do? Skunk me completely?" The large, trimly built man confronted her, feet spread apart in a threatening manner.

"Sorry, Coach, I just like to give it my all. What's the score?" She glanced away when she realized she had been trying to really kill the football coach of Middleton University in a game of handball.

"I don't even want to mention it aloud. You do realize that you're in the process of destroying a legend, don't you?"

She looked at him, quizzically. "I don't understand."

"I don't even remember the last time I lost on this court, and right now, you've got me down two games to none. And you're killing me in the third."

She smiled but said nothing, peering instead at the floor.

"Look, Nita, I asked you to play because I heard you were a whiz on the court. I wanted to see how good you really were, not how absolutely great a person could be at the game of handball."

"Gee, I'm sorry, Coach. I really am." She could feel her face turning red. Suddenly feeling embarrassed for him and herself as well, Nita looked up at the clock, which was protected by a heavy wire cage. "It's getting late. Maybe we should chuck it in. What do you think?"

Art Friend shrugged. "It's up to you. I know when I'm whipped. Where did you learn to play?"

Nita walked to the far wall, picking up a small hand towel she had tucked away. Wiping her face, she looked at Friend, who was waiting for an answer. She shrugged. "I don't really remember. I think it was my freshman year in high school."

"Well, whoever taught you sure did a great job. You're fantastic. Too bad there isn't big time college competition for handball. You'd be All-American."

Opening the door, Nita stepped through, waiting for the football coach. "I'm afraid I wouldn't have time."

"Why?"

"Too busy with my studies."

"All this and brains, too?" He smiled good naturedly. "Don't think I'm chauvinistic 'cause I'm not. You look like the type who can take a little joking. Am I right?"

"Oh, I guess I can, some of the time."

"What are you majoring in?"

She laughed. "I wish I were majoring in something. Actually, I'm working for a Masters in Phys. Ed."

"Your Masters? How old are you?"

"I thought you weren't chauvinistic."

"I'm not, but I thought you were maybe a junior in college at the most. Here you've already graduated and are working on your Masters. That's great. Really."

She laughed. "Dare I tell you of my Masters in English? Or the fact that I'm six hours shy of a Ph.D. in English Literature?"

Friend stopped short. "What? You've got to be kidding. You are, aren't you?"

Taking off her sweat band, she shook her

head, the curly, light brown hair swirling about. Her pale green eyes twinkled but she said nothing. If anything, she enjoyed shocking people with her academic background. At 28, she had accomplished as much if not more than many people much older than herself.

"Well, Miss Nita Galforth, let me be the one to admit that you fooled me completely. What else are you into, if I may ask?"

"Other than studying and keeping in shape, I'm training for the triathalon that's coming up soon."

Friend laughed. "It figures."

They walked along the corridor toward the main hall that would take them in separate directions toward the locker rooms. At five feet seven, Nita matched the football coach, stride for stride. Her sweat top did little to conceal her large breasts tethered inside by a tight, supportive bra. Her shorts could not hide the muscular legs that she referred to as "thunder thighs." A tiny waist separated those two physical features, and next to the muscular coach, Nita appeared most feminine.

"So tell me, Coach, now that the team is two and 0 for the season, is it too early to be talking about an undefeated season and post season bowl games?"

He snorted laughingly. "I suppose you play football, too?"

"No, but I am a fan. I also know a lot about you. All-American tight end at the University of Iowa before the Hawkeyes became a super power, you also played six seasons for the

Steelers before they became the 'team of the seventies.' Your record here at Middleton is fifty-nine and thirty-nine, which is not that bad considering the miserable state the team was in when you took over. I—"

"That's remarkable. It really is, Nita. I don't think the athletic director could reel off that much about me without looking it up. Or is that what you did? Look it all up before we played today?"

"I read an article about you several years ago, and I thought you were pretty interesting. I guess I just remembered it. I have a pretty good memory."

"I guess so." Friend stopped when they reached the main corridor. "Well, here's where we go our separate ways. Thanks for the lesson in handball."

"I'm sorry, Coach, I really am. I just like to compete, that's all. Want to try to get even?"

He grinned. "Why not, but let's wait until after the season is over. As you said, it might not be too early to think about the future of this team. The 'Smugglers' are pretty well-balanced. We might be able to take the conference this year. What do you think?"

Nita could not control the blush starting on her face. What a compliment! She was willing to bet anything that he never once asked the athletic director, or anyone else for that matter, such a question. "I think you're one helluva coach, Coach, and if this is the year, nothing will stop you."

"Judas Priest! A diplomat, too. 'Bye, Nita, and thanks again."

"Thank *you*, Coach." She turned to her right, hurrying down the corridor toward the woman's locker room. He was a nice man and she liked him.

Dave slowed down the truck, turning off Mississippi Drive and onto Campus Road that would take them to Middleton University. In the dark confines of the van, the boxes bounced about, each one emanating a soft growling sound.

Entering the locker room, Nita quickly undressed and, grabbing her bath towel, went to the shower room. Finding it deserted, she turned on the hot water and after tempering it with cold, stepped under the heavy spray. The jets of steamy water relaxed her muscles. Turning into it, she let it beat on her face. There were few things Nita found that were more restful or stimulating than a hot shower. She wondered if she should say something like that to Archer. She smiled. Archer would tease her about her priorities and make some little joke about their lovemaking having to take second place to a rush of hot water.

The soapy water swirled on the floor, spiraling toward the drain as she rinsed herself. The water running off her erect nipples fell directly to the floor. Turning off the spigots, she felt a chill. She reached for her towel and briskly rubbed down her body. With the white bath sheet tucked around her, she hurried back to the locker room. Once she had pulled on her jeans and slipped into a T-shirt, she hung up her gym clothes and closed her locker. After depositing the towel in the laundry bag near the door, she left the gymnasium.

The van backed carefully up to the side door of the John Thomas Science Building. Carefully removing the cases from the truck, Cricket and Dave loaded them on a cart, one on top of the other.

"Now all three are making that noise," Dave said when Cricket eased back on the handle and pushed the two wheel cart ahead.

"I wonder what the hell's inside. Nothing on the crates says anything about gas or careful handling other than the usual stuff. Just 'deliver immediately . . . by September 20th.' I guess we'll never know, unless we ask the guy we're taking it to."

"Right," Dave said, following the taller man into the science building.

Outside Nita relished the warm September air and sunshine. Walking briskly along the campus, she came to the inner edge of the quadrangle. Why would it be so deserted at this time of day? She looked at the campus clock in the Alan Ede Memorial Bell Tower. 2:20. Most of the students were in class, but despite the hour, there should have been someone other than herself crossing the quadrangle. A spooky sen-

sation rippled through her for an instant. Then
she saw a couple coming out of the Genevieve
Abolt Music Building and knew she had not
stepped through some sort of strange doorway
into a time warp. She smiled.

The quadrangle, dotted with trees around
the central Alan Ede Memorial Bell Tower, was
intersected with four walks, two at right angles
to the center and two that began at the corners.
As she made her way along the walk, she
wondered if Archer would be free now. She had
planned at least three games with Coach
Friend, but when he threw the towel in after
falling behind nine nothing in the third game,
she had come out of the gym at least half an
hour earlier than she had planned. She had told
Archer that she would stop by the lab around
3:00, but now she would arrive about 2:30.

A chill wound its way down her back when
she passed through the shade of three poplar
trees. She felt as if . . . as if someone were
watching her. Slowing her pace, she looked
around while trying not to be obvious. There
were no people in sight paying attention to her.
She stopped, turned completely around but saw
no one. How then, if she had that creepy feeling
of being watched, could someone be spying on
her without her seeing them? She caught herself looking up in the trees. Laughing at herself,
she turned to continue on her way. What had
she expected to see in the trees? Perhaps a wild
man following her?

"Hey, Doc?" Cricket asked, after taking the

last carton off the two-wheeled dolly. "What the hell's in these boxes that makes that noise? Sounded some of the time like leaking gas. Then it sounds like a dog growling."

The man in the white lab coat smiled. "Gentlemen, you've just delivered three king cobra snakes." He said nothing more, watching the men's reactions.

Cricket turned to Dave who had already paled. "Why the hell wasn't that stenciled on the cases? There should have been some sort of warning," the taller man said.

"Would you have brought them here as readily as you did?"

"Probably not."

"Actually, they're in plastic cages and couldn't possibly get out. Feel better now?"

Both men visibly relaxed, and after nodding, they smiled weakly and turned, leaving the laboratory.

Passing the Alan Ede Memorial Bell Tower, Nita changed paths, heading toward the John Thomas Science Building. There, she would meet Archer Buchanan. Archer's strong face came into focus in her mind, his dark eyes flashing in contrast to his prematurely gray hair. His black hair had begun graying in his teen years but had improved his already handsome appearance when, by the age of 27, it had attained its present shade of silvery pewter. His patience and kindness were the two attributes Nita found most appealing about Archer. Of course, she had been attracted by his physical charm at first but quickly had relegated it to a secondary place, once she had gotten to know the man and his inner self. It seemed as though the two of them had been waiting for each other. Archer, six years senior to Nita's 28, enjoyed competitive sports but not to the degree she did. He held his masters in biology and was working toward his doctorate in that field along with his teaching duties at Middleton.

Nita seemed to feel as much excitement about his upcoming project as Archer did. Soon he would be receiving several snakes from India as part of an exchange program that Middleton had become involved with and included sending at least one professor there for a year of teaching and lecturing. In addition, there would be personnel coming from India to Middleton but the thing that Nita felt most proud of was Archer's involvement. By the time he completed his studies of, and experiments with the snakes, he would be awarded his Ph.D.

She smiled to herself. She had to admit that she and Archer made a handsome couple. Both were in excellent condition, both were more than attractive in appearance and both were well above average in the intelligence department. At one point in her life, not too long ago, Nita had thought that she might remain single. She had had two lovers in her life. The first affair had ended in tragedy when he was killed in a car accident, and the other involvement just had not materialized to the point of fruition that would satisfy Nita.

When she had come to Middleton, it was to get her masters degree in Physical Education. Then, while teaching that subject at some college, she could further concentrate her efforts on completing her own doctorate in English Literature. Beyond that, she thought she might like to do some writing. At no place in her plans had she allowed for a lasting relationship of any sort. Then, she had met Archer and, although she thought of the phrase as the champion of all cliches, had fallen in love with him at first sight. The initial chemistry had worn off within six months, but during that time she had discovered the real person lurking behind the handsome Archer Buchanan.

Down deep, she knew he felt as strongly for her as she did for him. He had said so, but that hadn't happened until some time after Nita had sensed Archer truly loved her.

The one thing she wished for was someone with whom she could discuss such intimate matters. Both her parents were dead, and she had no brothers or sisters. Her father, Reverend Niles Galforth, had been killed in a traffic accident, struck by a drunken driver in downtown Chicago. That had been ten years ago, right after her graduation from high school. The event had been traumatic for her and her mother, Marietta. She had gone to college on scholarship and had maintained a four point grade average during the first three years. Then, her mother contracted cancer. Although Marietta had left a note, trying to explain her pain and her inability to cope with it any longer,

Nita had not been able to understand why her mother had killed herself right before she came home for spring break. Nita had found her mother's body in the kitchen, sprawled on the floor, clutching the note she had written to her daughter.

It had been the deaths of her parents that had made her turn to a physical fitness program. She had attacked her conditioning with a fervor that almost frightened her at the time. She had begun working out for an hour a day, following her father's death, quickly discovering she could build a resistance against tragic memories while building her body muscle tone.

When she found her mother, she had almost gone over the edge, grasping at the last moment the hand offered to her by Nick Cadler. Nick quickly took over, filling in the gaps that Nita's loss of family had created. She loved him completely, and when he too died in a car accident, she had consulted a psychiatrist for help. Along with the physical program she had developed for herself, one that was four times as long and strenuous as the one she had followed after her father's death, she became rock solid in her convictions, her personality and her body.

Since she had no one with whom she could discuss something as intimate as her feelings for Archer, she would have to rely on her instincts that had served her well thus far in her life.

When she came to Carver Hall, she turned at

right angles from the walk she had followed
from the Bell Tower and headed for the science
building.

Then, she stopped short. She couldn't
move. Someone was watching her. She knew it.
She could feel it. A sense of overwhelming doom
enfolded her, squeezing tightly until she
thought she would faint. What was wrong with
her? Commanding her body to respond to
orders, she moved one arm and then the other
before taking a step. How long had she stood
there like a statue? Had anyone seen her? Was
she losing her mind? What was wrong?

She turned, slowly making a full circle,
searching for someone who might be watching
her. She tried to recall if she had ever felt like
this before. Had someone watching her ever
made her react this way before? When she
finished her full turn, she shook her head. There
was no one she could see who might be paying
the least bit of attention to her. When she faced
Carver Hall again, she stopped, wincing when
she saw a tall, dark man, wearing a long-
waisted tunic leaving the entryway. He seemed
out of place, out of sync, with the campus of
Middleton University.

Nita watched him closely. Who was he? She
tried to recall if she ever had seen anyone like
him on campus. He certainly was from some
foreign country. She remembered having
visited the University of Wisconsin before
deciding on Middleton. There, at Madison, Wisconsin, she thought she had been transported
somehow to India when she encountered what

seemed like hundreds of women wearing saris and men wearing turbans. For some reason, Middleton had not attracted many foreign students, and the man walking toward her seemed totally out of place.

She wanted to divert her eyes without knowing why, wanted to turn and run away without knowing the reason. But she suddenly found herself powerless to do anything but stare at him.

She wanted to scream when he glanced in her general direction and for a split instant, their eyes locked. She felt raped. She felt violated. She felt he had, in that one quick glimpse, registered her entire life on his memory bank. He knew everything there was to know about Nita Galforth, and she didn't want him to know a single thing about her.

When he passed within three feet of her and nothing happened, Nita chastised herself. What was wrong with her? Why would she react so strongly to someone she didn't even know? More than likely the man didn't even see her other than as a person going in the direction opposite to his own. Now, that the man had passed without incident, she discovered that she still had the same eerie feeling coursing through her body.

A chill went through her as she passed the side of the John Thomas Science Building. All she could see were the dark eyes of the man she had passed—penetrating her mind and piercing her mental defenses before he peered into her soul.

She shook her head, rounding the corner of

the building. Inside, she'd be with Archer and things would be all right.

# 2

Archer watched the two deliverymen leave. When he was alone, he first looked at the crates before going to the telephone. After dialing three numbers, he waited for an answer.

"Al?"

Doctor Alfred Stewart's deep voice boomed in the earpiece. "Yes?"

Archer laughed to himself when he pictured the man. Contrary to the macho sound of his basso tones, Alfred Stewart stood about five feet seven inches tall, weighed 130 fully clothed and looked more like the intellectual type than he actually was. "They just arrived."

"Good, good. I'll be right down. Shall I bring Richard with me?"

Archer hesitated for a second before answering. Richard Roman, a professor of biology, did not care that much for Archer

Buchanan and Archer knew it. Why the man felt
any animosity toward him was beyond Archer's
ken, but if he chose to ignore Richard, the man
would undoubtedly have several nasty
comments to make. His alternative was simply
to have him come along with Al and take whatever snide remarks Richard would have. "Sure,
bring him along." Had he sounded too magnanimous?

Archer hung up and returned to the table
where the three wooden crates waited. Picking
up a nail puller he had had the foresight to
obtain earlier that day, he worked it into the
split between one end and the top. According to
the correspondence he had received from India
concerning the snakes, the cobras would be
housed in plastic cages, which contained air
holes the size of dimes—large enough to admit
air but not large enough to allow escape.

Wiggling the bar back and forth, he worked
it in farther until he could lever the end open.
Just then, the door opened, and Al Stewart and
Richard Roman entered the laboratory.

"So? These are the king cobras that are
going to make you and Middleton famous, eh?"
Al leaned down, resting one elbow on the table,
peering into the dark confines of the box. Al
Stewart, the likely choice to chair the biology
department when the election was held in a few
days, was affable and highly esteemed on
campus.

Archer knew he would certainly vote for the
man. Al had been more than instrumental in
backing the cultural exchange between

Middleton and India. Of course the government grants had financed the whole thing, but the idea, which had started with Archer in the first place, had been nurtured and brought to fruition by Al Stewart.

"Don't lean so close, Al," Richard said, his voice a bit hesitant and breathless.

"It's all right, Richard," Archer said. "They're safe inside a plastic cage."

"A snake is a snake is a snake," Richard fumed. "I wouldn't trust one any farther than I could pick up this building and throw it."

Archer smiled to himself. Richard came across just a bit effeminate and, although not homosexual, gave the impression at times that he might be hiding a secret. His life style did not help either. A bachelor, he lived alone, dating only on occasion, but more than likely, he would be seen alone in public or at social gatherings. Richard Roman stood an inch or two taller than Al. Archer, on more than one occasion, had chuckled at the incongruity of his own size and build next to the other two men. Archer's large frame appeared massive, but his muscle tone had not changed since he had left college as a student. Now at the age of 34, he felt he looked the picture of health and was proud of his physical condition. Towering over his two colleagues, he moved toward the other cases.

Pulling back on the second one, the thought of Nita suddenly popped into his mind. He had never enjoyed a person so much as he did Nita. Her total mixture of athlete and intellectual fascinated him. Here was a woman who could hold her own in a sports competition and also converse with the campus intelligentsia in more than one field. He knew he loved her and hoped that she loved him. As soon as he finished with his experiments with the king cobras, he would finish his paper and apply for the tests to complete his doctorate. Then, he and Nita could be married—if she would have him.

He finished opening the last crate and laid the tool aside. "Al? Will you and Richard hold the cases while I pull out the cages?"

"Sure." Al stepped closer to the table. When he saw Richard hanging back, he said, "Come on, Richard, what's the matter? You're not scared of a couple of little snakes, are you?"

Richard coughed. "I suppose it's the better alternative. He could have suggested I reach in and pull the cages out." He stepped closer to the table and tentatively grasped the wooden crate.

Archer found the handle on the end of the cage in the box and pulled. It easily slid out and soon rested in the sunlight pouring in through the west window of the lab. In quick order, he had placed the other two cages next to it. When the crates had been placed on the floor, he moved closer.

The snakes lay in different positions on the floors of the containers, brightly alert despite the long trip from India.

"Did you order the snakes from the zoological gardens, Al?" Archer looked up at the man who was perhaps 15 years older than himself.

"Yes. I think they arrived this morning. I'll check with my secretary." He turned, hurrying from the lab.

"I suppose you think you're going to make a lot of points with this show of experiments?" Richard glared at Archer.

"What do you mean?"

"If you think for one minute that you're going to be elected to chair the department, you're completely wrong, my friend."

Archer's eyebrows cocked as he stared at the smaller man, directing his penetrating gaze at him without blinking. "If you recall, Richard, I suggested that you be the one to travel to India on the exchange once Mr. Bahadur completes his term here."

"Of course, you did. And you did it simply to get rid of me. Admit it, Archer. You don't like me and you never have. These creepy snakes are your ticket to fame and fortune, aren't they?"

"They're my vehicle to attain my doctorate, if that's what you mean. And as far as disliking you, I think your opinion of me and my likes and dislikes are figments of your imagination."

"Just remember one thing, Archer. Al and I both have tenure with the school. It's not likely they'll grant any more to this department for quite some time. And as far as the chair is concerned, well, Al has the election locked up, and I'll be second in line after his term in office."

Archer realized that Richard's scope of life was limited to the school, campus activities and faculty politics. To him, holding the chair of the biology department and having job security were the epitome of life. To Archer, there were more important things. First of all, his work was usually left in the lab when he went home at night. He had Nita and her affection. Since they had met last year when she first came to school to study for her Masters, they had felt drawn to each other. Then, last January they had moved into an apartment and found complete happiness, a happiness that Richard Roman would not understand nor more than likely ever experience.

When the door to the lab opened and Al stepped in, Richard quickly said, "I don't understand why you need other snakes, Archer."

Archer ignored him, turning instead to Al. "Are they here?"

"They arrived shortly before noon. I can answer your question, Richard. A king cobra's diet consists solely of other snakes. Right, Archer?"

Archer nodded, the forelock of pewter colored hair bobbing up and down when he did so.

"Yuck," Richard managed, turning away to look out the window at the campus below.

Al and Archer stood close to the table, studying the snakes for several minutes without speaking. Two of the cobras, olive gray in color, seemed content to watch the three men, while the third, with yellow and buff colored crossbars, writhed back and forth the full length of its confinement, occasionally rearing up. When any of the three got too close, the cobras struck viciously, rapping their heads against the containers.

"What's the trouble with this one?" Al pointed to the more colorful snake. "Or are the other two the ones with problems?"

"The two that are satisfied with just watching are older, more mature snakes. The brightly colored one is pretty young, a juvenile really."

"How do you come off knowing so much about snakes, Archer?" Richard asked from the window after turning around to face the interior of the room.

"Truth of the matter is, I worked at the Chicago Zoo while I was going to college, and during a couple of summers while I was still in high school, I worked at a reptile garden in the Black Hills. I know enough about them to know how to handle them and respect them. Beyond that, caution and care are the main criteria in handling snakes of any sort." Archer turned from the more brightly colored reptile to the other two.

"Why king cobras, Archer?" Richard stared at Archer. Al leaned down closer to the cage nearest him. He moved back when the resident moved toward him in a threatening manner.

"First of all, king cobras are the largest, poisonous snake in the world. The apparent record in length, although it seems un-believable, is nineteen feet three inches. Lengths of twelve to fourteen feet are more the average. The amount of venom they produce is outrageous when compared to most other snakes that are poisonous. Therefore, the venom, which I want to do my research on, will be more readily available than if I were to use, say, rattlesnakes. Another point is the fact that while rattlesnake venom among others can be ingested without harm, cobra venom cannot. It's the perfect poison."

"Why do you want to work on something like that, for heaven's sake?" Richard walked toward the table but stopped six feet from it.

"As a biologist you should know that snake venom is a very complex protein compound. It's produced by cells lining innumerable small tubes, and like creeks feeding a larger stream, the venom is carried to the duct that takes it to the base of the fang."

"I know all that. After all, I'm not stupid." Richard stared derisively at Archer.

Choosing to ignore the short-tempered man, Archer continued. "Most poisonous snakes, in fact all of them, are immune to their own venom. I want to accumulate enough venom from these three specimens and then disect one or two to see if I can discover why they *are* immune, most especially in the manner in which the muscles are affected."

Richard chewed his lower lip. "What's the bottom line, Archer? What do you hope to learn?"

"Perhaps what I pick up here could be turned over to the research labs working on muscular dystrophy and other related diseases."

"Most worthy," Richard snorted.

"Hey, Richard, if nothing else, you get to go to India—or did you forget that your participation in that respect was contingent on this part of the exchange?" Archer smiled in a devilish way.

Without a word, Richard turned away again.

Archer knew he wouldn't leave because he didn't want to be talked about in his absence, not that Archer would have pursued the topic of conversation any further than he already had where Richard was concerned. Still, Archer could not help wonder why Richard Roman so intensely disliked him. He had his ideas but nothing that seemed definite or concrete. Richard's life style, his apparent loneliness, his inability to achieve success without having to work extra hard at it, all seemed to cause him to focus an intense dislike on Archer Buchanan who thoroughly enjoyed his own life style, was not the least bit lonely since Nita had come into his life and seemed to have things fall his way with only a modicum of work. Archer could understand Richard's behavior if that were the case, but he wasn't completely sure.

"Incidentally, Archer, have you heard from this Lal . . . ah, darn, what's his name again?" Al turned to Archer for help.

Archer smiled. Al had best master the man's name before he did arrive. "It's Lal Khan Bahadur. And yes, I received a phone call from him this morning. He's in town and will come by the lab today or tomorrow to check on the condition of the snakes."

"My God," Richard said, "you'd think those damned things were celebrities or something."

"They are, Richard, they are. Sort of. King cobras are the rarest cobra and not all that plentiful. I'd venture to say that you'd be hard pressed to find many in the state or in the whole southwest for that matter. They're just not that plentiful."

"Well, I don't like them. They're frightening." Richard turned away once again.

"Not so loud, Richard. They'll hear you," Al said good-naturedly.

"Not really," Archer said. "Snakes are deaf. They feel vibrations with their sensitive stomachs and sense vibrations and scents in the air with their tongues."

Al nodded. "You say that one of these grew to be over nineteen feet in length?"

"That's what I've been told but the average length is more twelve to fourteen feet, like these guys here." Archer pointed to the cages. "One thing that is peculiar to the king cobra is the fact they are the only snake to build a nest. They push up a pile of leaves and debris in the jungle, and after laying their eggs, the female and sometimes the male will stay close by and attack anything that comes near. Some people think that's why there are so many unprovoked attacks on people by king cobras. Others think they are just plain ornery and take out after anyone who happens by."

"What do you believe?" Al asked.

Archer shrugged. "Take your pick. I'll buy either one, but the first argument seems to be the more logical. What do you know of this Lal Khan Bahadur, Al?''

''Well, he's to lecture on the sociological changes in India in the last ten to fifteen years, hoping to make known some of the problems facing his country today. He's well educated and, as I understand from the material sent here by his government, quite a speaker.''

''Do you want to be here when he arrives?'' Archer directed his question more to Al than to Richard.

''It might be the most diplomatic thing, don't you think?''

''Well, as acting head of the department and a probable shoo-in for the chair, I think you should be.'' Archer emphasized the word ''you,'' noting that Richard still stood across the room, near the window. He wondered what the man intended. A quick jump out the window in the event one of the snakes got loose?

Archer smiled to himself and made a mental note to have at least three snakes here in the lab for the cobras to eat the next day when Lal Khan Bahadur arrived.

Nita hurried along the walkway toward the entrance of the John Thomas Science Building. She felt better now that her destination was in sight. Still, she wondered what had made her behave the way she had back near Carver Hall. Surely it couldn't be the man who had walked by her and barely looked at her. And there was that peculiar feeling of being watched. Pass it off. Forget it. Now that she was almost with Archer, she could face anything.

After entering the main foyer of the science building, Nita headed toward the staircase that would take her to Archer's third floor laboratory. Considering walking much more beneficial to her overall physical condition than jogging, she briskly made her way up the steps. When she reached the top floor, her heartbeat was no quicker than when she had been simply crossing the campus and quadrangle.

She stopped for a second outside Archer's lab, and after fluffing her hair, she turned the knob and walked in. Instantly feeling as if she were going to pass out, she grasped the door-jamb. What was wrong with her? "Archer?" she managed weakly.

Turning, Archer saw Nita, her face pale, her fingers clawing at the door frame. "Nita!" he cried, running across the room.

When he stood at her side, she regained her equilibrium and forced a smile. "I'm all right now. I don't know what happened." She took his proffered arm and entered the lab. When she saw the concerned faces of Doctor Stewart and Professor Roman, she wondered what she had looked like standing in the doorway, ready to collapse. At least, she had thought she was going to collapse.

"Are you all right, Nita?" Al Stewart asked.

"I . . . I'm fine, really. I don't know what happened."

"You're absolutely certain you're all right, Nita?" Archer asked, his concern evident not only in his voice but on his face as well.

"Really, I am. Look," she said, freeing her
arm from his grasp and whirling about in a
pirouette. As the room spun around, three
shiny, clear boxes caught her attention each
time she turned. What were they? She stopped.

Before she could turn to look at the table,
Archer said, "Look what arrived a little while
ago." He gestured toward the table and the
snakes in the plastic cages.

Turning, Nita stared, wide-eyed, at the clear
boxes and the king cobras inside. Her head felt
as if it were floating away from her body.

As one, all three cobras lashed out at her
with resounding knocks as their heads struck
the doors. The room, its windows, the boxes
with the snakes, the table and Archer's concerned face swirled into a hazy collage as her
eyes turned upward until nothing but white
showed. In slow motion, she sank to the floor in
a heap.

# 3

Nita relaxed in the overstuffed easy chair. She ignored the blind eye of the TV set staring at her. They had come home, once she had felt sufficiently strong enough to walk. She had no idea why she had fainted nor why she had experienced such weird sensations while walking across campus toward the science building and again after entering Archer's lab. She moved to get up.

"Hold it right there, ma'am." Archer entered the small living room from the kitchen, carrying a glass of milk. "I'm takin' care o' you-all, tonight, if'n you-all don't mind."

Nita smiled. Archer was doing his best to maintain a light attitude, but she knew he was worried and concerned. It showed on his face. When he was relaxed and placid, his face would appear almost languid. But now, tonight, it seemed everytime she looked at him, he was shooting covert looks at her, his forehead drawn together in a mass of wrinkles.

"I don't mind, Archer. In fact, I'm sort of enjoying it. I feel fine, and I wish you'd stop pacing around like a caged animal. You're beginning to make me feel nervous."

Plopping down on the ottoman at her feet, he looked up at her. "How do you feel now?"

"About the same as I did two minutes ago when you asked. Really, darling, I feel fine. I just fainted. It's not the first time I've ever done it, so, it's not that unusual." Reaching out she touched his hand resting on her knee.

"But you're in such fantastic physical condition. It seems so unnatural for you. Tell me about the other times you've fainted."

"I don't know if they would qualify as fainting spells. I sort of blacked out."

"How do you mean?"

"Well, for instance, when I was in high school, I had gotten into this argument with another girl. I don't even remember what it was about but we were pretty angry. At least, I was. I remember turning away from her and walking toward the rest room. For some reason she didn't follow. The next thing I knew, I was lying outside under the stars and it was about nine in the evening."

"What time had the argument taken place?" Archer got to his feet, moving around to the side of the chair to sit on the large arm.

"I don't remember exactly, but it was during school hours. In the afternoon."

"What did your parents say when you came home?"

"That's the strange part, now that I recall the whole thing. They didn't say anything, other than that I was ten minutes late in getting home from the library."

Archer stared at her when she looked up at him. "Had you been to the library?"

She shrugged.

"Had you planned on going to the library?"

"I . . . I don't remember."

"It sounds as though you were walking around in a fog, had been home, probably to eat your evening meal, went to the library, and your folks didn't pick up that anything was out of the ordinary. What do you think?"

Struggling to her feet, Nita stood, turning to face him. "I never really gave it much thought but now that you mention it, I guess the same sort of ideas passed through my mind at the time. I suppose they did, whenever I thought about it, which, I might add, hasn't been too often. See, I'm not really concerned."

"Well, I *am*. Sure, you're in fantastic health and condition, but you might have something wrong. I think you should consult a doctor before you do anymore training. What do you think?"

"I'm due for a complete physical in a week or so before the triathalon. I guess I could move the exam up a few days. If nothing else, it'll keep you happy and quiet." She smiled, putting her arms around his neck.

"At first," Archer said after they stopped

embracing. "I thought you might just be queasy at the sight of snakes. Not everyone can take them. Richard sure freaked out."

"He did?"

"Well, maybe freaked out is too strong, but he sure hung around the window, about as far away from the cages as he could without falling out. Maybe you're just squeamish at the sight of snakes. Are you?"

She shrugged. "I don't know. Again, I've never really given it much thought. I suppose I could be. Why are people so turned off by snakes?"

"Oh, I guess lots of reasons. The story of the serpent being responsible for Adam and Eve's eviction from Paradise is probably where it all started. Then, too, there are so many weird theories and misconceptions about snakes. Some stories and legends give them almost un-believable abilities—like milking cows, taking its tail in its mouth and rolling up like a hoop, flying, being wet and slimy. Chop its head off and the head and body will not die until sun-down. Of course, that one is true to a point. Both parts will live for thirty to forty minutes, and if the snake is poisonous, the head can still bite and envenomize. I could go on and on."

Nita shook her head, laughing. "I've never heard any of those."

"Face it, snakes are the most unusual creatures in all of nature. No limbs. Deaf as far as hearing is usually considered and no lids on their eyes. Actually, they're limbless lizards and

fall into the suborder *Serpentes*, which means
crawling animals."

"Ah, Professor Buchanan, could we do
without the lecture on snakes? I think I might
feel a whole lot better if you stopped."

"I'm sorry. I really am. I got carried away.
Forgive me?"

"Of course, you ninny."

"I do want to ask you one more question
about your past. May I?"

She nodded.

"You weren't by chance frightened by a
snake while living in Africa or India, were you?"

Pursing her full lips, Nita turned away. She
walked to the widow of their first floor apartment to look out on the quiet, deserted street.
"I doubt it. I was born in Africa, and we left
there when I was two years old. If I were
frightened by one there, I surely wouldn't
remember it. And we were in India for four years
or so if I recall what my Mom and Dad told me.
Again, I don't remember much of anything from
there."

Nita's brow furrowed. She hadn't thought
about any of her early childhood for a long
time. Every once in a while, before her parents
died, they would fondly reminisce about her
father's ministry in both countries, but he had
not wanted to return to the foreign missions for
some reason. Whenever it seemed the conversation would lead in that direction and the
reasons might be revealed, either her mother or
her father would change the subject, and Nita

would be left in the dark once more. When her father died, she and her mother seldom spoke of the distant past, preferring to concentrate on the later years when Nita could contribute her own memories to the conversation. Then, when her mother died of cancer, and Nita was all alone, she had no reason to wonder any longer about her early childhood. Now, for some peculiar reason, she wondered why her father had given up on the missionary work he apparently had loved so much at one time. She shook her head.

When he saw her response, Archer moved toward her. "Will you definitely have the physical as soon as possible? I'm really worried for you . . . for us. I don't want anything wrong with either one of us."

She embraced him. "Of course I will. I love you, Archer. I think I'd do most anything for you."

Nita pulled the examination gown around her backside, sensing that she had failed miserably in covering her buttocks. Whirling around to face the door when it opened, she confronted Doctor Juergens whose face revealed nothing.

"Well, Doctor? What's the good news? Or should I expect bad?"

"I've found nothing adverse in the lab work at all. Everything is absolutely perfect. In fact, I've never had the pleasure of examining such a perfect human specimen before in my life. What

do you do to maintain your physical
condition?"

"Without going into detail, I'm training for
a triathalon."

Juergens smiles. "That explains it. You
must be some athlete, Anita."

"It's not Anita, Doctor. My parents names
were Niles and Marietta. They named me after
both of them. *Ni* from Niles and the last two
letters of my mother's name, *ta*, gave them
Nita. I've been called Anita, Juanita and anything else that could be construed as being the
form from which Nita might be derived."

Juergens nodded. "Clever. At any rate, all I
can say is that your body condition and muscle
tone are excellent. Your lungs are in superb
shape. Your heart beat is sixty at rest and about
sixty-eight after two minutes of mild exercise,
which is simply great. Physically, I can find
absolutely nothing that might have led to your
fainting spell. You're certain you haven't held
anything back from me?"

"By anything, do you mean of recent
origin?"

"Recent, dim past, ancient history—whatever. Have you ever experienced anything that
could be interpreted as being out of the
ordinary?"

Nita thought how strange that just the
other night, when she and Archer were talking
about the incident in the lab, she recalled her
fainting spell in high school. But could that
have any bearing on the latest episode? The

same thing had happened in grade school, and if she remembered correctly, there was at least one other incident wherein she had experienced a time lapse. She looked at Doctor Juergens who seemed to be an understanding person. She remembered the doctor who had cared for her mother and how kind he had been at the time of Marietta's death. Somehow, Juergens reminded her of that man.

"I've had several fainting spells in my past."

"Tell me about them."

Nita explained each situation as best as she could remember, although the details were vague, and indistinct. When she finished, she waited to see what his reaction might be.

"I'm going to suggest a couple of other tests, Nita, neither of which will take very long but they will tell us a lot about your brain."

"My brain? What's wrong with my brain?" A sense of panic flooded through her.

"Nothing that I know of. Do you know of something?"

She shook her head, her eyes wide.

"Well, then, the best thing we can do is run these tests."

"What tests?"

"A CAT scan and an EEG."

"Are they necessary?"

"Well, we could x-ray your foot, but as far as I know the foot has nothing to do with fainting spells." He grinned impishly.

Catching his humor, she smiled back. "Well, let's get on with them, then."

"I wish it were that simple. You'll have to go to the University Hospital to have them administered. I'll call and arrange for them, if it's all right with you."

Nita closed her eyes for a second and thought of Archer. She'd do it for him. He'd feel better if every base were touched, and when the evidence came in and she was found to be one hundred percent healthy, he would be happy and so would she.

"How soon, Doctor, before I can get the results of the tests?"

While picking up the phone and dialing, he said, "I can tell the neurologist to give you the results right then if that's all right with you. Hello?"

She nodded as his attention turned to the telephone. When he hung up, he turned back to her.

"That'll be fine, Doctor."

"If you hurry over right now, they can work you in between regularly scheduled patients." He wrote down the doctor's name and where to find him and handed it to her.

She stood, extending her hand. When he took it in his, she said, "Thank you for seeing me, Doctor, I know you're busy, and I appreciate the quick response to my call."

"Well, we can't have you missing any class work or that triathalon. I don't think I'll be seeing you anymore. I'm sure the tests will be favorable. I'd tell you to take care of yourself, but it would be a little redundant considering your overall excellent physical condition."

"Thank you, Doctor Juergens."

By 4:00 o'clock that afternoon, Nita began fidgeting in the waiting room. She had had the EEG after the CAT scan and now had waited for almost two hours. Surely there couldn't be something wrong. How could there be? When she looked up, she saw the head nurse behind the closed glass panel. She'd have to be patient and think positive thoughts. Her impatience could lead to her becoming angry, and she didn't want that to happen. She hated it whenever she became angry. Usually, her anger was all out of proportion to the problem at hand. She would invariably feel like a fool after it passed and find herself having to apologize. She wished there were some way she could vent her anger without having to go through the embarrassment she usually felt after apologizing.

She picked up a copy of a woman's magazine, leafing through page after page of colorful advertisements and stories. Just as she found an article that might hold her interest, the panel slid open and the nurse called to her.

"Miss Galforth? Doctor Craig will see you now."

Dropping the magazine on the table, she stood and crossed the waiting room.

When she had settled into an easy chair opposite Doctor Craig's desk, he looked up at her. She wondered what lay behind his professional mask. Was he about to tell her some awful news? Or would he tell her . . .

"The CAT scan showed absolutely nothing wrong, as did the EEG. According to Ted Juergens, you're one healthy specimen from a physical standpoint. I guess the same holds true in a neurological sense as well."

"You mean I'm all right?"

"Precisely."

"Do you have any explanation for my fainting then?"

He shook his head. "What were you doing at the time?"

"I had just walked across the campus and up three flights of stairs to a lab in the science building."

"Did you feel winded or light-headed?"

"You mean from walking?"

He nodded.

"Not really." She hesitated. She had felt strange crossing the campus—as if someone had been watching her. As she recalled now, the sensation had been so encompassing that she *had* felt light-headed. Maybe she should tell him that. Before she could begin, he spoke.

"For someone as healthy as you, walking shouldn't trigger that sort of reaction. What did you do in the lab? Smell something that was bad?" He smiled kindly.

She shook her head. "There were three king cobras in plastic cages that were on a table. They were the first things I saw when I entered."

He laughed. "I'd probably have fainted, too. I can't stand the sight of snakes." He visibly shuddered at the thought.

Nita relaxed. Perhaps her reaction had been

perfectly normal after all. All she had to do was tell Archer the good results and everything else would be back to normal.

When Doctor Craig stood, she did the same, accepting his hand across his desk. "Best of luck, and I hope I don't see you in here anymore, young lady."

She smiled at the sandy-haired man and turned to leave.

When the John Thomas Science Building came into view, Nita assured herself that the sight of the cobras, if they were still in the lab, would not bother her. She pictured the reptiles in her mind. Actually, they were intriguing and surely not a threat, being contained in a plastic cage the way they were.

Entering the building she hurried to the third floor. Archer turned at the sound of the door opening. They embraced, and before releasing her, he said, "Well?"

Stepping away, she said, "Nothing. They found nothing."

"At all?"

She nodded.

"That's great. God, I was so worried."

A movement behind him caught Nita's attention and she focused on it. One of the king cobras had moved in its cage. She took a tentative step toward the table and stopped, turning to Archer. He smiled reassuringly and moved aside.

"Go ahead. Get the monkey off your back. Did the doctor tell you that it was probably the unexpected sight of the snakes that made you faint?"

She shook her head. "Not in so many words. The one doctor said that he would have probably reacted in exactly the same way."

"I guess a lot of people would. What are you going to do?"

"Well, I'm not going to get buddy-buddy with them, but I am going to look at them for a few minutes. Then we can go home and cele- brate my successful physical. All right?" She started toward the table.

"In time, we can go home. I've got to wait for Doctor Bahadur. He was supposed to be here earlier but called about an hour or so ago, saying that he wouldn't be able to get here much before five-thirty."

Without stopping, Nita said, "It's almost that right now," and continued toward the table. When she stood next to it, she looked down. The two older, darker snakes moved around the confines of the cages. When they became aware of her presence, both joined the younger snake, which was already rearing up. Nita found herself suddenly admiring the sheer beauty in the seemingly effortless movement of the reptiles. They were beautifully colored with darker bands of olive gray alternating with lighter ones. The third snake, the immature one, glistened brightly in the late afternoon sunlight as it poured through the window. The buff bands stood out in stark relief to the darker ones, as it reared up farther until its head touched the top of the three foot high cage.

Involuntarily, Nita jumped back.

"What's the matter?" Archer asked, coming up behind her.

"It . . . it looked . . . as if it wanted to strike me."

"More than likely it would have, too, if it weren't for the cage. Aren't they beautiful?"

Fighting to control a shudder she felt building deep within her, she said, "I hate to admit it but they are, especially this one." She pointed to the younger snake.

"He'll conform in time. They darken as they get older."

"Do you want me to wait with you or should I go on ahead and start supper?"

"Why don't you wait? I can help you with the meal. Besides, you'll probably have lots to talk over with Doctor Bahadur since you lived in India."

"For four years when I was a child." She lightly poked him in the ribs.

A soft knock at the door brought both of them around. Archer went to it, admitting the tall, dark man wearing a white, tunic-like jacket.

Nita froze for an instant. It was the same man she had seen the day she was coming to the lab, the same day she had fainted. She half-turned away when Archer and Doctor Bahadur introduced themselves to each other. She realized that she felt no adverse reactions such as the first time she had seen the man from India.

"Doctor, this is my friend, Nita Galforth. Nita, this is Doctor Lal Khan Bahadur of India."

Nita offered her hand which he took. He bowed from the waist and said, "I'm most delighted to meet you, my dear."

Nita noted the strange, dryness to his hand. For some reason, she had expected it to be wet or greasy. Withdrawing her own, she smiled. "Welcome to Middleton University."

Without acknowledging her welcome, he turned to Archer. "They arrived in good condition?"

Archer stepped aside, gesturing with his one arm toward the table where the snakes rested. "They're excellent. I'm sure much will be accomplished with them."

Nita watched Archer's face, catching out of the corner of her eye Bahadur's head bowing ever so slightly. When she turned enough to see him better, she found him staring at her. A chill zigzagged down her spine. She fought to regain her self-control and turned her attention to the snakes. At least they were confined in cages.

Nita sat astride Archer's body. Both gyrated in the final throes of their lovemaking. When Archer climaxed with her, they spiraled down to a more conscious level and, as he softened inside her, he smiled. She bent to kiss his face, and he encircled her upper body with his arms, rolling her to the side. Free of each other, he propped himself up on one arm. "I love you, Nita Galforth."

"And I love you, Archer Buchanan."

Snuggling down beneath the covers, Archer held her, one hand falling over her side to cup one breast. In seconds, his gentle snores rippled through the bedroom.

Nita smiled, content with the man in her life, and closed her eyes to fall asleep.

It seemed ridiculous to dance so wildly to the sound of the drum that seemingly filled her head with a soft muted beat. Nita tried to open her eyes. If she danced too much she might lose her sense of balance and fall. Struggling mightily, she forced first one, then the other eyelid up. She was in a crowd, dancing with an abandonment that frightened her. Shadows leaped, twisting and writhing against the trees surrounding the opening in which she danced. Firelight gave a macabre shifting effect to the scene. With whom was she dancing? She concentrated on her dancing partners, but they seemed to keep their faces turned away from her. She made an effort to catch a glimpse of at least one face, and when a nude man turned to confront her, she wanted to scream when she saw he had no face.

Looking down, she found herself unclothed not unlike the others. The tempo of the drum picked up, accelerating the rhythm until she feared for her safety in the wild, frenzied group. Arms were flung about, and legs kicked out in total ecstasy. A maniacal laugh threaded its way through the drum beats and the stamping of feet and the heavy breathing of the dancers.

Nita's eyes opened wide, staring into the darkness of the bedroom. Her body, covered with a film of sweat, trembled ever so slightly. She turned to see if Archer was awake but found him sleeping soundly. It had been nothing but a dream.

Turning over, she put an arm around Archer, pulling herself closer to him.

It had been nothing but a dream.

# PART II

## WITH A VENGEANCE

# 4

The members of the biology department broke into subdued applause when the vote tally indicated Doctor Alfred Stewart would be the chairman of the department for the next four years. Holding his hands up for quiet, Al smiled broadly.

"Thank you, thank you," he began. "I promise I won't speak for more than just a minute or two."

A murmur of approval ran through the small group.

"I just want to say that I think vast strides will be made in the near future, not because I'm chairman but because so many exciting things are happening and will continue happening during the next several years. As all of you know, Professor Roman will be going to India next spring and will be there for a full year

teaching and lecturing under the same inter-
change agreement that brought Doctor Lal
Khan Bahadur to Middleton University. This
agreement also brought the snakes that Archer
Buchanan will use in his research dealing with
venom. Along with the government grant that
funds his research and pays for Professor
Roman's stay in India and Doctor Bahadur's
stay here, the endowment fund is also giving
the department money for new equipment that
has been sorely needed for quite some time.

"Ladies and gentlemen, I don't know about
you or how you might feel about these things,
but, to put it frankly and concisely, I'm very
excited about the future."

Applause broke out again.

"Just let me assure you that my door is
open to each one of you at any time. Please
don't hesitate in coming forward to discuss an
idea or air a complaint. Again, thank you for the
honor."

To Archer, it was just so much rhetoric that
the occasion called for and that Al Stewart had
obligingly given. Sure, the next few years would
be exciting, but the ground work for all of it had
taken place over the last five years and now
they were bearing the fruit of those labors. He
smiled at Rosemary Ogleruk who taught freshman biology. Being overweight and wearing
glasses nearly half an inch thick did nothing for
the middle-aged woman's appearance. Her
blonde hair, severely pulled back in a bun at the
back of her head, seemed to point up her
spinsterhood like a badge of honor. When

Ogleruk turned away, Archer wiped the forced smile from his face and tried to ignore the fact that Richard Roman was coming in his direction.

"Well," Richard said quietly, "that's settled."

"You sound relieved." Archer eyed him for a moment.

"It's nice to know that some things are sacrosanct and unchangeable."

When he didn't continue, Archer said, "Such as?"

"Department head elections for one thing. Al certainly deserved the chair, and I'm glad he got it."

"You seem to put a lot of importance on something like that. Why?"

"Why? I'll tell you why. When one is associated with an institution of higher learning, one must be willing to make sacrifices. But along with those sacrifices must come a certain rigidity of fact and existence. The chair should go to the senior member with tenure. Then, the next in line should succeed and so on."

"What are you trying to say, Richard?"

"It would have been an insult to Al, the department and tradition had someone like yourself been elected."

Archer frowned. "I don't want the job, and everyone knows I'm not the least bit interested. I voted for Al, just like everyone else did for the most part. What is it about me that bugs the hell out of you, Richard?"

Richard turned his attention to Rosemary who was waddling toward the door. "I guess because you're so damned ambitious."

Archer forced a short, gruff laugh. "That's what bothers you. My ambition?"

Richard nodded.

Archer noticed a thin film of perspiration on the man's forehead. "I'm working for the University, buddy, not you. I don't feel I have to make excuses to you or tell you what my plans are, but I will tell you this much. If I put together the idea that is buzzing around in my head and it comes out in concrete form, I'll get my doctorate and then, if you want to go toe to toe and head to head for the chairmanship of the department, I'll be ready. Right now, I'm not. Besides, playing the game according to the unwritten rules, you'll be the next chairman, four years down the road."

Richard tugged at his coat sleeve. "I'm . . . I'm sorry, Archer. Really I am. I've been working under a lot of stress lately and I guess I sort of took it out on you. Now that Bahadur is here, I can begin making plans for next spring."

"Forget it." Archer snapped at the man for the weak reasoning behind his apology. Richard Roman had not been the least bit friendly to Archer ever since the latter had come to the school three years before. Turning, Archer walked toward the door of the meeting room, but seeing Al Stewart locked in earnest conversation with another teacher, Archer purposely changed directions and walked up to the two men.

"Congratulations, Al. I knew all along you'd get it."

"I guess I did, too. Funny how elections for this sort of thing take on a glow of familiarity over the years. Four years from now, Richard will be the chairman. Then, assuming you're still around, you'll probably be the heir apparent, but I wouldn't bet on it."

Archer looked at him, feeling his forehead knit in a frown. What had Al meant by that—*assuming you're still around*?

"I can see you don't know what I mean. If your work with the cobras works out and your findings match your hypothesis, you'll never stay at a school like Middleton. The 'U' would never be able to afford you." Al grinned, slapping Archer on the shoulder.

"Oh," Archer managed, before nodding. "At first, I thought you were going to lop off my head as your first act as chair of the department."

"I'm sure someone would do the same to me, if I did," Al said, turning his attention back to the person with whom he had been speaking.

Archer hurried from the room. He wanted to check on the cobras, make a couple of changes in his notes and then hurry home. Nita would be waiting for him.

"What are you looking so smug about?" Nita rushed to the door, embracing Archer as he walked in.

They kissed, and after parting, Archer smiled broadly at her. "Oh, I don't know. I guess

God is in his heaven and all's right with the world."

Cocking an eyebrow, she studied him. What could have happened to make him look so content? The election! That was it. He had won the election and was the new chairman of the biology department.

"Congratulations, darling."

"Congratulations? For what?"

"Why, for being elected chairman of the department. I'm proud of you. And here all along, you said you weren't the least bit interested in it. It's not nice to fib to people, especially the woman you claim to love."

Archer turned to face her after setting his briefcase on the floor next to the kitchen counter. "What are you talking about? What makes you think I was elected?"

"Why that silly little grin on your face says it all."

Crossing the room, he took her in his arms. "You're the one who's being silly. I wasn't elected. I didn't even get one vote. Why should I have? I told everyone that Al was the man for the job and that I wasn't the least bit interested."

Pushing free from his embrace, Nita stared at Archer. "Are you serious? I thought all along that the talk you were giving everyone about not being interested was all, you know, for show. Reverse psychology. You know—I'm not interested but wow, am I ever glad I won and I'll do a good job for everyone."

"Really, Nita, it wasn't anything like that.

I'm way too busy to want the title or the position at this point in my career. I wouldn't be able to do a good job even though the whole thing is practically nothing but show."

Glaring, she turned around, storming back to the stove. "That's not true and you know it. You're just trying to be magnanimous and cover up your hurt, aren't you?"

"Nothing of the kind. I'm glad Al got the job. He deserves it. He and Richard seem to thrive on that sort of thing—titles and prestige and junk like that. Hell, I don't. I never have and I probably never will. What ever made you think I wanted it?"

Turning over a chop in the skillet, she looked up at him. "Isn't it human nature to want to excel in one's chosen field? Wouldn't—"

"But I am—excelling in my field, that is. At least, I hope I will once I complete the experiments with the cobra venom and all."

"But that's down the road, in the future. What about right now?"

"Right now, I'm hungry and the chops smell delicious."

"Archer, I'm serious. What about now?"

"Well, if by now you mean the immediate future, I'm well into laying the groundwork for the experiments to begin. If I can ultimately explain why poisonous snakes such as the king cobra are immune to their own venom, I can perhaps discover—"

"Perhaps—maybe! There's nothing concrete in it, is there? You're poking around, looking for holes in the dark, aren't you?"

"The work is worthwhile. I don't think the United States or the government of India or Middleton University would have gotten involved if the idea was foolish."

Nita said nothing. What was wrong with her? Why was she attacking him this way? Of course he wasn't an athlete as such, conditioned to react to immediate stimuli, the way she was. Put a ball in her hand, lay out a course for a foot race or throw a challenge at her, and she was ready at an instant's notice to compete. Someone like Archer was trained to be positive before he spoke, think before he acted and check and double-check any data that he uncovered. That had to be the reason why he had not wanted to seek the chair. His work with the cobras had to take precedence over anything else that might come along. At least, he had not yet slighted her or given up paying attention to her. For that, she was thankful.

Dropping her head, she said, "I'm sorry, Archer. I just thought that you truly did want the position. What about in the future?"

"In time, if I stay here, I'm sure I'll be named chairman of the biology department. Really, it's no big deal. Are you all right?"

She shot a quick look at him. "All right? What do you mean?"

"You were getting pretty upset there for a few minutes when I was explaining the reasons why I wasn't interested and that Al had actually been elected."

"No, I'm fine. Really. I just got a little bent

out of shape when I realized that you hadn't been elected. That's all."

The subject was not mentioned the rest of the evening. After eating and reading the newspaper while Archer poured over some work he had brought home with him, Nita stretched when the bell tower in the quadrangle, two blocks away, struck 9:00.

"I'm ready for bed. How about you? You ready?"

Archer looked up. "It's not that late but I am tired. I guess a good night's sleep wouldn't hurt me, either." He closed his notebook and placed everything in the briefcase.

Nita checked the kitchen door, which they used more often than the front entrance because of proximity to the campus, and after turning out the lights, joined Archer in the bedroom. He had already undressed and was about ready to slip between the sheets when she entered. Sitting down on the edge of the bed, he waited for her to undress.

She pulled her T-shirt over her head, shaking it to free her hair and let it fall into place. After dropping the shirt on the floor, she undid her bra. Her breasts, jutting straight out, didn't move once she had taken off the restraining undergarment. Her tiny waist seemed almost too small for the swell of her hips and the large breasts. After she slipped from her jeans, she pulled off the bikini panties.

She knew Archer was watching her turn in front of the full-length mirror on the inside of the closet door.

"Archer, do you think I'm putting on weight?" She turned slowly, examining her reflection in a careful, calculating way.

Pursing his lips, he clicked his tongue after a moment. "Your thighs seem a bit bigger."

"My thighs? My 'thunder thighs'? You think they're getting bigger? My God, Archer, they're so damned big now that if I let them get bigger, I'll look like a cartoon character. Are you teasing me?" She turned to confront him and found him grinning from ear to ear.

"Your body, my dear, is probably one of the more perfect works of nature. Why you profess to a heaviness in the thighs is totally beyond me. They're perfect, just like your hips and everything else about you. Everything is perfect."

Crossing the room, she sat down on the bed next to him. Encircling his neck with her arms, she kissed him, her mouth open, her tongue searching for his. Lying back on the bed, they rolled about until she was on top of him. When they broke off the kiss, she said, "Thank you, Archer. Those were nice things to say, even though you say practically the same thing whenever I ask you about my thighs. I'm really concerned about them, you know."

"I know, but the whole idea is a great come-on to making love, isn't it?" He kissed her again when she brought her head down nearer to his. Reaching up, he caressed her solid, unyielding breasts and stomach. Her muscle tone amazed him—firm and yet, at the same time, as supple as anything he'd ever seen or felt.

Easing her over to one side, he positioned himself over her and kissed her, at the same time plunging his erect penis into her body. They worked their hips up and down in an increasing tempo and, once they had spent their energies, slowed to a stop, clinging to each other for a long while once they had finished.

Holding each other, they fell asleep.

Nita stared down at the figure of Alfred Stewart, Ph.D., newly elected head of the biology department at Middleton University. He was bound tightly with barbed wire, and his face, contorted in pain and rage, turned up to her.

"You're going to die, Doctor Stewart. You're not worthy of the chairmanship of the biology department. There are those who are so much more eminently qualified than you." She laughed wildly.

"But . . . what have I done to deserve this?" His voice pleaded in a whining whisper.

"Done? What have you done? You were elected in place of my Archer. That's what you've done, you intellectual asshole. Now, you'll pay and pay dearly for something so evil."

"But that's not evil. It goes with the job. Archer will be chairman in time. I'm sure of it. I promise you!"

"That's not *now*. I want him to be chairman *now*, you silly shit!"

"But he doesn't want to be the chairman.

I'm the chair.''

"I know, I know.'' She dragged out the words in an evil, insinuating way. "I'm ready to help you attain everything you ever wanted, Alfred dear!''

She found herself at a table, mixing powders and liquids in a mortar with a stone pestle. Someone, someplace, was laughing madly in a cackling, high-pitched falsetto, then she realized that the mirthless sound was coming from her own throat. When she finished mixing the concoction, she stepped back to the table on which Doctor Stewart lay, bound.

"So you wanted to be the chair of the department, eh?'' She dumped the mixture over him and a huge puff of smoke arose when it touched the quivering man. When the white, foggy cloud cleared away, Nita stared wide-eyed at the large Chippendale chair resting on the table where Doctor Alfred Stewart had lain bound mere seconds before. "Now, Doctor, you *are* a chair!''

Nita bolted upright in bed, her eyes wide open. The sudden jostling awoke Archer, who sat up next to her.

"What's the matter, darling?'' he asked, rubbing his eyes.

"I . . . I had an awful dream.''

"Want to tell me about it?''

She chuckled. "I guess it wasn't so awful. It was more silly now that I think about it.''

"Come on tell me, then we can go back to sleep. It's quite early yet. Barely ten-fifteen.''

She told him of the dream involving Doctor

Stewart, and when she finished they both broke into uproarious laughter.

"You . . . you . . . you have to learn to . . . to . . . to stop carrying a grudge like that, Nita." Archer gasped from laughing. "I never once thought of . . . of . . . you being the vind . . . vindictive type." He broke into another fit of laughter, and after several minutes, the humor of the situation withered and they settled back onto the bed.

Archer fell asleep immediately, but Nita lay on her back, staring into the darkness. She felt chilled even though the window in the living room and the one in the bedroom were open only a few inches. Slipping from between the covers, she went to the closet, fumbling in the dark for a blanket she knew was on the top shelf. When her hands closed on it, she brought it down, flaring it open over the bed. She crawled back into bed, snuggling next to Archer. She hoped she wasn't getting ill, catching a cold or something that would stop her from competing in the triathalon.

Perhaps she should have told the doctor about her occasional bouts of chilliness. It hadn't been going on too long, only since the day she fainted in Archer's lab. But now, as she recalled, there had been other times in her life when she felt cold when she should have been perfectly fine.

Turning over, she chastised herself for worrying about something that was nothing. She was in perfect health. Both doctors had said so.

She hugged herself in a tight embrace, relaxing when she began to warm up. Then, closing her eyes, she dropped into a dreamless void.

Alfred Stewart lay on his back, a gentle snore bubbling through the first floor bedroom. His wife's side, empty, was undisturbed next to him while a gentle September breeze nudged the sheer curtains into an impromptu dance. Outside the window a gentle rustling sounded for an instant but then stopped. After several seconds the sound came again and was accompanied by a thin silhouette on the drawn, cream-colored curtains, rising until the top of it was even with the middle of the open window. A bit more rustling sound filled the quiet night, and the shadow moved downward to the three inch open expanse below the window. The shadow became the slender head of a king cobra as it entered the bedroom. Sliding noiselessly onto the floor, the body, olive gray with dark bands, poured through the window. Once it had gained entrance, it lay perfectly still for several long moments, its tongue slithering in and out of its mouth, searching the air for information.

Bea Stewart, opening the car door with one hand, waved with the other to the members of the faculty wives' club.

"Congratulations again on Al's election," Mavis O'Rourke called.

"Thank you, Mavis." Bea slid into the front

seat. It was a shame that she had had to attend this meeting tonight. It would have been fun to go out for dinner and celebrate properly, but Al had insisted that she go. She knew he was proud but did not want to let on for fear of sounding pompous. She felt a great degree of pride for her husband and all he had achieved in his 49 years.

She turned the motor over and eased away from the curb, waving out the window with her left hand as she pulled away and returning the good-byes of the other women. In 15 minutes or so, she'd be home, and if Al hadn't gone to bed yet, they'd have a quiet glass of wine in passing for the election earlier that day.


Once it had scented the entire room, the cobra slipped its 21 pound bulk quietly, shadowlike along the floor toward the bed. When reaching there, the head rose, its hood spread, until it hovered almost five feet off the floor. The lidless eyes stared at the figure on the bed, while the snake's tongue constantly flickered in and out. Leaning over the foot of the bed, the cobra lowered its upper body to the covers, to undulate slowly toward the headboard. Its supple skin moved, allowing the ribs of the reptile to propel the body forward, its scutes grabbing the cotton material of the sheets.

Bea Stewart stopped for the traffic light that had changed to red, reaching out to tune in an FM station that played classical music all night long.

The king cobra opened its mouth, issuing a quiet hiss that was totally out of character for such a huge snake. The small fangs seemed to glint in the soft light from the digital clock on the nightstand next to Alfred Stewart's head.

Just then, the man moved a bit to one side, sensing the weight of something on the bed. Subconsciously concluding that it was more than likely his wife, Bea, who had returned from her meeting, he sank into a deeper sleep.

When the man stopped turning over, his neck lay exposed on the left side of his body. The snake glared at the small expanse of white in the eerie glow. It would have no trouble striking such an area, but instead of the swift lightning-like strike, it lowered its head and crawled closer, easing its upper body onto the man's chest. Bringing its head down to the throat, its mouth opened slowly and the fangs closed softly onto the yielding flesh. The man did not move. The snake bit down languidly, deliberately, without hurrying, without awakening the man, pumping its venom into his blood stream. Releasing his bite, the snake reared back until its head was a mere six inches from that of the man.

Turning off Brightly Avenue, Bea hurried along the shadowed streets of the neighborhood that bordered the campus. In ten minutes, she would pull into the driveway of their home.

Taking a deep breath, one that didn't seem to complete itself, Al opened his eyes, fighting the urge to scream when he saw the shadowy thing resting on his chest. What was it? Was he dreaming? He had to be dreaming. Something like that couldn't get into his bedroom. Where was his wife? He wanted to reach out for her but knew he would find nothing. Where was she? The meeting? Yes, the faculty wives' meeting tonight. He had been almost happy that such was the case since he could stay at home and not have to go out to some restaurant and celebrate. Being chairman of the department wasn't all that exciting for the most part.

But what the hell was on his stomach and chest? He tentatively moved one hand and heard the loud hiss in reprimanding answer. He thought it sounded like a small dog growling, only louder. It couldn't be what he thought it might be. It just wasn't possible.

His neck hurt. What was wrong there? He wanted to touch it and massage it for a moment but felt he couldn't without encouraging an attack from the thing on his chest. It couldn't be a snake, not one that large. The hooded head, as close as it was, scant inches from his face, appeared gigantic. But it couldn't be a cobra! It just couldn't be.

Of all times, why would he feel drowsy now? He fought to open his eyes but felt weak all over. Certainly that was understandable considering the situation in which he found himself. Anyone, the most powerful man or woman in the world, would get weak-kneed at a time like this. He could feel the sweat on his forehead building into drops until they started dribbling down the sides of his face. He wanted to wipe it dry but knew he couldn't. He swallowed. And swallowed again. Why was there so much saliva in his mouth? He swallowed once more only to find that his mouth still seemed full of thick mucus-like spittle.

Perhaps he could open his mouth a bit to somehow expel some of the water. He tried but his mouth wouldn't work. He wanted to scream out for someone to come and help him, to save him. He stared at the snake's hooded head that became suddenly fuzzy and out of focus. His head pounded painfully.

Al tried desperately to recall the little he knew of poisonous snake bites but found his mind befuddled with bits and scraps of information. From what he could deduce, though, he already had been bitten by the cobra on his chest.

He felt beaten, exhausted, totally weak. And still, somehow, he had to find the strength to throw the thing off him and run for help—but how?

Bea turned the last corner. In a few minutes, she'd be home. Nearing their house, she could see there were no lights, other than the one table lamp they usually left on when one or the other was out and would have to otherwise come into a darkened house. She turned into the driveway and braked the car to a halt without driving into the garage.

He had to do it. Now!

Al threw the covers back, leaping to his feet at the same time and taking the snake off guard for a split second. The cobra reacted in normal fashion, striking with a swiftness that defied description. The fangs found their mark in the man's ear, and he tried to scream, emitting only a bubbly gurgle from his saliva-filled mouth.

The reptile fell backward to the floor on the side of the bed away from the window.

Al's heart raced eratically, distributing the second dose of venom to all parts of his body. The darkened room swam in his vision as he spun about, falling first toward the bed and then toward the window as he fought to gain his balance. After several gyrations, his chest felt as if it would explode, and his arms, losing all sense of feeling, flailed about in the air. Spinning once more, he fell onto the bed, face up, foamy saliva running from his mouth. Then he quivered convulsively and died.

The snake sidled toward the window and rearing up, thrust its head through as the door to the kitchen opened and closed. Without hurrying because it had heard nothing, the snake oozed back outside, and just as the bedroom door opened and the light turned on, its tail slid through the window opening.

Bea Stewart took in the sight before her and, fighting the urge to scream, rushed to the side of her husband. Groping desperately for a pulse, she found none. She stared at his twisted face, held in a frozen mask of terror. What had happened? What had caused her husband to die with such a look of fright and horror carved on his face? Why had he died? His heart was good. What else could have killed him?

Then she heard it—just a slight rustling outside the bedroom window. Without thinking, she ran to it, pulling the curtains apart. Throwing the window wide open, she peered out. Nothing. She could see nothing. Then, for just a split second, in the light from the bedroom window, she saw what appeared to be a bare foot disappear around the corner of the house. The sound of running feet padded through the quiet, and Beatrice Stewart stared into the darkness of the night.

# 5

Archer stretched slowly, moving in such a way as to avoid awakening Nita. She had no classes until late morning, and although she had not expressed a desire to sleep in for a change, he decided it would be good for her. She needed her rest. In less than two weeks, she would be competing in the Inaugural Middleton University Mini-Triathalon for Women which was not sanctioned by the National Triathalon Association, because of its irregular sequence of events. Certainly he didn't want to be the one blamed for her not getting enough rest in the event she didn't compete well.

Nita's stamina and athletic prowess amazed him. He liked to play a game of basketball or work out on weights every now and then, just to keep his body tuned, but the way in which Nita attacked a project involving her

body or some degree of athletic ability almost
seemed to unnerve him. Her dedication coupled
with her overall physical condition and abilities
bordered on a fanaticism that he could understand only when he thought of it in terms of his
own dedication to his teaching or any other
work involving biology.

After showering and dressing, Archer
closed the door to the apartment without a
sound and walked in quick, energetic strides
the few blocks to the campus. The late
September morning air, brisk, clean and crisp,
invigorated him. Ten minutes later, he bounded
up the steps to the John Thomas Science
Building.

When he had unlocked the door to his lab
and stepped in, he was unmindful of the
attendant odors that had accumulated over-
night and to which he became so accustomed.
The room temperature, maintained at 74
degrees Fahrenheit for the benefit of the
snakes, differed greatly from the fresh outdoors
air. He walked to the windows, opening the
blinds to let in the early morning sunlight, then
he checked the cages of the king cobras.

The two older snakes reared up, their
tongues slithering in and out as they read the
scent of the man through the air holes of their
plastic cages. Both hissed loudly, and Archer
thanked science for the advent of plastic. When
he turned to check the third case, he froze. The
latch hung loose, and the door stood open half
an inch. With a good nudge from inside, the

youngest of the three reptiles could be free in a second. Reaching out, he stopped when the colorful snake hissed loudly and glided toward the door. Did the animal know it was within hair's-breadth of freedom?

Archer didn't hesitate any longer and, his hand flashing out, slammed the door and fixed the lock in place just as the cobra struck out. The sound of the snake's nose striking the plastic door sent a chill down Archer's spine. A few drops of venom trickled down the inside of the door. Stepping back, he became aware of a heavy film of sweat clinging to his face, arms and body. He gulped several deep breaths and leaned against the sill of the window, letting the warmth of the morning sun relax him.

Once he had recovered, he went to his desk and pulled out the journal he had started the day the snakes had arrived. After making an entry about the unlatched cage, he chewed on the tip of his ballpoint pen. How had the lock been left open? Who could have done something that stupid? Had it been him? No—of that he was most positive. Archer Buchanan was a creature of habits but precise controlled habits. If he felt he might not have checked on the cage doors before leaving last night, he would have purposefully gone back to that end of the room and double-checked to be on the safe side. More than likely, he would never know just how the door had become unlocked and left ajar, but in the future he would make certain that the doors were secured. Maybe he even should have another type of lock made up for the three cages.

The door of his lab burst open and Richard Roman charged in, his face white, his hands trembling.

"Have you heard?"

Archer looked up, startled by Richard's sudden entry. The man looked positively scared to the brink of death. "Heard? Heard what?"

"Al's dead. Al Stewart died last night."

The words registered, but in such a way that Archer thought he might have misinterpreted the few words Richard Roman had just spoken. "What? What did you say?"

"You heard me. Al's dead. His wife came home last night and found him on the bed. My God! What could have happened?"

Archer stood slowly, deliberately. He moved around the desk until he was opposite Richard who had plopped into a chair. Leaning back on his desk top, he stared at the man. "What happened?"

Richard shrugged. "I have no idea. Not a clue."

"Al was in good health, wasn't he? He never once said anything to me that hinted at any health problem."

Richard wiped his face with one hand. "As far as I know, he was in excellent health."

"What then? What could have been the cause of death?" Archer felt as if someone had punched him in the stomach.

"I suppose it could have been his heart.

Things like that happen, don't they, Archer?"

Archer studied Richard. He was groping for an answer, searching for a logical explanation that would suit his own scientific background. There was no way either man would be satisfied to accept it as just a natural death without cause. They wanted to know the reason.

"I suppose," Archer said after several minutes of silence, "there'll be an autopsy. There usually is when the cause of death isn't apparent."

"Yes, I . . . I never thought of that. Of course, you're right, Archer. My God! It's frightening. He was so healthy yesterday at the election. That was a stupid thing to say," Richard said before Archer could comment.

"I know what you mean, Richard. I guess something like this points out just how insecure life really is and that our futures at best are tentative and dependent on someone else's whims."

"What do you mean by that?" Richard stared at Archer in a peculiar way, his mouth twitching slightly.

"God. God really controls all of us, whether we like to admit it or not."

"God? Hah! I prefer to think of it as fate—kismet, if you will."

"Call it what you will, Richard, but a rose by any other name is still a rose. You call it fate and I'll call it God, and we can both soothe our conscience to the best of our ability with our own interpretations. But you know that basically I'm right."

Richard shrugged and stood. "Well, I've got to get going. I'm to meet with the Dean of Academics and find out what the department is to do now that the chairmanship is vacant again." He hurried to the door and left.

Archer pursed his lips as he thought about something he felt positive Richard Roman had been thinking about as well. Who would be the next chairman and, if it were Richard, who would go to India next year? Would the overall plan be in any jeopardy? Would his work with the king cobra be affected somehow?

The closed casket funeral and cremation was delayed by two days while an autopsy was performed. Bea Stewart, still in shock, attended both services and appeared to be in full control. Her two sisters had flown into San Carlos to be with her, and flanked by them, the widow managed to complete the awful ordeal of bidding a final farewell to her husband.

Two days after the funeral, Archer sat on his desk, making the latest entry in his journal when a knock sounded softly at the door. Turning in his chair, he looked up to see two men peering through the door window. He motioned for them to come in, even though he recognized neither.

"Doctor Buchanan?" the shorter of the two men said, entering the lab and crossing the short distance between them, his hand extended.

"I'm Archer Buchanan, but you have the wrong title. I'm just an associate professor."

"What do I call you then?" the man asked.

"How about Archer?"

"Fine," he said, flashing a toothy grin. "I'm Tony Alexander. Detective Sergeant Tony Alexander of the San Carlos Police Department. This is Detective Paul Adams. We'd like to ask you a few questions."

Archer's face screwed up. "About?"

"Among other things about the snakes you have here, as well as a few questions about Alfred Stewart. You knew him, didn't you?"

"Of course, I knew him. He worked with me. He was chairman of the department."

"I'd—"

"What do the snakes have to do with anything?" Archer broke in, realizing for the first time what the man had said.

"I'd like to see them. Where are they kept?"

Archer motioned for the two men to follow him and walked to the back of the room. "Right here. Why?"

The policemen stopped short of getting too close to the tables where the plastic cages sat. "Those are king cobras?" Alexander asked.

The three reptiles as one reared, striking out toward the strangers and bumping their noses on the plastic walls.

"How did you know that?"

"Richard Roman told us. You see, we've got a bit of a mystery on our hands."

"Mystery?" Archer looked intently at the spokesman of the duo and then at the other officer.

"It seems Alfred Stewart died of a massive dose of king cobra venom. We've already checked with the zoo, and they don't have any king cobras. In fact, your king cobras are the only ones for quite a distance around San Carlos. Now, you know why we're here."

Archer sat back on one of the lab tables. "What the hell are you saying? That one of these snakes got out of here, went over to Al's house and killed him? Then came back here and got back into its cage?" Archer mentally froze for a moment. *The unlocked cage.*

Alexander shrugged. "You tell us, Archer. We've got very little to go on. Anything you can tell us will be greatly appreciated."

"Such as?"

"Well, Doc Laffler, the medical examiner, said it would have to have been one big snake to pump all that venom into Stewart."

"How big did he say? Or how much venom?"

Alexander pulled out a notebook and flipped through it. Running a finger down one page, he said, "According to Doc, his computer estimated that the amount of venom isolated in the sample of blood he took would project out to about eight or nine hundred milligrams of dried venom."

Archer's face paled. "Are you kidding?"

Alexander looked up. "What's the matter, Archer?"

"That's preposterous. No one snake could produce that much venom at one time."

"That's the amount the M.E. came up with. Why is it preposterous?"

Archer stood, moving closer to the cages. "These three snakes here are pretty average in size. Each one is about eleven to twelve feet or so in length. They can produce about five hundred milligrams of dried venom at the maximum. You're saying that this Doctor Laffler found evidence of almost double that amount. Do you realize that would conceiveably mean a king cobra over eighteen to twenty feet in length. The longest one ever measured was nineteen feet, three inches. Are you certain this doctor is on the level?"

Alexander nodded.

The door to the lab opened and Richard Roman entered, a sly grin on his face. "Did they tell you, Archer?"

Bewildered by the man's attitude, Archer looked at Richard.

"Did they tell you what the medical examiner found?"

Archer nodded. How did the police come to approach Richard first? Was he already passing himself off as the new chairman of the department?

As if reading his mind, Richard said, "The switchboard referred the officers to me first. I guess—"

Archer turned to Alexander, breaking into Richard's explanation. "Did the examiner say anything else about the venom, the size of the snake or anything else?"

"Such as?" Alexander tried hiding the little smile he flashed at Archer, when he repeated the biologist's terse question of a few minutes before.

"Like how many times he had been bitten or anything else."

Again Alexander referred to his notebook. "He was bitten twice—once in the neck and once on the ear."

"Anything about the symptoms of cobra-ism?"

"According to Doc Laffler, all the visible, ready symptoms of the venom's presence in the body were there." He paused while turning the page of his book. "Excessive saliva in the mouth, localized edema, whatever that is, localized discoloration of the skin accompanied with blisters, localized necrosis. And apparently there was evidence that he was convulsing shortly before he died."

"Those are all classic symptoms, all right. Right, Richard?" Archer turned to Richard who quietly nodded.

"To answer your question, Sergeant," Archer continued, "edema is an abnormal collection of serous or thin watery fluid."

"So, tell me then, where the hell this cobra came from if not from here?" Alexander flipped the notebook shut and put it in his coat pocket.

Archer stared at him. That was the question of the day, and he again recalled the unlocked cage. How had that happened? Still, it couldn't have any connection since the cobra was still inside when he had arrived that morning. There was no way anyone could ever convince him that that particular snake had been out of the cage, gotten back in and let the door stand open a mere inch. It would have been completely impossible for the snake to have gotten back in through such a small opening. The snake itself was between two and two and a half inches in diameter. No, that was out of the question and he would simply file it away with other information for the time being. There was no reason to alarm anyone or bring his experiments under some sort of suspicion.

When the door to the lab opened again, everyone in the room turned to see the imposing figure of Lal Khan Bahadur filling the doorway.

"Do come in, Doctor Bahadur," Archer said, standing and motioning for the swarthy man to enter.

Striding across the room, he extended his hand to Archer. "Good morning, Mr. Buchanan." He peered at Richard, curtly nodding in his direction, and then turned his attention to the two policemen.

After Archer introduced them, he said, "Why not ask Doctor Bahadur about the things we were discussing, Sergeant." Alexander repeated the facts as he had learned them from the medical examiner and waited for the Indian's reaction.

Bahadur stocially waited after the Sergeant finished, apparently digesting the bits and pieces of information. Then, he said, "That, gentlemen, is quite a story. Of course, I do not doubt your word or integrity or abilities as observers, but what you are saying is quite fanciful at best." He turned to Archer. "Have you accumulated much venom thus far?"

Archer's face reacted to the question with an immediate grimace. How could he have forgotten? Of course, the venom that he was accumulating to conduct his experiments might have been tampered with and stolen. What if someone killed—murdered—Al Stewart with his collection of venom?

Noting Archer's consternation, Alexander said. "What's he talking about?"

"Have you checked it, Archer?" Bahadur asked.

Richard looked, first at Archer, then at Bahadur and the policeman before narrowing his eyes at Archer. "Well, Archer?"

"No, I didn't think about it. Come on, we can all check on it together." He moved to the front of the room where his desk projected at an angle against one wall. Behind his desk and to one side, a small locked refrigerator stood almost unnoticed. Pulling out his key, he unlocked the small cabinet and opened it. "There you are, gentlemen." He picked up a rack holding several vials of pale yellow liquid. "All I've accumulated so far is about six hundred milligrams, total, and you'll notice it's all here." He looked up into the face of each man surrounding him. Placing the container of vials

back in the cool interior, he closed and locked
the refrigerator.

"I didn't mean to sound accusatory,
Archer," Alexander said, "but I've got to touch
every base on this thing. It's pretty scary having
someone die of cobra venom right here in San
Carlos and not have a clue as to how it
happened."

Archer waved the lame apology aside. It
had been his own oversight to forget about the
collection of venom in the first place.

Alexander turned to Bahadur. "Tell me, sir,
what is your position here at the University?"

Bahadur, Archer and Richard explained the
essence of the exchange program.

"Have you ever heard of a king cobra being
large enough to kill a bull elephant?" Alexander
looked first at Bahadur then at Archer.

Archer studied the detective. He couldn't
have been much over 31. Boyishly handsome,
his straight blond hair was combed neatly and
his suit pressed and cleaned. He could have
been an accountant or an insurance salesman.
The last thing anyone would have suspected
him of being was a policeman.

Before Bahadur could answer, Archer said,
"Where did you come up with that idea?"

"Doc Laffler said the amount of the venom
could probably have killed a bull elephant. I'm
just curious to know if he was using an
expression or if it's really possible."

Bahadur smiled. "As a matter of fact, yes.
There have been reports from various provinces

in my homeland about king cobras. As far as killing a bull elephant is concerned, it happens quite regularly. One timber company loses two to three tuskers a year. It takes quite some time, about three hours, because of the pachyderm's bulk, but it is possible for a king cobra to kill such an animal. Why?"

"Well, according to Doc, the amount in Stewart's body was enough to have killed a bull elephant. That's all."

"If that's the case, Doctor Stewart would have died rather quickly. The normal span of time if left untreated would be much less than an hour, regardless of the build of the person bitten or how they reacted to the bite."

"Reacted to the bite? I don't understand," Alexander said.

"Normally, if the person lies quietly and is calm, the venom does not spread as fast as it would if the victim jumped around or ran about in panic. Do you understand? But with cobra venom . . ."

He nodded. "So how long, assuming the Doc's figures are right, did it take Stewart to die?"

"If his body had the equivilant of eight to nine hundred milligrams of dried venom, I would say perhaps ten to twelve, certainly no more than fifteen minutes."

Alexander shook his head. "Have there been any reports from the campus police about prowlers or break-ins on campus anyplace?"

"Why?" Archer coughed after asking the

one word question. He was as mystified as the
police, but for some reason he felt that
Bahadur's unflappable manner was almost
rehearsed. He hadn't yet decided if he liked this
foreigner. There were those visitors who had
proven to be most genteel and kind as well as
interesting, but then, too, there had been those
who had bad-mouthed the United States while
taking from the federal government. Those
hypocrites he had written off as unworthy of
attention. Where did Bahadur fall? Into which
category would Archer windup putting him?

"I thought perhaps someone might have
broken in here and messed around with the
snakes or venom or something."

Archer shook his head. "No. There've been
no break-ins here. You saw me unlock the
refrigerator where the venom is kept, and I have
the only keys. With the campus police and the
locks and all, someone would have to be pretty
darn clever to get in and out without leaving
some sort of trace." Archer's brow knitted
involuntarily when he again thought of the unlocked cobra cage. How *had* that happened?

Alexander handed each man a card with his
name and telephone number on it. "If you think
of anything or hear of anything that might help
our investigation, please don't hesitate to call."

Assured that they would, the young
policeman left with his partner following.

When they were alone, Archer looked at
Bahadur and then at Richard. How could he not
imagine that his experiments and the whole

exchange program might not be in trouble? With Al dead, Richard was the logical choice to be the new chairman, but Richard also was the candidate to go to India next year. If he knew Richard Roman, he would choose to be head of the department. What would happen then to the exchange? Who would go in Richard's place?

"I've already been to the Dean of Academics, Archer. He wants you to consider going to India in my place next year in the event I'm elected chairman."

"But what about my experiments with the cobras?" Archer glared at Richard for having been so damned efficient in his dealings with the Dean.

"You'll just have to postpone them for however long it takes." Richard smiled.

Archer turned to Bahadur. "What do you think?"

"I'm afraid I have no say in it, however I do know that my government expects someone in exchange for my stay here. You may have to forego your experiments for a while, Archer."

"What about the cobras?"

"Things such as that can be worked out, my friend." Bahadur smiled, his white teeth contrasting sharply with the dark, oily complexion of his facial skin.

Perhaps he and Nita could turn the situation into a honeymoon. Why not? If he had no choice but to abandon the experiments for the time being and go to India for a year, he and Nita should make it a honeymoon. They'd be foolish not to take advantage of the situation, but he would have to time everything precisely or run the risk of arousing Nita's anger. Her temper could get out of hand at times though she usually managed to control it.

At least he could continue his work with the cobras until next spring and possibly could make much headway by then. By then, he and Nita could have made all the arrangements for their wedding and yearlong honeymoon in far-off India.

That Saturday, after the Middleton "Smugglers" won their homecoming football game 53-0, Archer and Nita attended a faculty party at the Hiram Pins Lounge on campus. Archer still had not had the opportunity to broach the subject of a spring wedding and Indian honeymoon to Nita, but he hoped that once they got home that night, he would have the chance.

The talk at the party centered on the victory and the relative success of those former students who had returned for the weekend.

"Why don't we cut out of this place," Archer said quietly in Nita's ear.

"Not a bad idea. What've you got in mind?"

"Oh, a little conversation about something that involves both of us. Something that's pretty import—"

"Well, hello there, you two."

Archer and Nita turned as one to face a slightly inebriated Richard Roman. Archer glanced at Nita and smiled.

"Has Archer told you about the big change?"

Archer shot a quick look at Richard. He couldn't tell Nita—not now. He was going to tell her himself within fifteen minutes. He had the scenario all worked out.

"Told me what?" Nita asked, turning to Archer, a quizzical look on her face.

"Why, about his going to India?"

"What?"

"Well, my dear, you see, since Al is dead and the chairmanship is up for grabs and I'm the logical choice, as head of the department I won't be able to go to India. Archer's going in my place. Isn't that nice?" Richard drained his glass, a silly grin pasted on his face.

"I . . . I don't know what to say," Nita gasped. "I really don't." She turned to face Archer. "Perhaps you can tell me what to say under the circumstances. I thought we let each other in on every plan, every move, every career opportunity. What's this all about?" Her voice, suddenly cold, carried an edge of hysteria.

"I think we'd better go." Archer took her arm and started for the door. Surprised that she allowed him to lead her out, he took full advantage and beat a hasty retreat to the door, calling over his shoulder to Richard, "Thanks a whole lot, Richard."


"You had no right not to tell me, Archer,"

Nita said for what seemed like the hundredth time since they arrived at their apartment.

"I was trying to put everything together so that when I told you I'd have everything planned out in advance. You know, no loop holes or anything that wouldn't fit when we did talk about it. I wanted it to be perfect. I . . . I'm sorry."

"You wanted what to be perfect?"

At last he'd have the chance to explain it all to her. "I wanted to ask you to marry me and make the trip to India our honeymoon. It could have been absolutely perfect, but that stupid Richard had to spill the beans."

"There's one way that the trip might not take place." She grinned slyly.

"How's that?"

"If you were elected to the chair instead of Richard. Then, he'd have to go."

Archer shook is head. "I'm afraid it would be a bit obvious if I told everyone I was suddenly interested in the chairmanship now. I've told everyone the experiments were uppermost in importance to me, that they should vote for Al or Richard. Hell, I didn't care, but I certainly hadn't counted on Al dying."

"I guess you're right. When's the next election?"

"Week from Monday."

"The Monday after the triathalon?"

Archer nodded.

"Well, it'll take some time for me to think about getting married and going to India for a year." Nita smiled at him and threw her arms around his neck. "Look, Archer, I care for you deeply and I know that you care for me. Somehow, things will work out. They always do."

Without another word, he led her to the bedroom. After slipping between the sheets, they held each other and drifted off to sleep.

Shortly after closing her eyes, Nita dreamed of the gyrating shapes and shadows. The writhing dancers came into view, their bodies slick with sweat. For some reason she knew she wasn't with the dancers this time. She was watching them do something that seemed impossible. They were dancing on the walls on either side of her. She could just barely move her head enough to see on either side and make out the dancers bouncing and jostling up and down the walls. Then she slowly realized that the people dancing wildly about her were doing so normally but that she was lying down. She tried to move but couldn't. She was tied. Why was she tied down? She had to get away. Something dreadful was going to happen to her. But what? She had to get away before it happened. Struggling with all her might she tried to break loose but failed. Opening her mouth, she screamed.

Archer shot up in bed, turning on the nightstand light in the same movement. "What's the matter?"

Nita screamed again, writhing about on the bed, her arms pinned down to her sides by the sheet.

"Hey, Nita, wake up. Come on. What's the matter? Are you dreaming?"

She opened her eyes, looking from side to side, half-expecting to see the dancers but finding only Archer peering down at her. "What happened?"

"You tell me. I was sleeping soundly when all of a sudden you let out this ear-splitting scream. What's wrong? Bad dream?"

Freeing her arms, she sat up, unmindful of the sheet falling away to expose her breasts. Running her fingers through her hair, she yawned. "Something like that, I guess."

"Want to talk about it?"

Yawning again, she said, "I suppose. Maybe it'll go away then, if I do."

"Sounds like you've had it before. Have you?"

She nodded and told him of the dream dancers, shadows and shapes that wiggled through her sleeping mind. "You know, Archer," she said finishing, "somehow the dream seems familiar to me."

"You mean because you've had it before?"

"No. It's as if I'm remembering it, as if whatever it is that I'm dreaming, I've experienced."

Archer stifled a yawn and said, "That's pretty wild. Where've you been where they dance like that? For that matter, what else are they doing that you haven't told me? Anything?"

"No, it's pretty much the way I told it. At

first, when I had the dream, all I saw were the
shadows and shapes. Then, I was one of the
dancers. This time, I dreamed I was tied up and
couldn't move."

Archer grinned. "Tune in next week, folks
for the continuing saga of *Nita's Nightmares*."

Nita laughed but had to force it. "I'm sure
it's nothing."

Archer lay back on the bed. "Come on. Let's
get to sleep. I want to get up and go to early
Mass tomorrow." He turned out the light.

"I can see it now," she said lightly. "Saint
Archer the first."

"Want to go with me?"

"You know how I feel about religion and
such. Too much of it as a child and that was
enough. At least for now."

"Okay, you heathen, sleep well. Remember,
I love you."

"I love you too, Archer." She lay down next
to him and moved closer until their arms
touched. When Archer turned to face her, he put
one arm over her but she didn't move. In
seconds, Archer had fallen back to sleep and
Nita stared into the darkness.

What could the dream mean? Didn't all
dreams have meanings of some sort? If they
did, what did hers mean? She'd think about it
until it made sense. Perhaps she could talk with
someone and have the dream explained to her,
one of those people who knew how to analyze
dreams. Her eyes grew sandy and her lids
drooped. It had a meaning, but right now, she

was too tired to think about it anymore. Her breasts and chest rose and fell evenly as she dropped off to sleep.

# 6

Nita looked up to see the rump of the biker in front of her pumping up and down, not unlike the drive rods of a two cylinder motor. There was no opening. At least for now, there was no opening. She'd have to bide her time, wait for some of them to fall back, wait for her chance to move up in the pack of women bicyclists.

For the most part, she felt good. Her body didn't seem the least bit tired—yet. They had traveled about 20 of the 25 mile course, and her legs felt strong. That was one advantage of having "thunder thighs." She had developed lots of muscle that could propel a bike weighing only a few pounds. The next part of the race would be the most telling—the running race, 15 kilometers. She instantly changed her mind. Focus on the bicycle race. It was 25 miles of relatively smooth roadways with a few hills.

Without the hills, where would the challenge lie? There naturally had to be hills. They would separate the wheat from the chaff.

Suddenly, she saw an opening in front of her, and she shot through, passing at least seven women who had hesitated just long enough for Nita to make her move. Now was the time for a quick spurt, to leave some of them behind and concentrate on the riders in front of her. They were the enemy. They were the ones who had to be overtaken. If she didn't, she'd be nothing but an also-ran, and she couldn't live with that. Being an also-ran would not be acceptable to her standards. Failing to get her proper rest and sleep would be equally distasteful. And that she had done.

For the past week, since Homecoming Weekend, when Richard Roman had mentioned the fact that Archer might be going to India, she had not slept well. That stupid dream had not helped either, and it had occurred almost every night. Each time, something new was added. It was almost like watching a soap opera, waiting each day for a new miniscule piece of information. She didn't know which of the two had affected her ability to sleep, but she had not rested well, and since making her spurt past six or seven bikers to gain a position by herself for the time being, her legs were beginning to feel heavy. That shouldn't be. Her legs should simply work, do their job, propel the bicycle as fast as they could. If they were beginning to pain now, what would happen in the marathon. Forget the swim. Three miles and

almost 1200 yards would kill her if her legs were
beginning to hurt now. She'd never finish the
marathon. Forget it. She'd goofed pretty badly
to be hurting so soon.

Then she surged forward when she saw the
leaders, a pack of six bikes bunched together.
Her legs were forgotten, virtually working on
their own. They were on a slight decline, and the
leaders were resting, coasting down the hill.
She understood that reasoning. Stay with the
leader for now and don't wear the body out this
far from the finish line. There was too much to
be done this day so don't panic. Take it easy.

To hell with it! Nita pumped furiously down
the small hill, catching up to the leaders in less
than half a minute. Luckily for her, the drafting
rule had been set aside for this contest. Falling
in behind the last biker, she took advantage of
the situation and could feel her bike being
drawn along behind the rest. Great! She continued pumping but not as vigorously as those
in front. They were helping her rest now and still
keep her within striking distance of the lead.

She watched for the next mileage marker.
Within the next thirty seconds, she saw the
large two—two miles to go. That wasn't so bad.
She'd be able to make it without too much
effort, but she knew she'd be in a race with the
other six bikes in front of her when they got
within half a mile or so of the finish.

Where was Archer? He said he'd be at the
finish line of each portion of the triathalon.
That meant she'd be seeing him in minutes.
Thinking of Archer, she again wondered why he

hadn't mentioned the possibility of going to India. That made her angry every time she thought about it. She did believe him when he told her that he would like to make it a yearlong honeymoon, but why did she have such strong feelings for India? She felt fear and trepidation, intimidation and a sort of subdued anger whenever she thought of India and the possibility of going there for a whole year. Why did she have such a grab bag of emotions concerning it? Had something happened there? Possibly. But what? They had lived there for about four years when she was very small, but she remembered hardly anything about it. There were isolated flashes of memory that would accompany her reeling emotions whenever she thought of that country, but they were usually gone before she could zero in on one long enough to steady it.

If her parents hadn't died, she could ask them if something had happened to leave such a scar on her. But what could have happened? What? And why had her parents died?

When the roar of the crowd seared through her mind, she snapped out of her funk, finding the other bikers pulling away from her. Pumping frantically, she caught up to the sixth woman, easily passing her and heading for the fifth, whom she also passed without too much effort. When she tried overtaking the fourth one, it seemed as though the tall blonde had read Nita's mind and increased her own speed.

Determined, Nita lowered her head and pumped. Her thunder thighs would have to take

over. Keeping one eye on the rear end of the
blonde who was just to her right, she concentrated on her own legs. One! Two! One, two!
One, two, one, two, one, two! She sailed past the
fourth woman but was too far behind to
improve her position as the cluster of three
women headed across the finish line one or two
seconds ahead of Nita. Nita flashed across the
line, braking to a halt as soon as she could.

"Nita!"

She heard Archer call and looked around.
When she saw him coming toward her, his
pewter hair standing out in the crowd, she
stopped. Throwing one leg over the bike, she
walked the vehicle to the transition area and
put on her running shoes after disposing of her
bike. The start of the marathon run was close by
and she saw the women who had finished ahead
of her running in that direction.

"Gotta go," she cried to Archer, waving as
she ran toward the roadway.

Calling on totally different muscles now
that the run was well underway, Nita concentrated on her rhythm. Her arms, operating
like eccentrics on a steam engine, countered
the effort made by her legs, giving her body
momentum as she made each step, each stride,
each effort to move ahead. With the foot race
half over, she wondered how many were ahead
of her. There were those athletes who entered a
competition such as this because they were
good on the bicycle or in the running race or in
the swimming event. That type of athlete

usually burned out if they spent too much energy on their own speciality. Shortly after starting the second part, Nita had still been in fourth place, the same position she had held at the end of the bicycle race. Then a bunch came onto her, quickly passing her. She had recognized three of the women as swimmers, who were obviously having difficulty in pacing themselves. By the time they reached Lake Helpen at the end the Schuster Road running course, the swimmers would have worn themselves out.

As best as Nita could estimate, she was probably in seventh or eighth place, which wasn't bad. If she had to put a finger on one of the three portions of the triathalon and say which was her strong point, she felt she'd be hard pressed. She felt she was equal in all three without being overly strong in any one. In the end that might prove to be her salvation. She wouldn't wear herself out in any one part and would try to be strong in all three.

She'd like to do well and be invited to other such events, perhaps making it to TV some day. Something like that went with the territory and in itself was a lousy excuse to compete. At 28, she felt her physical condition was her strongest point, not her ability to outrun or outride or outswim the competition.

She took a cup of water from a man standing alongside the road, dumping it over her head. If felt good. The sun steadily climbed towards its zenith, and she estimated the time to be somewhere around 11:00. A woman moved closer to the edge of the road, holding out another cup of water. This time, Nita took a quick sip and splashed the rest over her head and shoulders.

Up ahead, she saw one of the women who had passed her a while back, sitting on the shoulder of the road, vigorously rubbing her left calf. Cramps. Nita mentally shuddered and passed the downed runner.

Her change over to running had been abrupt, and she felt bad that there hadn't been time to say something to Archer but knew he understood. Why hadn't he tried to fully understand her? Why hadn't he told her right away about the possibility of going to India? She had accepted his explanation that he wanted to think about asking her to marry him. That would have accelerated their plans by several years. They had talked of marriage, and she knew that one day they would undoubtedly be husband and wife.

Would they be happy in India? Why didn't she like the idea of going to that country? Had something happened there to make her dislike it so intensely? Her father had given up his missionary duties about that time. Had she picked up his unhappiness over something that might have happened there? What was in India that had so affected Nita Galforth at the age of six to make her feel so strongly about not wanting to go there at age 28? Was something evil there? Something evil waiting for her?

Nita spurred herself forward. Using her aroused anger as a force, she pictured something evil and ugly behind her, running after her and trying to catch her. Her body, reacting to the shot of adrenalin that coursed through her veins, moved ahead as though running fresh instead of having covered almost ten miles.

Rounding a bend, she saw the leaders several hundred yards ahead. From her own rhythm and by watching the strides of the runners ahead, she knew she was gaining. Was that group the leaders? She counted. There were five women. She had passed one who had dropped out. That meant, since she had started in fourth place, and three had passed her, she must be in sixth position and all the leaders were right ahead of her and she was gaining on them.

Checking her strides to prevent herself from burning out, Nita settled into a graceful run, matching the leaders, step for step, trying to measure hers to be a bit longer than the longest of those ahead.

She felt good; she felt strong. She also felt the anger about Archer's reluctance to tell her and the strong emotions brought on by thinking about India. Perhaps it was best that she did feel the way she did, especially if she turned it to her own advantage during the triathalon. She had hoped to be closer to the lead at the end of the foot race since she was not a swift swimmer. A powerful swimmer, yes, but not that fast. She had promised herself to try to stay with the leaders. If she could do that, her superior conditioning might win out in the

long run if she succeeded in pushing the leader
to her limits and make her overextend or even
drop out. She didn't know if her reasoning was
sound but she thought it made good sense.

Still, here she was 50 yards behind the
leaders—another woman dropped out and Nita
shot by her—and the end of the foot race was
getting near. They had a grade to climb along a
hillside before dropping down to the lake level
and the finish of the run. Perhaps they'd lose
one or two other runners then. If that
happened, she'd be satisfied, but she would be
angry with herself if her reasoning did not pay
off. Maybe she should move up a bit and get a
little closer. She increased the length of her
stride and began gaining.

The hill loomed ahead. Halfway up, another
runner dropped out, collapsing along the side
of the road. Running in the shade of the hill
helped Nita tremendously, and she was
thankful for the people lining the road, armed
with ready cups of water. One over the head, a
sip from the next, then dump it over the head
and shoulders. She took a third, throwing it on
her neck. The cool water flowed down her chest,
over her heaving breasts only to warm and mix
with the sweat on her body. After coming across
the top of the hill, Nita started down the other
side. It was so tempting to pick up speed and
lose control of the downhill pace. She fought
that urge and in seconds was on the level,
pumping her legs toward the leaders, who were
but 15 yards or so ahead.

Nita felt strong, good, in control. There was

one final turn and then the race to the lake shore where the third and final leg of the event began. She could smell the water and sense a slight change in the air as she neared the small lake.

The evil something was gaining on her, and she renewed her effort. Ten yards separated her from the third runner. Eight yards. Seven. Six. Five. Four. They crossed the line.

She was still running fourth—not bad—but could she possibly improve on it in the swimming competition?

"Nita! Over here!" Archer called, waving to her from the side of the portable dressing tent.

She rushed over to him, grabbing the towel he offered as she entered the tent.

The water felt cool and refreshing. She was thankful they saved the swim until the end, even though it should have been the first event. If she finished dead last, the swim would revive her no matter how exhausted she might be, and she would still feel alive and fresh. She was in fourth place, and concentrating on her arm strokes and kicks, she had no idea if she were moving ahead, gaining or falling behind. She thought the three women ahead of her were not spectacular swimmers. Most of the others had dropped out or were someplace behind her. That was good. If the women in front of her were not known for their swimming abilities, she might still stand a chance. She continued, scissoring her legs even faster. Still, her anger bubbled beneath the surface of her conscious-

ness that controlled her body and its swimming
motions. Fourth. Would she be satisfied with
fourth? How could she be? Winning was what
counted. Fourth? She wouldn't be able to face
herself in a mirror, much less Archer or anyone
else she knew.

Her mind blacked out the competition and
erased all thoughts of Archer. Her body felt as if
it stopped functioning all together. She felt constricted for some unknown reason. What was
happening to her? Was she suffering a painful
cramp? What would happen if she were? She
tried to recall the last time she had had a cramp
but couldn't. Her condition almost precluded
the possibility, but now, she wasn't aware if she
were suffering a cramp or drowning. Drowning?
Could she be drowning? Her mind felt too alert.
If she were in trouble, the helicopter overhead
would notify one of the nearby chase boats that
she was having difficulty in moving.

She closed her eyes and waited to see what
would happen next.


"This is Airspotter One to Chase Boat One."

"Chase Boat One to Airspotter One. Go
ahead."

"I've lost visual contact with one of the
swimmers. I don't know if she went under or
what might have happened. She was closest to
swimmer three where Boat Two is about twenty
feet or so away. Have Boat Two check on her.
She was about forty feet back."

"Airspotter One, this is Chase Boat One. We
read you. Chase Boat Two, do you see the fourth

swimmer any place?"

"We heard Airspotter One's report. We're checking on it now."

Chase Boat Two moved away from the third swimmer, toward the place the helicopter crew last saw the fourth swimmer.

"Chase Boat One, this is Airspotter One. The glare of the sun on the water is preventing me from adequately looking for the missing swimmer. I am, however, seeing something, but I don't think it's the swimmer. It looks more like a long piece of rope in the water. It's about twenty-five feet or so ahead of the first woman. Like I say, the glare of the sun is preventing me from seeing it adequately. Can you check it out?"

"Airspotter One, this is Chase Boat One. I read you. We'll check it out."

While Chase Boat Two looked for the missing swimmer in the place where the helicopter last saw the fourth place contestant, Chase Boat One maneuvered ahead of the swimmers to check out the piece of rope. Something like that could injure a swimmer, or a swimmer might panic, become entangled in it and go under before anyone could help.

Chase Boat One looked about the area pointed out by the chopper, and as the first three swimmers passed, the men in the boat could not see anything.

"Airspotter One, this is Chase Boat One. We haven't seen anything. Do you still see it?"

"Rodger. We see it about seventy-five yards ahead of the first swimmer now."

"Are you certain that it's the same thing?"

While the crew in the helicopter scanned the water below, searching for some indication that there might be more than one piece of rope in the area, Chase Boat One rejoined Chase Boat Two.

"Hey," one of the men standing in Boat Two cried out. "We didn't see any swimmer back there. Do you think one of us should dive and take a look?"

"Probably wouldn't hurt," one of the men from Boat One said. "Be careful of the other swimmers coming up from behind. There should be about six of them back there."

"Gotcha."

Chase Boat Two turned and headed back to the last place the helicopter crew had spotted the fourth place swimmer. One of the men slipped a tank on and went over the side.

Chase Boat One continued monitoring the first three swimmers and waited for the helicopter to call in.

"Chase Boat One, this is Airspotter One. We don't see anything at all now. The lead swimmer has about one hundred fifty yards to go before touching bottom. We'll stay in touch. We don't see any piece of rope from up here any . . , Hey, wait a minute. Jesus Christ, I don't believe it. There's a swimmer coming out of the water up ahead. I didn't see her at all. I mistook the number two swimmer for first place. I give up."

The radio on Chase Boat One went silent, and the crew continued monitoring the girls they followed.

*   *   *

The crowd roared as Nita walked from the water. What had happened? She had finished, thank God for that. At least she could hold her head up and be proud of that fact. Triathalons at best were nothing but a physical drain.

She looked up. Archer was running toward her.

"You won! Won!" he kept repeating. "Nita, you've won."

She stared at him. How could that be? She didn't even remember swimming a stroke the last 20 minutes or so. Archer smiled broadly, pride for her accomplishment written all over her face.

"How did I win?"

"Pretty handily, I'd say. The next swimmer is about forty yards off shore yet. Congratulations, Nita!"

She looked at him, confused by everything he had said. How had she won the triathalon when the last thing she remembered was being a poor fourth?

The judges approached her. Now they would disqualify her for some reason. But for what reason? She had no idea. Smiling broadly, they offered her their congratulations.

Thoroughly bewildered, Nita accepted the congratulations and the trophy. She vaguely heard the main judge saying something over the P.A. system about the first being the best and that Nita Galforth's name would be engraved on the permanent trophy as the first winner of the Middleton University Mini-

Triathalon for Women, along with her time of two hours 21 minutes and 31 seconds.

Nita looked at Archer who was beaming from ear to ear. Forget it. She had won. That's what counted. She knew she hadn't done anything wrong other than lose control of her mental faculties toward the end of the swim, but she knew that something like that was possible. She had read of athletes who were so determined on finishing a race that they would take hours to do it, subject themselves to unbelieveable and tortuous pain, seldom remembering any of it until well after the event had been over. In a way, she looked forward to the time when she would recall everything. The only thing she remembered was blacking out and feeling like she was being squeezed in a vise or something like it.

The one thing she wanted to concentrate on now was going home, showering for several weeks and sleeping for at least half a year.

Nita opened her eyes. Archer, fully dressed, was just about to open the bedroom door. Where could he be going? She tried to focus on the alarm clock but couldn't make out the fuzzy numbers.

When he realized she had awakened, he stopped, facing the bed. "I'm sorry, Nita, I didn't mean to awaken you. How's my champion feeling?"

"What time is it?"

"A little after seven."

"What day?"

"It's just Sunday. I'm going to Mass. You go back to sleep. 'Hear?"

She incoherently mumbled something and dropped back to sleep.

Archer smiled and closed the door without a sound.

Nita's eyes flew open. The slithering shapes were back. And the dancers. She could hear the soft beat of the drum weaving its hypnotic rhythm, and somewhere off in the distance she could hear the strange laughter.

She looked about, surreptiously stealing glances to either side. The dancers seemed to be gathered around something, flailing their arms about and stamping their feet on the ground in time with the drum's erratic beat. She moved closer. She had to see what they were dancing around. For some reason, she felt as if she should turn and run as fast as she could. Her legs hurt, her chest heaved, and every breath seemed to burn. Her arms pained her with an intensity that brought tears to her eyes.

When she reached the dancers, she joined them, throwing aside all caution. Moving like they did felt good. She no longer ached the way she had. She could feel the breath of the dancers, but when she turned to see who they were, the same faceless heads turned toward her.

Every now and then, she caught a glimpse of a table or dais of some sort that seemed to be the center of the dancers' activities. She moved in closer, hoping to see it better. When she reached the inside ring of dancers, her back was momentarily to the platform. When she turned, she screamed.

A small girl, tied hand and foot, her dress torn from hem to neck exposing the child's nakedness, lay on the platform.

Nita stopped dancing and stared at the bizarre sight. The girl looked from side to side, her eyes wide with fright, large tears running down either side of her face. Nita felt her own eyes welling with tears, then she swallowed the second scream that formed. She suddenly realized who the girl was. *It was she.* It was Nita lying on the table. No, it wasn't a table. It was more like . . . like an altar.

Nita wept. What was going on? Why was she, as a child, tied up and put on an altar? What was going to happen? Who were these people? She turned to look at them again and saw a man approaching the dais.

What was he carrying in his hand? Nita peered closer but couldn't make out the object. When the man stood next to the bound girl, he reached out, stroking her hair. Then without hesitating took several strands and pulled them out. The girl yelped in terror and pain.

Nita wept openly. Her own head hurt where the man had pulled the hair out. Why had he done it? Why?

Archer unlocked the apartment door and tiptoed in without making a sound. When the latch clicked into place, he breathed easier. First, he'd check on Nita to make certain she was still sleeping. She deserved her rest after the Amazonian effort she had made the previous day.

He smiled ruefully. What would the situation have been had he been the one physically and mentally exhausted? Would he have gotten up and gone to church? To Mass? He nodded. Of course he would. Such things were important to him. That was the only point of contention between Nita and himself. He felt in time she would come around to leading a more religious life, but he could also understand her feelings about organized religion and the participation she had had to undergo when she was growing up with her father as a minister. Not unlike Caesar's wife, she had to be beyond reproach. It would be awful having to grow up like that. It must have been awful for Nita. For that reason, he would not exert pressure on her now or anytime in the future. Still, he hoped and prayed every day that she would come around to his way of thinking about religion.

Pausing outside the door to the bedroom, he opened it, lifting on the knob to keep the weight off the hinges and prevent any undue noise. At first, she appeared simply to be sleeping on her back. Her breasts rose and fell in even motion, but every once in a while she sobbed, and then he saw the tears streaming down the sides of her face. He entered the room, stood over her and leaned down. She was crying, weeping quietly in her sleep. Should he awaken her? Deciding against it, he stood upright just as she opened her eyes.

Nita screamed when she saw the figure of a man standing over her.

"Hey, it's all right," Archer said soothingly, sitting on the edge of the bed.

The tears continued flowing, her breath broken every once in a while by a sob.

"What's the matter, darling?"

She peered at him, her eyes wide. "I . . . I guess I was dreaming. It was awful, Archer."

"Want to tell me about it? It might not seem so awful if you talk about it."

She looked at him, trust filling her face, and told him about the dream and how she had been having it for the last several weeks. When she finished, he held her tightly to him.

How strange that the dream kept expanding, giving more information each time she experienced it. What could that mean? He had no idea. Maybe he should suggest that she talk with someone about it. But who? She seemed content to simply let him hold her now. To whom could he refer her?

Nita trembled, and he held her more tightly.

Could something be happening to her? The dream was manifesting itself constantly. If it made her cry in the middle of sleep, it was something that should be confronted and dealt with before it grew out of proportion and control.

Archer watched Nita as she fell back to sleep. He had to do something. But what?

# 7

Archer, dressed only in his bikini briefs, stood framed in the doorway to the bathroom. "Well?"

Nita sat up in bed, stretching. "You don't give up, do you?"

"In this situation, I'd never give up. You know that."

She nodded.

"So what's it going to be? Morris or Brown?"

Shrugging, she threw one leg over the side of the bed. "I thought a lot about it last night before I went to bed. I think Father Brown."

Archer failed to conceal the smile that crossed his lips for a second. "I'm happy you've made a decision."

"I thought you might be happy, especially if it were Father Brown."

Archer sat down on the edge of the bed,

next to her. "I won't deny that I wanted you to meet Father Brown, but the thing I'm most happy about is the fact that you're going to get some help."

"Will he be willing to help a non-Catholic?"

"Sure. Why not? He's one of the chaplains for the U. He won't turn his back on anyone."

"Well, I've got lots to do today." Nita stood, grabbing her robe from the foot of the bed. "I've got to meet with a reporter from one of the news services today for an in-depth interview. I've got some stuff to do at the gym and," she added, leaning down to kiss Archer, "I've got to make an appointment with Father Brown."

Archer watched her go to the bathroom door and close it behind her. They had discussed the dream yesterday until they both were tired of talking about it. Both had agreed that there must be some rational explanation and that Nita should seek out some sort of professional expert who could give it. The one thing they also had agreed on was the time involved. They didn't want a long, drawn out situation and felt that they might find the best solution right there on campus.

"What about Doctor Morris?" Archer had asked.

"Who's he?"

"Sterling Morris? Head of the psychology department. He maintains a small practice and is quite good from what I've heard."

"But I thought we didn't want to drag it out. Wouldn't someone like him want to go through every little step? It could take ages."

Archer frowned. "What about religious help?"

Nita jumped to her feet. "Why religious? How could someone like that do something for me?"

"Hey, take it easy. It was only a suggestion. I know you're not that keen on religion and what have you. I'm sorry I mentioned it."

"Who did you have in mind?"

Archer looked at her. It was just like her to refuse and then turn around and want to know more. "Father Roland Brown. He's the Roman Catholic chaplin here at the U."

Nita cocked an eyebrow. "You trying to swing me over to your side?"

Archer smiled. "Someday, maybe, when you're ready. But the reason is simple. You need someone to talk with, someone who can calm your anxiety about this dream. I don't know that much about dreams and such, but I do know that one simply doesn't dream on the installment plan over a long period of time. I'm sure they don't work that way."

"I know what you mean, but can this priest really help me? Is he trained in stuff like this?"

Archer shrugged. "I don't know if he's trained in the field of dreams. More than likely, he's not. He is—"

Nita interrupted him. "Then why go to him?"

"He is trained to talk with people and help them through moments of crisis. Wouldn't you define your—our—situation as a sort of crisis?"

"I guess so."

"All I want is for you to be at ease about this thing."

"It doesn't bother me that much."

"That's easy to say, but when I come home and find you weeping in your sleep and sobbing . . . well, it's getting to you whether you want to admit it or not."

"Archer?" She turned, her green eyes unblinkingly fixed on him.

"What?"

"You don't think I'm crazy, do you?"

"Of course not." He moved to her side, embracing her.

She snuggled in closer to him, sighing deeply.

"Will you do whatever Father Brown suggests?"

"What's that supposed to mean?"

"What if he recommends you visit with a psychiatrist or something. Will you do it?"

"I . . . I don't know. Maybe."

"We both know you're physically sound. You passed your physical with honors. You won the triathalon without too much trouble. What else do you have to worry about? Other than me?" He forced a laugh and stopped when she didn't pick up on his attempt at humor.

"What about the blackouts?"

"If they were a problem, the doctors would have said something. Wouldn't they?"

Nita shook her head. Her voice cracked when she said, "I . . . I don't know."

Archer grabbed her by the shoulders, turning her to him. "What's happened?"

"I . . . I . . ." Nita coughed, clearing her throat. "During the swimming portion of the triathalon, I think I blacked out."

"What? That's impossible. You won. You came from behind to win. Besides, the chase boats or the helicopter would have seen you, wouldn't they?"

She shrugged. "All I know is I don't remember anything from the time I was well back in the race, fourth place, I guess, until I was walking out of the water."

Archer studied her for a long, intense moment. "What happened? Tell me everything."

"That's just it. There isn't anything to tell. I was swimming along. I was sort of angry with myself for not being closer to the lead, but I kept up my pace. I wasn't about to panic and blow my energy on a quick spurt. The only hope I had of winning at that time, was the possibility of the three swimmers in front of me dropping out. They didn't, as you well know. I . . . I think I went under the surface."

"Did you stop swimming?"

A puzzled look crossed her oval face, mixing with her usual autocratic expression. "I think I did." She stared into space.

"Then what happened?" Archer asked.

"I felt as if I were being squeezed. As if I might be drowning, but I've never been in that situation so I really don't know."

"What do you mean by 'squeezed'?"

"Squeezed. You know. Like something was around me pushing in, hard." She stopped and looked at him.

"That's it?"

She nodded.

Archer sat back. "Strange, to say the least. Be sure to tell Father Brown all of this. I think he'll probably suggest you see someone. Please, Nita, for God's sake and ours, do it if he does."

"I will, darling. You've convinced me."

"And everything about the dream, too?"

"I'll even tell him that I was dancing naked. You know, that's the one thing that really stops me. The dream is almost too real the way I remember everything, too real I think, to be a product of my subconscious."

"What do you mean by too real?"

"There's no symbology. I remember enough from the psychology courses I took in my freshman and sophomore years in college to know that. Archer?" She peered at him, a concerned, almost frightened look crossing her face. "What if the dream is a memory, a memory of something I actually experienced?"

"You've got to make a decision as to whom you're going to talk with about this, Nita."

"Can I sleep on it tonight?"

Archer nodded.

"I promise you, by tomorrow morning I'll have decided who it'll be. All right?"

"That's fine."

Both had lain awake for a long time that night, lost in their individual thoughts but concentrating on the same thing.

Nita watched the short, sandy haired man

behind the desk nervously light a cigarette. Off
in the distance she heard the Alan Ede Memorial
Bell striking the half hour. At least this man of
God was prompt. She had made her appointment with him for 4:30 that afternoon, and both
he and she had been on time.

"So, Miss Galforth, tell me about this dream
you've been having."

Nita launched into as complete and
detailed account as she could, and when
finished she discovered that the priest had
fallen asleep. Fine. That was just fine and
dandy.

"That's some dream," he said without
opening his eyes. "I hope you didn't think I'd
fallen asleep. I sit with my eyes closed a lot of
the time because I broke my glasses and I find
that the bright light of day really bothers me if I
don't wear them."

Nita reprimanded herself quietly and
waited to see what else he might say.

"As far as offering you any ready
explanation, I can't. I'm not really trained in the
field of psychology as such. I'd suggest that you
seek out professional help in that field if you
want to fully understand your dream."

Nita felt defeated. She had thought a few
minutes with someone like Father Brown might
solve the whole thing. She had been wrong to
have chosen him.

"Archer tells me you were born in Africa or
some such place."

Nita smiled graciously. "Yes. We lived there
for only two years. Then, we went to India for

four years or so.''

''Then back here?''

Nita nodded. ''My father was a missionary but gave it up when we returned to the States. We lived at a series of parsonages over the years until I . . . I lost my father. My mother died a few years after that.''

''I'm sorry for your losses. You're alone now?''

She nodded. ''Of course I have Archer.''

Father Brown lit another cigarette. ''Filthy habit but there are worse ones I could develop, I'm sure,'' he said with a short harsh laugh that was followed by a cough. ''Archer's a nice man. You've done well in selecting him.''

''Selecting him?'' Nita frowned.

''I've a theory that the successful marriages are those made up of women who let the man think they've made all the right decisions. My theory is seldom wrong.''

Nita dwelt on the theory for a moment, and then smiling broadly said, ''You might have something there, Father.''

''If I might suggest, Nita, Doctor Sterling Morris, the head of the psychology department here at Middleton. He conducts a small private practice and . . .'' He stopped when he saw Nita smiling, ready to break into a laugh. ''What's the matter? Did I say something funny?''

''Doctor Morris was Archer's first choice. I picked you.''

Father Brown snapped his fingers. ''Darn, another loser, eh? Let Archer think he was right

all along. You'll prove my theory right, if you
do."

"I will, Father, and thank you for your
time." Nita stood, and when the priest did the
same thing, she turned and left his office.

By the time Nita arrived home, it was
almost 6:30 and Archer had their evening meal
well under way.

"What have you been up to?"

"I saw Father Brown."

"And?"

"Nothing. He couldn't help. He suggested
that I see Doctor Morris."

Archer dumped the hot water off the pasta
he had been cooking. "I hope you will now."

"I probably will. I don't seem to have much
choice. It's either that or have you riding me
about the dream the rest of my days. Besides,
I'd like to know what it means, assuming it has
a meaning."

"I would too," Archer said, shaking grated
cheese on the meat. After dashing a few spices
on, he set the two plates down. "Chow's on."

They ate in silence, and when she finished,
Nita said, "I'm ready for bed. My body is still
scolding me from Saturday. Do you mind?"

"Hey, take care of yourself. If you're tired,
go to bed. I've got some reading to do and a few
notes to transcribe. I'll be in in a few hours."

"Want me to help with the dishes?" She
stood, moving around the table to him.

"No, there's just a few. Besides, the

experience will do me good. When we're married, you can nag me into doing the dishes all of the time."

Leaning down, Nita kissed him.

"G'night," he said quietly as she left the small kitchen.

"G'night."

After washing the dishes, Archer went to the living room and opened his briefcase at the small desk. He'd transcribe his notes first then do his reading. After looking over the notes of his last week's efforts, he began writing them in a precise hand into the ledger-like notebook. He stopped when one entry caught his attention. "One door unlocked." The memory fleshed out with the three word note. How had that happened? He hadn't had much time to think on it because of Al's death, and then after the funeral and cremation, the triathalon had taken over his time. Sure, he had been working, but he was behind on his notes. Now, he sat back, chewing on the top of his pen. There was no rational, or for that matter irrational, explanation to the unlatched cage door. Thankfully, the cobra had not bumped the door and found it open. There was no telling what might have happened if it had.

Redirecting his attention to the book, he continued transcribing his notes into a more permanent form:

"The one thing I find absolutely amazing is the fact the snakes, all three of them, seem to recognize me. The first

week they were in the lab, they struck at
anything that moved. Now, because I'm
around the most, they seem to almost
ignore me with their attacks. I've noticed
they still strike at Richard Roman and Nita
Galforth whenever they come into the lab,
but they watch me with their unblinking
eyes. Whenever I turn to look in their
general direction, I find them with their
attention already fixed on me. I've read
and been told that king cobras exhibit a
keen sense of intelligence. I'm beginning
to believe it."

After finishing his notes, Archer picked up
the books he intended to peruse that evening.
By 10:00 o'clock, he yawned and closed the last
book. There was so much material he had to
study, and he wondered if he'd ever get to the
point of disecting one or two of the reptiles to
search for the answers he needed to solidify his
hypothesis.

He stood, stretched and walked to the bedroom. Nita lay on one side, sound asleep. For
that he was thankful. She had been magnificent
in the triathalon, but the price she had paid
since then was every bit as large as the amount
of energy she had invested. She'd be ready for
bed on the early side of the evening for at least
several more nights. He undressed and slipped
into bed. Nita, clothed in a thin nightgown, did
not react to his presence. Archer lay on his back
for several minutes, hands behind his head. He
was happy. He had Nita and her love, he had his
experiments to work on, and he had a relative
amount of security at the school. Of course he

didn't have tenure, not yet, but he felt he would in the not too distant future, especially since Al's death. He had had tenure, and Richard had tenure. Other than that there were none in the department. If they wanted to offer it to him, he'd take it naturally, but he didn't need it, not at this point in his career. Al had said something about the U. being lucky if Archer decided to stay—high compliment indeed.

Archer turned on his side, facing Nita's back. Closing his eyes, he fell asleep.

Nita turned on her back, subconsciously aware of Archer's presence next to her. She slept soundly, deeply, but moved a bit when the sound of the drums began beating in her mind. The dancers followed the steady rhythm, and for several minutes she joined in with them but then found herself unable to move. She felt restrained, and when she opened her eyes she found nothing ahead of her but darkness. On either side, she could see the dancers on the wall in her periphreal vision. She was lying down. The drums grew louder and she tried to move but couldn't. Her arms were tied.

A huge, evil face loomed in her vision for a moment, and the face laughed at her—a strange, high-pitched, scary laugh. She saw a hand, probably belonging to the man with the ugly face, reaching out toward her. He pulled her hair. It hurt. Why had he done that? When his hand came away, she saw that he held several long strands of her dark blonde hair, and he was still laughing. She was frightened.

She was scared to death. Where were her
parents? Why weren't they there? How had she
come to be in such a place?

The drums grew louder and the dancers'
gyrations increased. The man, who she could
still see standing at the bottom of the table on
which she was being held, leered at her. He held
a knife and was reaching out toward her again.

*Dear God in heaven, don't let him hurt me.
Don't let him cut me. That will hurt something
awful. Please, make him go away. Please let my
Mommy and Daddy come for me. Please, God,
please.*

The knife came closer and with a quick
move, she felt her dress being cut away. Now,
she'd really get it. That was her church-meeting
dress. She only wore it there. Her mother and
father would be furious, but it hadn't been her
fault. They'd understand. They had to understand. That awful, ugly man had cut her dress,
and she looked at him and shuddered. It was all
his fault. He was so ugly and mean. Now what
was he doing? He had a doll. A doll? Was he
some kind of crazy person? Playing with a doll?
Boys didn't play with dolls. Neither did men.
And this man was playing with a doll. But what
was he doing with the doll? He had stuck some
of her hair into the head of the doll and was
wrapping a piece of her good dress around it.
He had to be crazy.

She felt hands grabbing her, and Nita
awoke, screaming into the pillow that partially
covered her face.

Trembling, she sat up. Archer hadn't heard

the muffled cry. Thank goodness for that. She quickly promised herself that Archer would not be told of this new part of the dream. He'd only worry, and for that she was grateful. For a long time, after her mother died, she wondered who would ever worry about her again. Then, after meeting Archer, she knew the answer to that question, but she didn't want him to be upset and worry needlessly. She'd already made up her mind to call on Doctor Morris. She'd tell him but no one else. The only bad thing happening to her right now was her losing a little sleep. She could stand that. Besides, she felt she could lie down and fall asleep immediately, if she had to.

She turned to look at Archer who still lay on his side, facing her. He was so handsome, but underneath those good looks she found the qualities that she had decided were necessary in the man she wanted to love. His kindness, his intelligence, his concern for others, his sense of humor, his independence all combined to make Archer Buchanan the ideal man for her.

A smile crossed her lips when she thought of Father Brown's theory. Perhaps he was right. It took a lot of give and some take in marriage to make a successful union. If she had to go through life letting Archer think some of the ideas were his when they weren't, she could do that. But from what she knew of Archer, and she felt she knew him as well as she ever would at this point in her life, she would seldom if ever have to resort to that form of marital chicanery. They would have a good life and a good marriage.

Reaching out, she stroked his bare arm. She thought of falling asleep again, but did she want that? If she slept, she might dream again and learn more and wake up screaming loud enough to awaken Archer. Then, she'd have to tell him everything. She couldn't lie to him and hold anything back.

*"To sleep, perchance to dream?"*

Where had she heard that before? Who had written it? She was tired. Lying back on the pillow, she stared into the darkness. She'd lie here and stay awake. Once Archer got up, she could go back to sleep. She needed her rest; she needed her sleep. She yawned. Her lids fluttered and closed.

Nita slept soundly.

# 8

An almost warm breeze washed over the campus of Middleton University and Barolo Lecture Hall. Sociology students, whose assignments were to attend the lecture of Lal Khan Bahadur, along with the curiosity seekers who disliked television and those people whom the aloof Indian had befriended, walked toward the auditorium.

"I'm still not that keen on going to this," Nita said, gently elbowing Archer in the side.

He grimaced. "Hey, you didn't have to come. I'm the one who is more or less obligated. He was the one in India who acquired the snakes."

"And I'm with you, you know. *Quo vadis?* Whither thou goest? Who knows, maybe I won't feel so icky around him if I hear him speak." Nita smiled at Archer who stopped frowning the instant he saw her facial expression.

Once inside, they took seats in the middle of the small hall and waited for the lecture to begin.

President Charles Lane introduced the speaker, and after the ripple of applause died down, Bahadur waited dramatically for 30 seconds before beginning his talk.

Nita studied him. She had never really taken the time to look at him closely. The first incident wherein she had seen him had been but a brief, passing glimpse as she walked by Carver Hall and he was coming out. In Archer's lab, she had been more concerned with her attitude toward the king cobras, which seemed to strike at her whenever she was too close to the cages. She didn't take the time to peruse the foreigner then. Here in the lecture hall, after a relaxing meal with Archer and with no distractions around, she took her time to appraise the man from India.

His dark swarthy skin appeared oily, which seemed to emphasize the deep wrinkles around his eyes. If she had had to give points for his most arresting feature, it would have to have been his eyes. The one time she had looked at them she had first thought they were black, but changed her assessment to a very dark brown. While he spoke from the podium, she categorized his eyes' qualities as being shrewd and calculating as well as piercing, their strongest element. She felt if he were a stage hypnotist, he'd do well on a nightclub circuit. In contrast to his arched brows, which grew low and close to the eyes, his eyelids appeared drooping, almost in a hooded way, seemingly to protect his penetrating gaze.

Nita watched, fascinated by his mouth as he spoke. It appeared grim, and while the upper lips were thin, she had to look closely to see if he actually moved them when he said something that seemed to dictate an accompanying smile. When they did curve into a grin of sorts, she noted his eyes did not reflect any joy.

More intent on the speaker than what he was saying, Nita caught snatches of his talk— poverty, birth rate, death rate, unemployment, threat of communism from different areas surrounding his country. She found she could not or did not want to concentrate on his speech. Instead, she found herself fantasizing about being with him alone. What would happen? How old was he? She zeroed in on his age, trying to determine it, but concluded after a long while that he had to be somewhere between 30 and 130. She simply could not pinpoint an age for him. She'd hold off making that decision until she had an opportunity to view him up close, and she felt that chance would come because of Archer's association with Bahadur. When she thought of him touching her in an intimate way, she shuddered, then suddenly realized his talk was finished, the crowd was applauding and some were even beginning to leave.

"Well?" Archer looked at her, waiting for some response.

"Well what?"

"What do you think of Doctor Lal Khan Bahadur and his dissertation?"

"Want me to be truthful?"

He grinned, watching her sense of impish humor about to manifest itself in her answer.

"His appearance held my attention more than his talk did." She wasn't lying. If her life depended on giving a reasonable account of what the man had said, she would have to think up some prayers before they executed her.

"Yeah, he's not your average university prof, is he?"

"What did you think?"

"So much rhetoric. Who can argue with anything he said? It's all true. If anyone ever reads a newspaper or watches TV, the answer is obvious—his talk was a bit on the hackneyed side. Incidentally, I don't have anything to worry about, do I?"

"Worry about? I don't understand." Nita stared at Archer. What was he talking about?

"Bahadur. His appearance. You said you found it more fascinating than what he was saying."

"I didn't say say fascinating. I said it held my attention. Hey, next to you, he's a candidate for Mr. Ugly of the universe. You don't have a thing to worry about."

"That's a relief. Let's go to the reception for him backstage. Maybe you'll change your mind if you can study him up close." Archer ducked Nita's half-hearted swing and moved to the aisle.

A group of students had corraled Bahadur by the time Nita and Archer reached backstage, and they went instead to the punch table. Armed with a paper cup of the sweet drink, Nita and Archer waited at a comfortable distance from the knot of people. One by one, satisfied they had received an answer to their questions, the students drifted away and out of the building.

When Bahadur stood alone, he saw Archer and Nita. "Well, my friend, Archer, what do you think? Did I make a strong case for my country and its situation?"

"You certainly did, Doctor. I'm sure many of the students had their eyes opened to the conditions in India."

While Archer and Bahadur spoke, Nita caught herself scrutinizing the dark man. Whenever he directed his attention to include her, she felt her hair react at the base of her skull. There was something positively over-whelming about the man but she could not quite define it. She continued staring at him, all the while feeling ill-at-ease and nervous.

"Tell me, my dear . . . ah, Nita, isn't it?" Bahadur was speaking to her.

"Yes, Nita," she heard herself saying. She had to get back in touch with her senses and reflexes if she were going to be included in the conversation.

"I sense that you are uneasy about some-thing. Perhaps a bit on the nervous side. Is there something I can do for you?"

Nita felt her face redden. Was he a mind

reader as well? "I'm all right. Really."

"Come come. While I practiced psychology in India, I developed a sixth sense for picking up on people's feelings and states of mind. You have something bothering you?"

"I'm sorry, Doctor," she said. "I feel uncomfortable when you look at me. I feel as if you're looking right through me and that you know everything there is to know about me."

Bahadur chuckled. "I'm sorry. Again, my practice in India."

"I wasn't aware that you were a psychologist, Doctor." Archer's expression advertised the fact that he was impressed by the additional information.

"I was a psychologist before I studied sociology."

"May I ask why you chose to change professions? Or do you still practice psychology?"

"I think everyone in their daily lives practices some form of psychology, whatever their limited abilities might be, my dear friend, Archer. If you mean do I have a formal practice, I do not have one here. At home, I limited myself to a few patients, just to keep myself in practice, so to speak."

He smiled again, but this time Nita noticed that while his mouth curved, his eyes remained as fixed and cold as—as—She shuddered. She was about to compare his eyes to those of the king cobras in Archer's lab. Still, she congratulated herself on noting that his smiles were not always sincere.

"What prompted you to move into sociology, Doctor?" Archer fixed his own stare on the Indian, waiting for his answer.

"Ah, yes. You see, my dear Archer, as a psychologist I could help but one person at a time. Sociology allows me to help my entire country. It is in a way a sort of psychology of the masses."

Archer nodded but said nothing when he noticed that Bahadur was again staring at Nita.

Nita felt she had to say something, but what? Under the circumstances she could hardly comment on his talk since she had not paid much attention to it. She had to ask something, say something. "What do you think of Doctor Morris?" Now where had that question come from? Without noticing the reaction of Bahadur and Archer, she analyzed her own thought processes. She was supposed to contact the head of the psychology department, wanting to solve the meaning of her dream. Bahadur was a psychologist. All she wanted was his opinion of the man with whom she was to meet and discuss her dreams.

"Why . . . why do you ask?" Bahadur seemed taken off-guard. "Who is Doctor Morris?"

"He's chairman of the psychology department here at Middleton." While he spoke, Archer studied Nita, searching for the reason behind the question.

"Why do you want to know my opinion of the gentleman?"

She was stuck. Why had she asked something so stupid? Now she'd have to tell him something, but what? The truth? It couldn't hurt. She found Bahadur studying her, but for some inexplicable reason, she suddenly found herself completely at ease, almost drawn to Bahadur.

"I'm going to tell him about a dream I've had. It's nothing important."

"Ah, but dreams are very important. I could talk for hours on them but I won't bore you." Bahadur nodded to Nita.

"Have you done much work with dreams, Doctor?" Archer asked.

"At the time I gave up my practice to move into sociology, I was studying dreams and how they might be a reservoir of helpful information to the individual."

"Maybe you're the one Nita should talk with—that is if you'd agree." Archer turned to Nita to find a frown wrinkling her forehead.

"That would depend on Miss Galforth," Bahadur said gallantly.

"Oh, I don't . . . well, that is . . ." Nita stammered. What else could she say but yes under the circumstances? Darn that Archer. Why had he said that? For a fleeting second, she had entertained the same thought but had discarded it as being too risky—too risky to be in a closed room with this dark man, alone, unprotected, defenseless against his staring eyes.

"Of course, if you don't want to, you don't have to, my dear."

·   At least Bahadur recognized the fact that she would have to agree to make the meetings workable.

"There isn't anything else that you haven't told me, is there?" Bahadur waited for Nita to answer, occasionally glancing at Archer.

"Well, the dream," Archer said when Nita didn't answer, "has been reoccuring for the last few weeks. Each night, a little more is unveiled."

"Each night? Interesting. And I find 'unveiled' to be an interesting choice of words as well, Archer. Go on." Bahadur spoke without taking his attention from Nita.

"She's also had several blackouts in her life."

Nita placed a hand on Archer's arm. Enough was enough. Sure, Archer was worried about her. Sure, he had this complex of wanting to be a big brother to someone. But why her? They had been lovers for well over a year. She hardly wanted his attention as a concerned, worried, big brother. She knew that he loved her, but his whole attitude right now smacked too much of his only being her big brother.

"Perhaps some physical reason?" Bahadur said. "I find it most difficult to imagine that one so lovely or healthy appearing could have some dark secret that would affect her such as the way you are telling me."

"She's had—"

"I've had a complete physical within the last month and passed everything, including a

CAT scan and an EEG when the doctor learned of my blackouts. There's nothing wrong with me physically." Nita glared at Archer for a moment before reading the concern and worry on his face, now that the subject had been broached.

"Perhaps it is nothing," Bahadur said. "Perhaps with my knowledge and expertise in dreams and their understanding, I might be able to allay any problem resulting thereof."

Nita turned to Archer. She had to talk with someone, for Archer's sake as well as her own. The way in which the dream was revealing itself a little at a time was beginning to irritate her. Maybe this man could help her understand it. If she did that, the dream might very easily go away. What if the head of the psychology department wouldn't talk with her? She couldn't afford the expense or the time of regular consultation with another doctor away from campus. If she said no now, would Bahadur agree later in the event Morris wouldn't or couldn't help her? She focused a smile for Bahadur's sake and faced him. "Would you be willing to talk with me?"

She sensed Archer relax as his shoulders slumped almost imperceptibly.

"Of course, my dear. When would be convenient for you?"

Nita shrugged. "I have no idea as to your schedule. When would be good for you?"

"I am an early riser. Would tomorrow morning about eight be good for you?"

Nita ran her next day's schedule through her mind. She had no commitments until 10:00 o'clock. "Yes, that would be fine. Where is your office?"

"They have given me a small room in the administration building."

"Carver Hall?"

"Yes."

"Well, I guess I'll see you tomorrow morning then, Doctor." Nita offered her hand, half-expecting it to come back dripping with grease. Instead, she found a warm, dry hand holding hers for a farewell that lasted only a brief moment.

After leaving Bahadur, Archer and Nita walked across campus in the direction of the Alan Ede Memorial Bell Tower and the quadrangle. It was the most direct route to their apartment. When they rounded the curved walk that skirted the modern sculpture, *Man At Work And Play*, they saw the John Thomas Science Building. A light shone from Archer's third floor lab.

"I must have forgotten to turn out the lights," Archer said more to himself than to Nita.

"But it's late. Wouldn't the custodian have turned them out when the floors were swept?" Nita asked.

"Hm? Oh, yeah, I suppose that could be. Maybe they didn't turn them off. Come on, it'll only take a moment to go up and turn the lights out. I don't want my cobras thinking there's no night tonight."

"You speak of them as if they knew the difference." Nita matched Archer stride for stride as they changed their direction, heading toward the science building.

"They are intelligent, as snakes go."

"Did you give them an I.Q. test?" Nita failed to camouflage her humor and laughed a bit.

"Not as such, but I've heard stories about them, and in the little while that I've been around them, I've noticed different things that tell me the stories I've read and heard are true."

"Such as?"

"They get to know the people who are around them. At first, they struck at me every time I walked by the cages. I'll tell you, it gave me some pretty good starts for a while. Now they only strike at strangers. They also seem to know which day they get fed. The morning of the day they're to receive food, they become very active as if working up an appetite. They're not, I know, but it seems that way. Then too, they know which side of the door opens and position themselves close whenever I have to run a wire in to pull out shed skin or put their prey in to eat. They're really remarkable."

"Aren't other snakes like that?" Nita asked, stepping through the main entrance of the science building.

"Not really. I wonder who left the door unlocked? If it's the custodian, he's going to have to answer for it."

They hurried upstairs, stopping at the door

to peer through the window. Someone, a man, stood with his back to the door, facing the cages that held the cobras. Archer opened the door and entered.

"How did you get in here?" he asked.

The man, startled at the intrusion, jumped and turned in the same motion. Richard Roman blushed, his embarrassment complete when he saw Nita behind Archer.

"I used my keys."

"Your keys?"

"Well, I picked up Al's ring today. Since I'm in line for the chairmanship, I thought I'd get his keys and make a few rounds. Archer, how in hell did one of these snakes get out, go all the way to Al's house, get in, kill him and get back here without being seen? I don't understand any of it." He turned back to face the cages again. Instantly, all three snakes, which had lain down when Richard turned his back, rose as one, facing him.

Archer stepped around Richard, standing between him and the cages. The snakes looked at Archer and lay down.

"See what I mean, Nita?"

Nita nodded.

"What's that mean, Archer?" Richard's voice sounded gravelly, as if he were exhausted or hadn't slept much.

"We were talking about them when we were coming here to investigate the lights. I was telling her how intelligent king cobras are. Did you see how they recognized me and lay down when I blocked you out of their view?"

"Well," Richard huffed, "if they're that intelligent, why couldn't they have killed Al then?"

"I said they were intelligent as snakes go. They're not whiz kids. What you're saying is out of the question and completely impossible. Besides none of these snakes could have venomized Al with that much poison by themselves. And don't modify your theory by saying more than one did it. It's just not possible."

Richard stared at Archer. "But—"

"How would they have unlocked the cage, for one thing?" Archer paused. After Richard had told him about the death of Al Stewart, the thought of the unlocked cage had been relegated to the back of his mind until the police arrived a few days later. Since then, the thought had been practically dormant. Now, he had recalled it and was about to dismiss it when Nita spoke.

"For that matter, how did they get to the ground floor, assuming they could somehow get out of their cage? This is the third floor and the door to the hallway is usually locked, isn't it, Archer?"

Archer nodded, moving to one side.

The three cobras fixed their attention on Richard again, and the man turned around to follow Archer. "If these didn't kill Al, then what did? Is there another cobra around here loose?"

Archer shrugged. "The police said they checked with the city zoo and found out they didn't even have a king cobra or any kind of cobra for that matter. It's probably a mystery that will never be solved. Besides, the amount of venom in Al's system, which the medical examiner estimated, would seem to indicate one hell of a big snake."

"How big?" Nita asked.

"Well, his estimate computed out at eight hundred to nine hundred milligrams of dried venom. One of these can yield about five hundred to maybe five fifty milligrams. These are about eleven to twelve feet long. Our mystery snake would have to be eighteen or nineteen feet long."

Nita shuddered.

"Would that even be possible, Archer?" Richard asked, his face blanching at the thought.

"The record for years was eighteen feet, four inches, until one was found in the Phillipine Islands, I think it was, that measured nineteen feet three inches."

"Good God!" Richard whispered.

"Records are made to be broken. Someday, if one is let alone long enough, a twenty footer will come along."

"I hope I'm not around," Nita said softly.

"So back to my question, then. What killed Al? A giant king cobra?"

Archer shrugged. "I don't know. Come here, Richard, I want to show you the venom I've collected since the snakes arrived."

Nita locked her attention to the cages. She

could not help but admire the sinuous beauty of
the reptiles in the three cages. Fascinated, she
watched as the two older ones moved about as
if they were suddenly nervous. The younger
brighter colored cobra slithered back and forth
in rapid motions before rising up to face Nita.
Beautiful! They were actually beautiful. Of
course if they weren't in the cages, she would
have to consider the danger they represented,
but they were safely locked away. While she
stared at the youngest snake, it slowly lowered
its body to the floor of the cage and moved to
one side where it gathered together in an
apparent hopeless mass of loops and coils.

"You ready to go, Nita?" Archer called from
the front of the room.

Turning, without taking her eyes completely off the reptiles, she said, "Uh-huh."
Then, breaking her captivated stare, she turned
around and went to Archer.

Richard seemed as though he weren't
going. "I'm staying," he said when he saw the
quizzical look on Nita's face, "for a few minutes.
I'll turn off the lights."

Archer and Nita left, walking slowly down
the steps. When they reached the outside, Nita
took his arm.

"He's pretty confident that he's going to be
elected."

"He should be. I told him I'd vote for him."
Archer squeezed her hand on his arm.

"Why don't you want the chairmanship? I'd
think that it would be a goal for you."

"It is, but not now. I've got to do my work with the cobras and write my paper, get it published and finish my work toward my Ph.D. Then, I'll feel I have enough time to head the department."

Nita snorted under her breath. Why couldn't Archer be more competitive like she? She'd try to do everything at the same time, but Archer was competitive only to a point. When they played handball, he'd do his best to beat her, but his best usually came out second. Why couldn't she understand his reasoning? If she tried, maybe she would, but she felt Archer Buchanan was a much better person, teacher, diplomat and researcher than Richard Roman could ever hope to be.

"The air's getting a little cool," Archer said quietly.

Nita agreed with a nod of her head but continued contemplating the enigma with whom she was in love. She shuddered, and Archer put his arm around her.

"What's the matter with me?" Nita looked up into Archer's face.

"I don't know what you're talking about?"

"I couldn't be coming down with a cold, could I?"

"What are you talking about?"

"I feel chilled."

Archer pulled her closer to him. "I noticed that you shivered a moment ago. Do you feel all right?"

"That's just it. I do. But lately, I've noticed

that temperature changes seem to . . . well, not exactly bother me but I seem to notice them."

"Notice them?"

"You know. If I'm walking in sunshine and then go through some shade and it's considerably cooler in the shade, I notice the difference."

"Most everyone does, if they take the time to pay attention to such ordinary things."

Nita fell silent, and when Archer didn't offer anything further, she was content to walk along in silence, comfortable with his arm about her.

When they reached the apartment, Archer unlocked the outside door and after turning on the entryway light, stepped back for Nita to enter. After locking the door, Archer joined her in the kitchen.

"How do you feel now?"

"I still feel a little chilled. I'll be all right."

He stepped closer. "I know of something that will warm you up. In fact, it'll warm both of us up."

She smiled, moving closer to Archer. They embraced after kissing, then walked out of the kitchen, arms around each other. Archer turned off the light, and they made their way to the bedroom.

Nita reached out, unbuttoning Archer's shirt and helping him slip out of it. Undoing his belt buckle, she opened his slacks and pulled them down over his hips. When he stepped out of them, she threw them on to a chair and slowly stood, running her fingertips along his legs, pausing momentarily at his shorts. She pulled them down and he stepped out of them as well.

"Socks, I don't do," she whispered softly as she stood once more, running her fingertips along his legs, tracing a twisting path through the hair. When she stood upright, her hands continued dawdling at his penis and scrotum, fondling, caressing, barely touching yet communicating her desire through her evocative contact.

Archer's arms enfolded her for a brief second before reaching down to the hem of her blouse. Pulling it up, he slowly lifted it over her head. When she was free of it, Nita gave a shake of her head and her light brown hair fell into place. She stepped back to allow Archer freedom of movement to reach the clasp in front of her bra. When he had unfastened it, it fell away, exposing her breasts, her nipples taut and upright.

The bra flew through the air to land on Archer's pants, and he dropped to his knees, unfastening her slacks at the side, pulling them down over her hips. After her bikini panties followed, they embraced, both nude.

Moving to the bed, Archer hesitated for a second, making a move to take off his socks. Nita interfered, pulling his arm and upsetting his balance. He plummeted to the bed, where they rolled back and forth, embracing, kissing, their tongues seeking hidden spots that were best explored by kissing.

Nita lay on her back, and Archer lightly bussed her mouth, moving his lips from side to side, farther each time until he was able to touch each ear in turn with his mouth. Then, he slowly touched her on the neck, nibbling just a bit to let her know that he was neither doing it from rote nor merely providing a functional service. Then he examined her firm breasts with his lips and tongue. Concentric circles led outward and then in to focus on the hardened nipples standing high in the center of her pink aureoles.

Leaving her breasts, he kissed his way to her navel, poking his tongue in as a gesture of things to come. Nita, her emotions seething, reacted by stroking the back of Archer's head as he moved farther down, kissing her lower stomach, brushing past her pubic hair. Running his lips down one thigh, he chewed at the tight skin, almost unable to make a purchase with his teeth because of the well-muscled leg. Moving back and upward, he kissed one thigh and then the other in a quick back and forth motion, each time moving in closer and closer to her vulva. When he kissed it, she writhed on the bed, moaning, her ecstasy almost complete.

Rising, to straddle her body, Archer lifted one leg while she spread hers. He lowered himself until his erection pressed against her belly. They kissed, their tongues fighting an age old duel, each promising the other the ultimate in physical release. Raising his hips, he allowed

Nita to guide his hardened penis into her body. Both reacted instantly, and the rhythm, established immediately, rocked the bed as they demonstrated each aspect of their physical love.

When they climaxed together, their bodies shuddering, delighted, released, both Nita and Archer lay together, coupled, spiraling down from the heights of their lovemaking.

"I love you," Nita breathed in his ear.

"And I love you." He jabbed his tongue into her ear and she reacted with a little shiver.

"You still cold?"

"Not on your life, mister. I feel positively great, as if I were skydiving and winning an Olympic gold medal all at the same time."

"Wow," he said quietly. "And I did all that to you?"

Nita propped herself up on one elbow, looking around the room. "It must have been you. I don't see anyone else around that might have had anything to do with it." She giggled.

"What's so funny?"

"You didn't take off your socks."

Sitting up in bed, Archer removed them. "I wanted to, but somebody wouldn't let me as I recall."

"I wonder who that might have been?" She tousled his hair and he lay back, next to her.

"I really do love you, Nita."

"I know. I love you just as much. I think it's sort of nice that although we have a good sex life, it isn't the only ingredient in our relationship that makes everything work."

He nodded. "I know exactly what you mean. When we get around to making everything nice and legal, we'll know what richer and poorer means when it comes to this part of married life."

Nita frowned for a second and then nodded.

Reaching over, he turned out the nightstand light and focused his attention on Nita again. He slipped one arm under her neck and they kissed deeply, reverently. "Good night, my darling."

"Good night, Archer. I love you. Always remember that."

"Hey, how could I forget?"

Nita missed the broad smile on his face as he lay down next to her. In turn, Archer had missed the look of concern on her face when she had made her good night to him.

Within minutes, he was snoring quietly as he fell into a deep sleep.

Nita lay on her back, staring into the darkness. What had Archer said? Something about "richer and poorer?" Richer? Richard. Richard Roman? She reacted instantly. She disliked the effeminate man, not for his affected way of acting at times but because he could be down right nasty to Archer. The way he lorded his tenure over Archer was disgusting. The way he looked on himself as the new chairman of the biology department was equally distasteful to her. He needed a good comeuppance of some sort. She imagined Richard's reactions to the

election wherein Rose—what was her last
name?—heavy-set, funny-looking Rosemary
Ogleruk was unanimously selected to head up
the department. Richard had somehow not
gotten a single vote. Even his own had been
changed and given to Rosemary. She pictured
the heavy-set woman in her mind. The hair on
her upper lip seemed to be heavier in Nita's recollection, while thick tufts sprouted from
around her neckline. Her arms were exceedingly
hairy, and when she reached up to take off her
thick-lensed glasses, Nita stifled a scream when
she saw Richard Roman confronting her.

Turning on one side, Nita purposefully
redirected her thoughts to Lal Khan Bahadur.
She was supposed to meet with him tomorrow morning at 8:00. She had to get to sleep or
she wouldn't know what she was saying when
she met with the Indian.

Dropping off to sleep, Nita's last thoughts
were of Richard Roman and how she hated him.

No sooner had she fallen asleep than the
drums began. She saw the dancers and their
shadows, which were cast by the huge fire,
leaping and cavorting on the trees. She tried to
move but her arms were pinned down to her
sides. She felt cold and wiggled just enough to
see that her dress had been torn open and she
lay exposed to the dancers and the man
hovering over her. His wide, maniacal grin
dominated her vision. She tried to look away
but each time found herself drawn back to him.
He pointed a stick with a tiny skull on it directly

at her, jabbering something. When she looked away from his ugly face, she concentrated instead on his hands. What was he doing? Rolling something back and forth between his palms. It looked like the doll he had previously shown her. But what was he doing with it? It was becoming longer somehow. It must be made of clay. She did that all the time with her own clay set that Santa Claus had brought to her last Christmas.

She felt as if she couldn't breathe—and Nita sat up in bed, sweat pouring down her bare breasts, dripping onto her thighs. The dream! That damned dream again! She had to get up. Why did she feel so short of breath? Her upper body pained immensely. Sliding out of bed, she half-stumbled, half-ran to the living room. She didn't want to awaken Archer. He'd only worry. She would sit in the easy chair and relax. That would help.

Her arms pained her as well as her chest, and the sudden thought of heart attack crossed her mind. Could she be having a heart attack? The thought of her recent physical examination seemed to rule that out. No, that was impossible. She had received such high compliments from the doctors concerning her physical condition that it couldn't possibly be a heart attack. Then the memory of having read about Burton Lazowsky, the all-pro linebacker shoved aside her sense of complacency. He had had a complete physical by the team doctor and dropped dead of a heart attack in the waiting

room as he left. The doctor had raved about
Lazowsky's terrific shape, lamenting that sometimes the body will completely fool everyone.

Was that it? Was her body fooling her into
thinking she was a great physical specimen
only to knock her over with a fatal heart attack?

Nita hugged her upper body. The pain
seemed less severe when she did that. She
shuddered. She was cold. Returning to the bedroom on tiptoes she pulled out her nightgown
and slipped it over her head, then put on a robe.
That was better. She felt a little warmer but the
pain continued. Again, she wrapped her arms
around her upper body and the pain lessened.

She had to get her mind off the ache. Maybe
she should call someone or get Archer up. The
pain seemed to be throughout her entire body,
and from what she knew of heart attacks, the
pain concentrated more in the upper chest and
shoulder and arm areas. Her legs hurt equally
as did her midriff. It couldn't be a heart attack.
Think about something else. What? The dream.
It had been the dream that had awakened her.
What had been added this time?

She pictured the Shaman or whatever he
was called, darting in and out of her mind's eye,
swooping down close to her face, jabbering
something in a strange language. He laughed.
He chanted his gibberish while doing something with his hands. What? Rolling the doll,
which obviously was made of clay, back and
forth in his hands.

What could any of it mean? Perhaps Lal

Khan Bahadur would be able to explain it. She certainly hoped so. She didn't like the idea of lying in front of the dancers and the wild man with the doll, with her dress ripped open and her body exposed. She didn't like any part of the dream.

Nita lay back in the easy chair, unable to find a comfortable spot. She moved to the couch and lay down. That was better. Adjusting her body to the contours of the pillows, she closed her eyes, but the pain was still there. Pulling her legs up, she hugged herself tightly. It should have lessened but didn't.

Off in the distance, she vaguely heard the bell tower in the quadrangle toll the hour of 11:00. Then she closed her eyes and dropped into a deep sleep.

Richard stood 15 feet away from the nearest cobra cage. He had studied the snakes, staring at them and returning their fixed, baleful glare. Occasionally, one of the three would hiss loudly and Richard would jump. The hiss, the loudest of all snakes, sounded more like a growl of anger from a small to a medium-sized dog.

Shaking his head at the unexplained death of his colleague and friend, Richard turned. Staring at the three snakes would not solve the mystery, nor would it do him any good. He hated snakes. They made his skin crawl. He grinned. That was a strange way of thinking about it.

The Alan Ede Memorial Bell Tower struck 11 times. At least, he didn't have to worry about getting up early in the morning. His first class was at 10:00 o'clock so he could sleep in if he wanted, and he wanted to very much. The last few nights he had not rested that well. Things hammered at him, keeping him from falling asleep—Al's death and the upcoming election. He wanted the chairmanship so badly that if by some quirk of fate he didn't win, he didn't know what he'd do. The prestige was important to him, but down deep he knew that the position was only for show.

For another 15 minutes, he watched the snakes before deciding to leave. He turned off the lights and locked the door. When he reached the ground level, he walked out into the brisk night air after locking the front door behind him. He was getting home later than normal but he anticipated the sleep he would enjoy once he got into bed.

Changing direction once he started walking, he decided to take a shortcut, across the bluff overlooking the football stadium. It was a clear cloudless night, and the moon was just rising over Carver Hall. The walk would make him even sleepier, and he would have no trouble getting his rest. The air, just a bit on the cool side, was still warm for early November. By next month, the air would get crisp, and shortly after the first of the year the warming trend would begin once more.

Richard enjoyed his bachelorhood even

though there were times he wished he were
married and settled down. He thought of Archer
Buchanan and Nita Galforth. She was a
beautiful woman and had a body like none he
had ever seen. He wondered what she would
look like without clothes. That lucky Buchanan!
He seemed to have everything going for him. Of
course, he didn't have tenure and he wouldn't
be the next chairman of the department.
Richard had those and he was delighted to have
them.

He stopped walking for a split second. He
thought he had heard something. Looking
about, he found the area deserted. No one. Just
himself. Why did he suddenly feel as if he were
being watched—or maybe, followed? He could
see no one. Still, he had had the creepy feeling
of being followed or watched ever since leaving
the science building.

He continued walking but could not shake
off the sensation that he wasn't completely
alone. He shook himself all over as if trying to
dislodge the paranoid feeling but couldn't do
so.

Leaving the sidewalk that would lead to the
street paralleling the far side of the football
stadium, he headed toward the bluff.

He stopped. He had heard something again,
like leaves rustling or being blown about in the
wind. But there was no wind. And there were no
leaves on the ground where he was walking.
There were no trees.

He hurried toward the top and stopped

once more. There was the same noise. He
turned but could see nothing, no movement,
nothing out of the ordinary. However, he
couldn't shake the idea that someone might be
following him. His hair crawled at the back of
his neck, and he ran one hand over his thin
face. Turning around, he hurried, half-running,
half-walking. He wanted to get home. He didn't
like the feelings he was experiencing. Maybe it
was his imagination but he doubted it. The way
he was reacting was not normal for him. He
seldom felt threatened in a physical way.
Emotionally reacting was entirely different.
Perhaps that was why he had never married. He
felt emotionally threatened by the women he
knew. But physically? He doubted it. Nevertheless what he felt right now were physical
reactions, as if someone were about to pounce
on him. He had never placed himself in that sort
of situation and found the experience most
nauseous.

Reaching the top of the bluff, he paused to
take in the view of the football field and horse-
shoe-shaped stadium 85 feet below. The moon
cast icy blue light on it, creating blacker than
black shadows. He was just about to turn and
leave when he heard the growl behind him.
Spinning about, he screamed.

It hadn't been a growl but a hiss, a loud hiss
from the gigantic king cobra slithering toward
him. It couldn't be. It was huge. Gigantic. What
could it be doing here? Why hadn't anyone seen
it? Or reported it? He had to run, but could he

outrun it? The only way he would ever know was to try.

He spun on one heel but before he could move, the snake struck at him, missing. Richard stood perfectly still, while the cobra moved toward him. The snake was still 15 feet away, its strike having missed by a considerable margin. Then he recalled something Archer had said about the cobra's ability to strike as far or a bit farther than the snake's head was above the ground. No wonder it had missed so badly. Taking a tentative step backward, Richard found the snake moving forward swiftly. He'd have to move faster than that to escape it.

Out of the corner of his left eye, Richard could see the football field below. To his right, he might stand a chance running down the hill he had just climbed. He'd be able to move faster going downhill than on the level behind him.

As if reading his mind, the snake moved to his right, cutting off the downhill route.

Richard kept his eyes on the giant reptile that now lay a scant ten feet in front of him. The head, its small hood flared, rose from the ground, higher and higher until the lidless eyes fixed on Richard. Richard couldn't tear his attention from the sight. He felt hypnotized, even though he knew such stories of snakes mesmerizing their prey were not true. Richard stood six feet tall, and the snake's head was opposite his. That meant the cobra could strike a distance of six feet or so. If he kept more than that amount of distance between him and the reptile, he'd be all aright. He took a step backward to ensure the stability of the distnce, but the snake moved forward.

Richard froze. The damned thing seemed to be taunting him. He took another step.

The snake moved again, closer this time.

Calculating the distance now at less than eight feet, Richard took a big step back, kicking up dust in the sparsely grassed area in which he stood.

Again the snake moved, closing the distance to six feet.

Richard had to get away. Without thinking, he turned and ran off the bluff. Startled by his fall, he was unable to scream and struck the asphalt track surrounding the football field head first, smashing his neck and back.

The snake stood poised for a long moment after Richard Roman disappeared and then, lowering its upper body, glided soundlessly away into the night.

# PART III

## FROM THE PAST

# 9

Archer was aware of the pounding but it was off in the distance, far removed from the safe haven of bed and sleep. Concentrating on it without opening his eyes, he groped for Nita. Maybe she had heard it as well and could investigate. What was it? What was that pounding?

His eyes flew open when he realized that someone was knocking on the kitchen door of the apartment. "Nita?"

No answer. Her side of the bed was empty. Where could she be? Maybe she had heard it and was already answering the door.

But the pounding continued. Throwing back the sheet, he reached for his robe and, slipping into it, stumbled to the hall.

The knocking was coming from the back kitchen door. "Hold it! I'm coming," he called, his voice croaking. When he passed the entrance to the living room, he stopped short. Nita was lying in the middle of the room, naked. Should he check her first or quiet the incessant knocking by answering the door?

"Hold it, I'll be there in a minute." Running to Nita's side, he crouched. "Hey, Nita, what's wrong? What are you doing in the living room, bare-ass naked? Hey, come on, wake up, we have company." Archer shook her shoulder, gently at first then more roughly when she didn't respond immediately. "Wake up, I've got to answer the door. Come on. Get up. You have an eight o'clock appointment. Remember?"

Archer left the living room, hoping Nita would have the good sense to stay in there once she realized that they had company. Hurrying to the kitchen door, he opened it and saw two men; one seemed familiar.

"Mr. Buchanan. I'm Sergeant Alexander, San Marcos Police Department. We'd like to talk with you."

Archer studied their faces. It definitely was not a social call. "What can I do for you, Sergeant?" Archer surreptitiously glanced at the clock over the sink. 6:30? It would have to be awfully important to be aroused at this hour.

"May we come in?"

"Sure, but you'll have to stay in the kitchen. What's up?" Archer looked from one to the other, finding no clue at all as to the purpose of their visit.

"We need your identification of a body that was found this morning," Alexander said simply.

"A body? Whose?" Archer felt weak-kneed. Who had died?

"Professor Richard Roman's body was found on the track at the football stadium this morning by early morning joggers."

"If you know it's Richard, why do you need my identification?"

"Just formalities. He apparently has no family, and the switchboard suggested we contact you since you're apparently the senior member of the biology department now. Is that correct?"

Archer's mind raced. He and Nita had just been with Richard last night. What had happened? How had he died? "Huh? Oh, yeah. I guess I am—now. What happened to Richard?"

"We think he fell from the bluff at the one end of the stadium." Alexander closely watched him.

"But . . . but he was alive just last night. He was fine. How could he have fallen?" Archer's mind raced. At least he hadn't died like Al did. This would not cast any suspicion on his research or the reptiles in his lab.

"You saw him last night?"

"Yes."

"Why don't you tell us about it on the way to the morgue. We'll wait while you dress."

"What? Dress? Oh, sure," Archer said, indicating they should sit down while he changed.

"So he was in good spirits last night when you and Miss Galforth left him?" Alexander asked, half-turning from his seat next to the driver.

The car slowed to turn into a driveway that led to the back of Saint Joseph's Hospital and the city morgue, which was housed there.

"He was still disturbed over Al's death. He was wondering how so much snake venom could have been introduced into his system. So have I, for that matter," Archer said matter-of-factly.

"We all have, Mr. Buchanan." Alexander got out when the car stopped and opened the back door of the sedan, letting Archer out of the back seat.

They walked into the building without further conversation, and when the attendant greeted them, the sergeant asked for Richard Roman's body.

"He sure was broken up in that fall, Sarge," the thin man said. "The M.E. finished a while ago for the time being, but he'll be back and open him up then."

"Did Laffler say what the cause of death was?"

"Multiple fractures of the neck and spine. 'Course the legs and arms were done in, too. He said he'd be back around nine this morning and finish up. You'll get your full report just like always when he's done."

"Where's the body now?"

"Still on the table. I'm supposed to leave him there until Doc finishes with him. Come on. This your witness?" His head motioned toward Archer.

"This way, Mr. Buchanan," Alexander said, nodding in answer to the attendant's question.

They entered the white examination room. Archer immediately saw the covered body on the center table. He felt a shudder run down his spine. It would be bad. How could it be anything but bad?

Without hesitating, the attendant whipped off the cover and Richard Roman's terrified face stared at the lights over his dead body.

"Well?" Alexander asked, staring at Archer, waiting for some indication that it was indeed Richard Roman.

"You know it's Richard, Sergeant. Am I through now?" He turned, his head feeling just a bit light.

"He had no family from what we can gather. Is that right?"

"I didn't know Richard that well, but yes, from what I know, you're right on that count. Why does he look so . . . so horrified?"

Alexander shrugged. "I thought maybe you might know. After all, you and Miss Galforth were with him last night."

"What's that supposed to mean?" Archer suddenly thought of Nita lying in the center of the living room, nude. Had she gotten up? He hoped she had. She had an 8:00 appointment with Bahadur at his office. Perhaps he should have made certain she was awake. But, why had she been lying nude on the floor?

"Tell me everything that happened and then maybe I can tell you what I meant by it."

Alexander indicated they should leave and followed Archer from the antiseptically clean room. "In fact, why don't you go with me to the site where the body was found. You can tell me on the way."

Archer shrugged. It was almost 7:45 and he wanted to be at the lab by 8:00 or 8:30 anyway.

"Sure, why not."

After repeating everything to the sergeant, Archer took a deep breath when he finished. He hoped that he wouldn't have to tell the story again. Twice was enough. He glanced at Alexander who drove the car. His partner Officer Paul Adams had stayed at the morgue to wait for Doctor Laffler.

"Let me ask you this," Alexander said, parking the car as close to the stadium as possible. "Could there be a connection between Roman's death and Stewart's death?"

"Wh—what?" Archer stammered. That idea was preposterous at best. One man died of poison and the other fell to his death. How could there possibly be a connection? He voiced his question to the policeman while they walked down the stadium steps to the track. Stepping under the police barricade of yellow ribbon, Archer followed the short stocky man. An outline of the body as it had landed, marked in white, stood out in bold relief against the black path.

Archer looked up at the top. It was high all right. He had never paid much attention to it before now. Anyone who fell from it would certainly die. There could be no question of that.

"Just how disturbed was he when he talked about Stewart's death?" Alexander walked about, head downward, searching for anything that might enlighten him and help explain the death of Richard Roman.

"He and Al were friends, pretty good friends, I guess. Of course, he was upset by the way in which Al died. Hell, we all were. You've got to admit that dying the way Al did is pretty strange and would have to be traumatic to his family and friends."

"So, how disturbed was he?"

"He was staring at the cages with the king cobras inside, dwelling on the question as to how they got out, went across campus, got into Al's house, killed him, and got away and back to the lab without being detected. He—"

"Do you think that's what happened, Mr. Buchanan?"

Archer shook his head. "Of course not. I told you that before. Besides, the venom was intact in the refrigerator the morning you were there and one of the cobras couldn't have killed Al by itself."

"What do you mean?"

"I told you that, too."

"Tell me again."

Archer repeated the same reasoning he had given that morning when the police had investigated him, his lab and the three king cobras. When he finished, he waited for Alexander to say something.

"Let's go up to the top of the bluff."

"What?"

"We can look around up there. Maybe the other officers missed something." Alexander turned and started back toward the car.

Archer had no choice except to follow him. He looked at his watch. He could afford to humor the detective another 30 minutes or so but then he had to get to the lab. Running one hand over his face, he decided he could get away without shaving since he had just shaved last night before attending Bahadur's lecture.

Bahadur! Nita should be with him by now. He certainly hoped everything worked out all right there.


On top of the bluff, they crossed another yellow barricade and walked around, silently looking for some reason why Richard Roman fell to his death.

"You realize, Mr. Buchanan, that you're a suspect."

"I'm what?"

"A suspect. You seem to have a motive."

"A motive? Me?"

"This may not be the smartest police procedure I'm following right now, but why don't you just tell me everything and get it off your chest. You'll feel a lot better."

"You're crazy, Alexander. You know that?"

Alexander shrugged. "I've been told that before but I'm still running around without a keeper."

"Why would I want to harm my colleagues?"

"I like your choice of words. Harm instead of kill. Nice touch."

"I don't have to take this. You haven't read me my rights. I don't have an attorney here. I don't have to talk to you, unless you formally arrest me on charges and then only if I have a lawyer with me."

"You know the law pretty well, Mr. Buchanan, but I want you to put yourself in my place for a few minutes. The newly elected chairman of the biology department dies of a huge dose of cobra venom. The man who is third in line for the chairmanship, as I understand it from the Dean of Academics, is now second and also just happens to have three king cobras in his charge. Then, the man who is more than likely to be elected to the same position, turns up dead at the foot of a bluff. The morning after, I might add, visiting late at night with the number two man in the department, who is now number one. If you were me, Mr. Buchanan, who would you suspect?"

Archer felt his throat go dry. Wasn't it all circumstantial? Of course, it was. This Alexander was fishing, poking around in the dark, hoping tht the situation he just outlined was correct and that the suspect, Archer Buchanan, would knuckle under and confess in a fit of jangled nerves.

"If you really did your homework, Sergeant," Archer said icily, "you'd have learned that I don't really give a damn about the chairmanship and that my only interest right now is the work I'm doing with cobras.''

''Oh, yeah, I know that. But wouldn't it make a great smoke cover if the situation I outlined were actually correct?''

''You admit then that I had nothing to do with it?''

''No such thing. Everyone is a suspect until the perpetrator is under lock and key.''

''But you don't know for a fact that either man was murdered. Or do you?''

''We have to leave every option open. I'm not ruling anything out.''

''Look, Sergeant, in time I'll be elected to the chair, if I stay around here long enough. I know that. Right now I'm not interested.''

Alexander turned, head bent to the ground, covering again the same territory he had walked over earlier.

Archer did the same thing, just to see what the man might be viewing, and froze. Why hadn't he seen it before? He looked from one side, then to the other. It was totally unmistakeable to the person who recognized the spoor. A large snake had been here sometime recently. But when? Archer looked around more. The double wavy line in the soft dirt lay at right angles to the bluff. How big could the reptile have been? He eyed the distance between the parallel lines. They were quite far apart—almost three feet. Footprints of the police marred the smooth portion between the lines but the markings were those of a snake.

Archer shuddered. The snake could be upward to 17 or 18 feet in length.

The thought of the dried cobra venom found in Al Stewart's body shot through his mind. Had Richard encountered the snake up here and, frightened beyond reason, fell from the bluff? Or had the snake attacked him and he fell trying to avoid the strike?

Now what should he do? Tell Alexander and get him off his own back? But then the investigation might jeopardize the experiments with the snakes. If his own speculation proved to be true, there was nothing to be gained by telling the police. They'd continue their investigation without the information. Besides, he wasn't 100 percent certain the markings had been made by a reptile.

"Well?" Alexander called, breaking into Archer's thoughts. "Come on, I'll take you home."

"No need to, Sergeant. I'll walk across campus to my lab from here, if that's all right with you."

"Sure. Just stay in touch. I'll do the same if I need anything."

Archer turned, striding away from the bluff toward the campus walks. If his observation proved to be correct and there was a snake that huge, where was it right now? Was it hiding? Obviously. But where? Did someone own it? Who in their right mind would want to keep that large a snake—the most poisonous snake in the world because of the amount of venom it could produce? Secondly, who would keep one and let it roam around by itself? Maybe someone had a snake that big, which might have gotten away, and the owner was too frightened of the consequences to report it. Just who would have a snake like that and be able to keep it a secret?

He entered the John Thomas Science Building and ran up to the third floor. When he turned the corner that led to his lab, he bumped into Lal Khan Bahadur.

"Good morning, Doctor."

"Mr. Buchanan? Why didn't Miss Galforth show up for her appointment with me this morning?"

"I'm not sure. She was just waking up when I had to leave. I mentioned the appointment but she still might have been asleep. I'm sorry for the inconvenience."

"It's not an inconvenience. I was rather looking forward to talking with her. She seems to be a most fascinating person. Perhaps you could tell me something about her."

"Let's go inside my lab, Doctor."

"Very well."

"The police got me up rather early. I had to identify the body of Richard Roman."

"Really? What happened?"

Archer felt his neck hair crawl. The man seemed almost indifferent to the idea that Richard was dead. He told him of the incident that morning, only because he had been asked about it, but the manner in which he had been asked was almost as indifferent as asking about the weather or the outcome of a sporting event.

Once they were inside, Archer turned to face Bahadur. "Perhaps I should call her first. Then, if there's a good reason why she didn't keep the appointment and wants to reset it, you can."

"That is an excellent idea, Mr. Buchanan."

Archer dialed his home number, half-expecting not to get an answer. After five rings and right before he intended to hang up, the phone was answered.

"Hello?" Nita sounded as if she had just awakened.

Archer looked at his watch—past 9:15. Could Nita be sick that she hadn't gotten up to keep her appointment with Doctor Bahadur?

"Are you all right, Nita?"

"Who is this?"

"Wake up, sleepyhead. It's me. Archer. Are you that tired you don't even recognize my voice?"

"Where are you? What time is it?"

"I'm at the lab and it's going on nine-twenty."

"What? I don't believe it. How could I have slept this long?"

"Where are you? Still in bed?"

"Yes. And I might ask you what you did with my nightgown?"

Archer frowned. She sounded serious but what she was saying came across like a game between lovers. "You went to bed without it last night, my dear." He dropped his voice to prevent Bahadur from overhearing.

"No. I got up after you went to sleep and put on my gown. I felt cold."

"Thanks. That's not saying much for me. You realize you missed your appointment with Doctor Bahadur."

"Oh, God. I'm sorry, Archer."

"Don't apologize to me. He's here."

"Apologize for me. Apologize profusely. Tell him I overslept and will contact him to make another appointment if he'll still see me."

"I'm sure he will. Take care. When will I see you?"

"I'll stop over after I'm awake and showered. All right?"

"That's fine, darling. I love you."

"Bye."

She hung up, and Archer smiled when he turned to Bahadur. "If it's all right with you, she'll contact you and set up another time. She overslept."

"That'll be fine, Archer. Could you tell me a little about Nita and her family and background?"

"Such as?" Archer stared at Bahadur, whose dark complexion stood out even more when his white tunic was taken into account.

"Where are her parents? What sort of background does she come from? What she is like and so on?"

Archer told him of her dead parents and the little he knew of her early life abroad. When he mentioned her physical abilities, Bahadur at first seemed highly interested but dismissed them when he learned that she was into sports. He mumbled something about women's true place, and when Archer finished, said, "I am very impressed, especially about her life in Africa and India. I am naturally a bit prejudiced but I find that part of her background makes her most intriguing to me. Most Americans, especially women, seem rather shallow when it comes to the everyday rite of living and learning. I shall find talking with her most enjoyable, I am sure. Here," he said, handing Archer a small card. "I have written down my office number and my home telephone number. Have her call me one place or the other."

Archer took the card and breathed easier once the man had left the lab. For some reason—perhaps it was the undigested news that Richard Roman was dead—he felt relieved to be alone. He wondered about Bahadur's seeming indifference to the news of Richard's death.

Turning he went to his desk and unlocked it. He had wasted enough time for one day.


"It's not very funny, Archer." Nita glared at him, attempting to hide her humor and act angry.

"I had nothing to do with it. I swear."

"Oh, you did, too. I found them laying on the couch, very neatly laid out to their full length. The gown was inside the robe and the robe tied shut. Very funny, Archer. The next time, I might catch my death of cold. Then you won't be able to laugh and deny it."

"Watch my mouth, Nita. I had nothing to do with it. When I was awakened this morning, I found you on the living room floor, in the buff, sound asleep. You explain that to me."

Nita wrinkled her forehead. That was right. She had gotten up and gone to the living room when she began hurting. Why hadn't she thought of that before? But why had she taken off her night clothes? That was the real puzzler. And the manner in which she found them was equally mysterious. As if she had put them on and then taken them off at the same time without unfastening the tie.

After telling Archer about her nighttime prowlings and avoiding the part about her chest hurting badly, Nita asked Archer for all the details regarding Richard's death, something she should have done when she first got to the lab a little past 10:30.

When he finished, she said, "Of course I'm sorry, but I'm just as happy for you, darling. Congratulations."

Archer stared at her. "Congratu—? Are you serious? Richard is lying, all broken up, on a slab at the morgue and you're congratulating me? For what?" His voice was edged with an iciness that seldom came forth, cutting through the distance separating them.

"Won't you be elected chairman of the biology department now?" She sounded puzzled, confused, as if she didn't fully understand the workings of such a situation.

"I don't know. Maybe. But I'm not going to actively seek it. If the school wants me to accept the position on an interim basis, I'll consider it, but my work must come first." Archer looked up from his desk top, half-expecting to find her smiling down at him. Instead, he found himself alone and discovered Nita standing near the cages. He opened his mouth to speak but only watched her, silently. For someone who had fainted the first time she saw the cobras, Nita had certainly recovered sufficiently to be able to stand next to the cages and stare at them. Then he noticed the cobras themselves. They were reared up, as if to attack. By now, they should have struck at Nita, but they merely balanced themselves, weaving back and forth. When he looked at Nita, a chill ran down his spine. She was smiling at the snakes.

# 10

Archer stared at Nita. She seemed to be in a trance. The snakes stood, rearing as high as the confines of the plastic cages would allow. Nita faced them, her head slightly bent to put her line of vision on a plane equal with theirs. What the hell was she doing? It appeared to Archer as though she might be communicating with them, if such a thing were possible.

"Nita?"

No answer.

"Nita? Are you all right?"

"Hmm?"

"I said, are you all right?"

She jerked as though experiencing a seizure of some type. "What?"

Archer ran to her. Turning her away from the cages, he said, "Are you all right?"

Nita looked at him, an expression of

befuddlement on her oval face. Running a tongue over her lips, she said, "What happened?"

Archer's face screwed up. "You were staring at the snakes. You looked like you were in another world."

"I . . . Good grief, I don't remember. Archer, am I going nuts? I have a serialized dream. I wake up in the morning and can't remember where I put my nightclothes. I come in here and, according to you, stare at three lethal snakes and don't remember doing it. Am I going crazy or what?"

"I think it's the what. I don't think you're going crazy, to use your term. Bahadur will straighten you out on your dream. Anyone can wake up in the morning and be disorientated. And, let's face it, this is the first time the cobras haven't struck at you and you had a chance to see just how beautiful they are." He smiled reassuringly.

"Beautiful? I don't think so. They are fascinating and, you know you're right, they didn't strike at me. Why?"

"They're beginning to recognize you. Cobras are like that—king cobras, that is. They're singularly intelligent."

"Singularly? I don't understand."

"I've mentioned it to you before. They exhibit characteristics other snakes aren't capable of, such as recognizing people."

Nita shuddered. "Maybe they're just marking their first victims once they get out of their cages."

Archer laughed. That was more like the Nita
he knew, ready to make a joke about something
serious. "Now, I want to ask you something," he
said turning to walk back to his desk.

"What's that?" Nita followed and sat on the
edge of it while Archer plopped heavily in the
swivel chair behind the desk.

"What did you mean by congratulating
me?"

Nita frowned for a moment, brightening in
recollection after a few seconds. "Why for being
the first in line for the chairmanship of the
department."

Archer scowled. Why did she persist in that
line of thinking? Why couldn't she understand
he didn't care if he was ever elected? Maybe he
should tell her what the police were thinking,
then she might stop her incessant pushing. If
he wanted the chairmanship, he would have it
when he was ready. Not now, not with the
experiments hanging over him. He wanted
those to be successful, not because he might
gain a modicum of attention but because of the
potential good that could come from such a
breakthrough. Still, if he told her of Sergeant
Alexander's reasoning, she might become truly
concerned. He would enjoy her full commit-
ment but that was an awful way of gaining her
support—by being accused of murder.

"That's what you said before and I think it's
awful."

"Awful?"

"Considering Richard died just last night or
early this morning after we were the last ones to

see him alive, it—"

"We were? How do you know?"

"The police seem to think he left here, started home and, for some stupid reason, fell off the bluff. That makes us the last ones to have seen him."

"You told the police?"

"Of course. Why not?"

"They'll suspect us."

"Not us."

"Who?"

"Me." Why had he told her?

"You? How can they suspect you? You were with me."

"I know. That might be the one thing holding them back although they didn't ask for an alibi."

"What did they say?"

"Not they. He. Sergeant Alexander hinted broadly that I had something to gain by Al and Richard both dying when they did."

Nita blinked. "The chairmanship?"

Archer nodded.

"No wonder you think it's awful for me to say what I said."

"Not for that reason alone. I simply don't want the job. I wish somebody, especially you, would believe that. I've got too many involvements to have the job now."

"But what if they elect you. Will you turn it down?"

Archer shrugged. "I don't know. I'd take it on a temporary basis until someone else could

take over." He just wanted everyone to believe
him when it came to the importance of his
experiments outweighing the chairmanship of
the biology department.

"What are you going to do about Bahadur?"
He reached out taking Nita's hand in his.

"I'll call him today. I promise." She freed
her hand, marking her left breast with a cross.
"I'll make another appointment and then you'll
not have that to worry about any longer."

"Nor will you."

She smiled, a sense of relief seemingly
washing over her for an instant. "What time will
you be home?"

"Late. I've got several long-running
experiments to conduct today. I should have
been going at it for the last several hours and
haven't even begun. First the police dragged
me out of bed this morning, then Bahadur
showed up when I got here, telling me how
naughty you were. Then—"

"Then I came in and kept you from your
work. I can take the hint. I'll go. About what
time can I expect you?"

Archer shrugged. "Ten. Maybe eleven.
Maybe earlier. You go to bed. Don't wait up for
me."

"All right." She stood, waiting for him to
come around the desk to embrace her. When he
did, she said, "It must have been awful having
to identify Richard. Was it bad?"

He nodded. "Anytime anyone has to view
the remains of someone they knew and . . ."

Richard's twisted face exploded in his mind's eye. He shuddered.

"What is it?"

He told her of the mask of terror gripping the dead man's face.

"I wonder what caused that. The fall?"

"I don't know, but it must have been awful. That's a terrible way to die—falling. Knowing you're either going to die in an instant or be horribly crippled and maimed the rest of your life."

"Will you be all right?"

"Yeah, I'm fine. Really. Don't worry about me."

"Okay. If you want to talk or want me to come around, just call. I'll be home by midafternoon."

"I will."

They kissed and Nita left.

By 9:30 that evening, Nita felt wide awake. Maybe she'd wait up for Archer. She wasn't that tired that she couldn't sit up and watch a little television. Turning on the set, she ran through the channels and settled on a Gary Cooper movie. The black and white flickered steadily as Cooper walked through shadows and bright sunlight, six gun in hand. Unable to get into the movie storyline, Nita's mind wandered, her eyelids growing heavy. Her head dropped forward onto her chest and she wiggled about, searching for a comfortable position. When she found one, she fell into a deeper sleep.

The television set continued softly emitting gunshots and shouted dialogue but the sounds fell on unhearing ears as Nita drifted through the shadows of her dream. The dancers and their familiar specter-like shadows writhed in accompaniment to the muffled pounding of the drum. The maniacal face of the man, the only person there she could see who had a face, darted down close to hers, laughing, jabbering in some strange language, occasionally showing her the doll figure with a piece of her dress wrapped around it and several strands of her hair stuck into the round head. He squeezed it, rolling it back and forth in his dirty hands. Then she could hear someone crying—deep, deep sobs that seemed to tear at the very fabric of her soul. Then, she realized it was she who was weeping, terrified, frightened beyond words. Horror struck at her like an angry viper.

Suddenly, she felt hands grabbing at her. Whose hands? She tried to see but tears welling in her eyes made everything all wiggly and slithery. She couldn't make out anything any-more. Who was grabbing at her? They held her so tightly, yet at the same time the hands felt gentle. Their gentleness gave her a sense of security she had not sensed ever since she had left her mother. When had that been? Where had they been when they became separated? She fought with her overwhelming sense of fear, desperately trying to let the feeling of security that she felt from the hands override her fright. But nothing she tried seemed to work.

Then, off in the distance, the loud clap of a cannon sounded.

Archer lost his grip on the door and it slammed with a loud bang. Cursing himself for having been noisy, he hoped Nita had not heard it and awakened. He was exhausted. The experiments had gone well but it would be several days before he knew the exact outcome and results.

When he approached the living room, he saw the lights and heard the television set playing quietly. Peering in, he saw Nita sitting up, rubbing her eyes.

"Hi. Did I wake you up with the door? I'm sorry if I did."

She looked up at him confused. Where was she? What had happened? What had she heard? It had sounded like a cannon report. She focused on Archer. He had just said something about a door. Had he slammed one and had she heard it, interpreting it as a cannon?

"What's wrong, Nita?" He sat down on the couch next to her and gently took her hands in his. "Is something the matter?"

She looked at him, wanting to scream. She felt she owed herself one good scream because of the nightmare she had just experienced. "The dream," she managed hoarsely and coughed.

"Again? Did you call Bahadur?"

"Yes, but he wasn't at either number. No answer. I'll call tomorrow."

Archer could feel her tremble as she spoke. "Are you all right?"

"I . . . I want to talk."

"About?"

"About the dream. There was more tonight and I want to talk about it while it's fresh in my mind. Okay with you?"

"Of course. Go ahead."

Nita launched into a detailed account of the entire dream, adding the last new addition—the hands, grabbing her in a rough way but at the same time exuding a sense of gentleness and security. She looked up at Archer. "What do you think of that?"

Archer shrugged. "You were saved. Right?"

"I don't know. I think maybe that's what it means. What do you suppose the man who laughs and talks in a foreign language is doing with the doll?"

Again Archer shrugged. "Tell me everything."

"Well, it looks something like a voodoo doll. He always puts a piece of my torn dress around it and pokes a few strands of my hair in the head of the figure."

Archer nodded. "It does sound like a voodoo doll of sorts but you were never exposed to something like that when you were little, were you?"

Nita shook her head. "Not that I know about. Of course, I don't remember anything like the dream, either. Does the dream have to be something from my past?"

"I don't know. It could be. Or it might be symbolic of something in your life right now or something that's going to happen. I remember that much from Psychology One when the subject was dreams and their hidden meanings."

Nita stood, crossing the room to turn off the television set.

"Do you think the hands were helping you or holding you for further rites in the ceremony?"

Nita shrugged.

"Do you have any idea as to whose hands they might be?"

Nita shrugged again.

"Could they have been your father's hands?"

"I . . . I don't know. Maybe. Why my father's?"

"He was the man in your life when you were small. Right?"

"I guess so."

"Do you remember anything like this at all from your childhood?"

Nita shook her head and turned away. "I don't think I do. How much do you remember from your childhood?"

Archer flashed a brief smile. How like her to rationalize by bringing him into it. Perhaps she wanted company in her misery. "Do you recall anything at all about an altar or a doll or drums or anything that's in your dreams?"

Nita spun about to face him. "No! No! No! I don't remember anything like it at all. Nothing.

Don't you think I've racked my brain trying to recall something, no matter how insignificant? But I tell you there's nothing."

Archer went over to Nita and wrapped his arms around her from the back. She turned in his embrace, snuggling in closer to his body.

"Archer, I'm very frightened. I've had a sense of foreboding recently, and I don't know why. But the first time I realized it was the day the snakes arrived."

"You mean when you fainted?"

"No. Before that. When I was coming toward the science building. I felt very uneasy as if . . . as if . . ."

Archer waited. When she didn't continue, he said, "As if what, darling?"

"I don't really know. That's just the problem. I can't seem to get a handle on anything lately."

Archer frowned. What was happening to their world? A few weeks ago, he had everything mapped out—the experiments, completing his doctorate, Nita and he getting married. Now, she was balancing on the edge of something that he didn't even want to think about. This, coupled with the police seeming to think he might be responsible for the deaths of two of his colleagues, brought a sense of disaster to Archer.

He held her at arms' length. "Do you remember anything about this morning?"

"This morning?" She looked at him, tears running down her puzzled face.

"When you awoke nude? Remember?"

"Oh, that." She smiled. "I hadn't really given it much thought. Why?"

"Do you remember having had the dream last night?"

She looked over his shoulder for a moment. Then, shaking her head, she said, "I don't think I did. Usually, I recall when I do. It usually wakes me up. I . . ." She turned away. Last night. The pains in her chest and body. Why hadn't she thought of that before just now? Should she tell Archer? Dare she tell him? What would he do if she did? It might be best to keep it to herself for the time being. She felt perfectly fine. In fact, she felt so good all day long that she hadn't thought much of the awful constricting pressure until just now.

"You don't remember lying on the floor of the living room, nude?" He cupped her chin, turning her face to his.

"Uh-uh. Really. I sort of recall you telling me to get into bed and talking to me, but the first thing I remember from this morning is waking up in bed without anything on, wondering why you had taken my gown off."

"Darling, will you promise me to call Doctor Bahadur first thing in the morning?"

For his peace of mind and for her own sanity, she knew she had better consult someone who might have the answers to the myriad questions flooding her mind. "I promise, you big old meany." She chucked him under the chin, trying desperately to lighten the mood. Somehow, she felt she had failed miserably.

They went into the bedroom and were soon
lying in the dark. Neither spoke, but Archer's
mind raced furiously with worries over Nita and
her well-being. Every once in a while, Sergeant
Tony Alexander's face pushed into his
thoughts, and he would blink the unwanted
image away.

Nita lay on her back staring into the darkness. She imagined the type of room Lal Khan
Bahadur might have at the Administration
Building. His dark face, the hooded eyes staring
at her, formed in her imagination. His head
narrowed, thinning down until it took on the
shape of one of the king cobras at Archer's lab.
She pictured the three reptiles, confined in their
plastic cages. Their sinuous beauty and effortless way of moving filled her mind. They were
fascinating, absolutely fascinating.

Turning on her side, she stared into the
darkness for a while before dropping off to
sleep.

# 11

Nita dialed the last digit of Lal Khan Bahadur's telephone number, laying aside the slip he had given her, and waited for the connection to be made.

When the receiver on the other end was lifted, she heard his resonant voice. "Hello, this is Doctor Lal Khan Bahadur speaking."

"Doctor? This is Nita Galforth."

"Ah, yes, Miss Galforth. How are you this morning?"

"Fine, Doctor. I hope you've forgiven me for missing our appointment?"

"Of course. It is only human to forget something now and then or to perhaps oversleep. It was, after all, an early appointment."

'There shouldn't have been any reason for me to miss it. Normally, I'm up quite early every morning."

"Nevertheless, it is over and finished. Let us not dwell on it any longer. When can we get together, Miss Galforth?"

Nita frowned. Since the next few days were quite free, she could see him just about anytime he wanted to see her. "Why don't you make it convenient for yourself. The first few days of next week will be open for me for the most part."

There was no immediate response, and Nita assumed he was looking at his appointment calendar. "Would the day after next be acceptable to you?"

"Monday? What time?"

"Would right after lunch be appropriate?"

"One o'clock?"

"That is very good. I will look forward to seeing you here in my office at that time Monday."

Without another word, he was gone and she heard the disconnecting click in the earpiece. Laying the phone in its cradle, she stared at nothing for a long moment. If the appointment with Bahadur didn't work out, she would make another with someone else. Archer's desire to solve the dream and be rid of it must have been contagious since she too felt very anxious to solve it, now that she'd made an appointment with the swarthy Indian.

Snapping out of her momentary funk, she turned to go to the kitchen and have a glass of juice before leaving for the day. The jangling of the telephone brought her to a quick stop, and retracing her steps, she answered it.

"Hello?"

"Long distance calling Nita Galforth."

"This is Nita Galforth."

"Go ahead."

"Miss Galforth? I'm Duffy Ryan, coordinator for the Southern California Triathalon Association. We would like to formally invite you to participate in our Ironman competition for men and women next month. Would that be possible?"

Nita could not contain the smile of pride spreading over her face. She wanted to laugh and scream and shout all at the same time. She could hardly believe her ears. Was the man serious? Was the call on the level? "Ah, anything is possible, I guess, Mr. Ryan. Could you tell me more?"

"You are interested?"

"Of course."

"Then rather than run the risk of omitting something on the telephone, I propose to send you complete information and the application form. Is that acceptable to you?"

"Yes, of course. Do you have my address?"

"Not really. I got your number from the University switchboard. Could you give it to me?"

After giving her address, Nita said good-bye and hung up. Clapping her hands, she leaped into the air. She could hardly wait to tell Archer, but she didn't want to do it on the telephone. She'd wait until he got home tonight. They could celebrate. She could hardly believe it. She knew the event Ryan was speaking of—most prestigious, with national television coverage on a major network. It was an opportunity of a lifetime and she wanted to start training for it as soon as possible, though the last thing in the world she wanted to do was overtrain. Whistling a happy tune, she went to the kitchen for her glass of juice. Her workout this morning would be more fun than ever.

Archer felt uncomfortable sitting across the desk from the president of the university. Off to Archer's right, Dean Joshua Helgens sat upright in his chair, one hand resting on the smooth walnut top.

"The reason for this meeting, Archer, is to explain to you the actions the president would like to take in regard to the biology department."

Archer felt his face screw up. What was the dean talking about? Why include him? He didn't need time away from the lab to attend stuffy meetings that for the most part would not concern him.

"May I, Dean?" Charles Lane, president of Middleton University asked, taking off his rimless glasses to stare first at Helgens, then at Archer.

"Of course." Helgens sat back in his chair, an expression of relief crossing his face.

"What Dean Helgens started to tell you, Mr. Buchanan, was that I should like to invite a few biologists that I know to interview for positions that are suddenly open here at Middleton. It is certainly no reflection on you as a biologist or researcher or teacher."

"I don't understand what you mean by no reflection on me, sir." Archer looked at the president who quickly diverted his gaze to the dean.

"Perhaps it was a bad opening, Archer," he said, coughing a bit. "I'm sure that you will be granted tenure one day in the not too far distant future, but I want the University to interview several candidates to fill Alfred Stewart's and Richard Roman's places."

"I'm still a bit confused. Why tell me all of this? I'm not the least bit interested in the hiring practices of the University at this time. I—"

"What do you mean by 'at this time,' Archer?" Lane put his glasses back on.

"I'm very involved in my experiments with the king cobras and all that that work entails."

"I think you missed the key word. Tenure. We have no one in the biology department with tenure now which makes that arm of the science department rather tentative at best. We could suddenly start having a turnover in personnel and that would not be good. We need continuity in the department for the benefit of the students. You will be granted tenure, I'm sure, in the future, but not now. We have to get two biologists who have credentials, woo them by offering tenure and get them to sign contracts. We can hardly go on without those two vacancies being filled—and filled soon."

Dean Helgens coughed and looked at the president as if seeking unspoken permission to speak. When the president sat back, deferring

to him, Helgens said, "The election that was to
be held, wherein I'm sure Richard would have
been elected, will not be held. We just didn't
want you to be upset because of it. We
appreciate your work and experiments. You're
young and proving yourself every day."

"Of course you are, my boy," Lane said,
standing to move around his desk.

Archer thought for a moment that the
short, older man was about to attack him but
the wide grin on his face told him differently. He
stood and the president clapped him on the
back.

"This is by no means a reflection on you,
Archer. We must hire these people. We have no
choice. One of them will be appointed chairman
of the department for an interim period, then
sometime in the future, an election will be held.
Who knows, perhaps you'll be elected." Lane
forced a laugh and Dean Helgens joined in.

Archer felt like telling them to go to hell. He
couldn't care less about campus or depart-
mental politics. They could hire the devil
himself as far as he was concerned. Why they
wanted to take him away from his work just to
tell him this was beyond him. He didn't give a
damn for tenure, not at this point in his career.
He had the government funding for his experiments, and even if they wanted to fire him and
be rid of him altogether, they could, but he'd
take his experiments, his king cobras and his
funding to another school. They probably had
forgotten that the grant had been given directly
to him and not to the school.

"Gentlemen," he said, taking the hand President Lane offered, "I can certainly live with whatever decision you make. Of course we need two more people. I'm much to busy to be involved in chairing the department. Please don't feel that you have to consult me because I happen to be the senior member now."

After shaking hands with Helgens, he turned and left the opulent office of the president. He had to get back to the lab. He had work to do.

Because of the meeting with the president that morning, Archer's whole day ran late and he didn't arrive at the apartment until well after 8:00 o'clock. The instant he saw Nita's face, he knew something good had happened. Perhaps she had met with Bahadur and knew the meaning of the dream.

"You certainly look like the cat who ate the canary. What's up?" He kissed her lightly on the mouth and, stepping back, waited for the good news.

"I'm going to be formally invited to participate in the nationally televised Southern California Ironman Triathalon next month." She smiled broadly, waiting for Archer's reaction.

"That's fantastic, Nita. Congratulations. I can hardly believe that I know someone who's going to be on television."

"Oh, Archer, I'm so happy. I don't know what to do or say or how to act or anything."

They hugged.

"How was your day? You're awfully late. Did everything go all right today?" She peered at him, waiting for an answer.

"I had to go to a meeting that I didn't want to go to this morning, throwing my whole schedule off. That's why I'm late."

"Meeting?"

"At the president's office." Before she could say anything or jump to a wrong conclusion, Archer quickly explained what happened. He instantly saw Nita's euphoric state change, her face clouding.

"Does that mean you won't be getting the chairmanship of the department?"

"Hey, who needs it right now? I'm so busy it's unbelievable. I'm just glad they didn't say something about taking over Richard's classes in addition to my own."

"Who's idea was this? Dean Helgens?"

"The President's. Why?"

"Just curiosity, I guess. I'm really unhappy about this, Archer."

When Archer looked at her he saw her anger, seething just below the surface. "Incidentally, did you call Bahadur?"

Shifting gears, to cover her feelings of frustration, she nodded. "I'm to see him Monday. You know, Archer, you *will* be head of the biology department."

"In time, in time. But not now. I don't have the energy or the time to do three things. Class-work and the experiments are more than enough to keep me going." He looked at her again. This time she seemed overly confident, but about what, he couldn't determine. The triathalon next month? Or did she know something about the biology department situation that he didn't? "Just why are you so adament about my being chairman of the department?"

"Because, silly," she said, crossing the room to embrace him, "I want to be married to the head of the department. Don't you want me to be a triathalon champion?"

"Of course I do. Say, is this a proposal? It sure sounds like one."

"No. Well . . . yes. I mean . . . maybe it is. Why?"

"I just want to know how I should act when I'm asked, that's all." He shook his head and kissed her again on the mouth.

"If you want me to be successful, why can't I want you to be the best in your field?" She looked up at him, her face serious.

"Look, Nita, if you don't make it as a triathalon athlete or win any more events, I can live with it."

"I can't."

"You can't what? Live with the fact that I might not ever be head of the department or that never winning would be traumatic?"

"You know what I mean. Don't go to extremes." She turned her back to him.

"Why all this sudden urge for prestige?"

She turned back to face him. "I guess it's my competitive spirit."

"Well, if you're throwing out conditions for

marriage, then I will, too."

"Such as?" she asked, looking away, not knowing what to expect.

"I won't marry you, Miss Competition, unless you see Lal Khan Bahadur and put your dream away forever."

"Hey, come on, I'm seeing him. I've got an appointment. But, what if I can't get rid of my dream?"

Archer's demeanor changed instantly to one of a more serious nature. "You will. With Bahadur's help or some psychologist's help, you'll get rid of it. You have to get rid of it. I'm afraid it's already affecting our relationship somewhat."

"How?"

"Well, for openers, I think I'm more concerned about it than you are. It could act like a wedge between us and drive us apart, and I don't want that."

"Neither do I, Archer," she said moving closer to him.

They embraced and he felt her tremble ever so slightly. "Are you cold?"

"A little. Why?"

"I felt you tremble when we hugged." He reached out, laying a hand on her arm. "Your skin feels cold, too."

"Well, it is almost the middle of November, and I've got short sleeves on. I'm bound to be a little cool."

"I wonder how you'd react to an Iowa or Minnesota winter. You'd probably freeze solid until spring. Want me to turn on the space heater?"

"Not really. Just hold me in bed tonight. That'll keep me warm."

"You just got yourself one heater for bed-time."

They ate their evening meal and, after studying and reading a while, went to bed a little after 10:30. Both fell sound asleep in minutes. A few minutes before midnight, Nita threw the covers off and hugged her chest without waking.

The November moon rode low in the inky black sky, casting long shadows with its yellow light onto the campus. Barely a breath of air moved through the trees bordering the quadrangle, and when the bell tower tolled mid-night, several of the few remaining lights in the women's dormitory went out. No movement of any kind could be seen on the campus at this hour, no movement other than the slow, sinuous motions of the king cobra as it made its way across the quadrangle. It felt sluggish in the cool night air, barely able to make a decent rate of progress. When it reached the base of the tower, it stopped. Flickering its tongue in and out, reading the messages borne on the ether, it turned its head from side to side. It had sensed something, something warm-blooded, coming toward it near the tower steps.

Moving off the concrete walkway, it lay in the grass, before again raising its head to a height of five feet to read the air with its tongue while also paying attention to the miniscule vibrations it felt on its stomach scales. Definitely, some animal was approaching. The snake could not afford to be found. It had to find cover. But where?

Extending its full length on the ground, the king cobra lay still, waiting.

"I don't think we should stop, Chuck," the girl said quietly. For some reason she felt if she spoke louder than a hushed whisper, everyone on campus would hear, and the fact that she had gone out with Chuck Lastner would become common knowledge. She didn't want that, especially since she still held hope that Pete "Tuna" O'Mara, the football team captain, would ask her out. She didn't want a hunk like Tuna thinking she was dating someone like Chuck Lastner, a nice guy and brainy but sort of weird. She had had fun on the date and they had laughed at some of his intellectual jokes, but now she wanted to get home without being seen.

"Aw, just for a minute, Pam. We can sit on old Alan Ede's Memorial and look at the moon. Isn't it beautiful?"

"What? The moon or Alan Ede's Memorial?"

He laughed. "See? It's contagious. A joke can be made about most anything. I hope to be able to write for a TV show someday."

"You told me that."

"Oh. Well, here we are. Let's plunk for a

minute." He took her hand, leading her toward the steps that surrounded the base of the tower.

Pulling her down next to him, he tipped her head, kissing her on the lips. His tongue forced its way into her mouth and she fought to gain her breath.

"Come on, Chuck," she said hoarsely, "give me a chance to get my breath." She made a move to stand but he pulled her back.

With his arm around her shoulder, she relaxed for an instant until his hand fell on her left breast. She wanted to groan. If he started doing something like that and he hoped it led to bigger and bigger things, just where did he expect to consummate the act? Here on the steps? She didn't have enough padding to do it on concrete. In the grass of the quadrangle? It was dewy wet now and she didn't want to catch cold. She'd just as soon go home and go to bed—alone.

"I've got to get going." Pam stood quickly, but he rose with her, grasping her arms.

"One more kiss and then it's home for you, my sweet." He kissed her on the lips and neither caught the undulating movement in the grass as the king cobra slithered away from the tower.

When the cobra came to the street separating the campus from the bordering neighborhood, it stopped, raising its head above the ground but keeping next to a tele- phone pole to prevent its silhouette from being noticed by passing cars. There was not much traffic after midnight, and when no cars passed for several minutes, the king cobra lowered its upper body to the ground and moved across the street. The blacktop felt cold, and the snake grew more sluggish with each movement of its long body.

Successfully reaching the other side of the street, it made its way parallel to the campus for one block and then headed down the first street it came to.

Every once in a while the reptile stopped, reading the air currents with its tongue, looking at the house in front of which it reared, the round pupils of its large eyes taking in each detail of the building. Then, it would continue on its way, searching, looking.

When it reached a two story house, it raised up, hissing loudly. A stray cat, which lurked in the bushes surrounding the house, watched, its yellow eyes reflecting the moonlight. At the sound of the loud hiss, the cat broke from its cover, dashing around the corner and out of sight.

The snake was alone. Studying the house, the cobra slicked forward through the dewy grass, keeping its head five feet off the ground. Investigating the windows at the front of the house, it found none open. It moved around the corner, stopping at a window that looked out on the driveway. The sill, at least six feet off the ground, posed no challenge for the 19 foot snake, and it simply raised its head to that level, instantly picking up the warmer current of air flowing from inside the house. The head went forward but the window was open only two inches, not enough entryway for the snake's body, which was almost three inches in diameter. Forcing its head in further, the window raised a fraction of an inch, then another and another until it had been raised sufficiently to permit the king cobra entrance.

Without a sound, the long body began sliding through the window until the tail disappeared into the darkened interior.

# 12

A mantle clock struck the quarter hour, its Westminster chimes singing through the darkened living room. A faucet in the kitchen dripped, plopping water into a filled pan. After several minutes, the grandfather clock in the front hallway, sounded the quarter hour to the melody of the Whittington chimes.

The king cobra, vaguely aware of the soft nighttime sounds around it, picked up the vibrations through its body and tongue as it made its way through the downstairs. After checking each room and finding nothing that would satisfy its search, the reptile paused in the hallway, its head raised. The eyes, their large pupils dilated, scanned the shadows. Nothing.

Prowling swiftly with its vigor renewed in the warmth of the house, the cobra moved back through the rooms once more, diligently searching each nook. When it finished, it found itself back in the front hallway. Its tongue, zipping in and out of the closed mouth, searched desperately before the snake suddenly froze, its eyes fixed on the stairway that led to the second floor. Picking up a gentle rumbling from that direction, it slithered toward the bottom step, where it raised its head off the floor. Lying down on the steps, it tried to move but found it difficult at best. Discovering it almost impossible to make a purchase with its scutes, it zigzagged its length to enable a few folds of the sinuous body to rest flat on different steps. Repeating the process, it slowly made its way to the second floor.

The cobra skimmed down the warm, carpeted hallway, stopping at each open doorway. Those that were closed were treated as part of the wall and ignored. The open doors were checked by the huge snake rearing up, tongue examining the air coming from inside, before lowering itself to the floor and moving into the interior of each room. Once carefully examined, the cobra would abandon it. Then, it would move on to the next and repeat the procedure.

The next to last doorway held the attention of the king cobra longer than the others. Within the confines it sensed living, warm-blooded creatures. The door, open no more than a few inches, didn't move when the reptile entered. Once inside, it reared up, examining the darkened bedroom. Snores rumbled through the night, and the sleeping man and woman lying on the king-size bed, their back toward each other, were blissfully unaware of their visitor.

Its hood flared as far as it would go, the snake hesitated, its eyes studying the quiet forms before moving to the man's side. Peering down on the sleeping man's face, the cobra seemed satisfied and lowered its body carefully onto the bed. Once it had situated itself between the man and woman, it crawled toward him. Rearing for an instant, the reptile lowered its body until, draped across the man, half of its body rested on each side.

The right arm, bare to the middle of the bicep, lay exposed along the topside of the sleeping man's body. The snake's head inched nearer until the tongue could check it without touching it. Sensing the flow of blood mere millimeters below the surface of the skin, the cobra opened its mouth, extending the lower jaw as far as possible. After the hypodermic needlelike fangs were poised over the large vein in the man's inner elbow before puncturing the soft skin, the snake bit carefully. Hanging on but unhurried, the snake pumped its murderous venom into the victim's system. The man barely moved at the slight discomfort.

Almost exhausting its supply, the snake withdrew, settling its head, the hood extended, on the man's side, close to his face. In minutes, the pain usually associated with the bite of a king cobra took hold, and the man reached up, enfolding the reptile close to his own body, to massage the wounded arm. In his sleeping stupor, the man suddenly sensed the presence of something and opened his eyes. The glow from the digital clock on the nightstand barely lighted the area but threw enough illumination to show the man what he was hugging close to his own chest.

Opening its mouth farther, the snake hissed loudly, its growling sound booming through the darkened bedroom.

The man's scream began as a whispered word, "God!" then rose slowly in volume, pitch and degree of panic. "Good God! Jesus, what's on me? Jenny, wake up. What is this thing on me? Jenny! For Christ's sake, wake up. What's on me? Oh, Sweet Jesus. It's a *snake*!"

Reacting more to the degree of fright in her husband's voice than to his actual words, the woman sat up, fumbling for the switch of the table next to her side of the bed. Instantly flooded with light, the bedroom took on an incandescent quality, blinding both the man and woman. When her eyes had adjusted to the light, she turned and took in the awful sight of her husband, frozen with fear and hugging a gigantic snake to his chest. She screamed, her long, wailing cry piercing the quiet night. She then reacted instinctively, throwing back the covers and leaping from the bed.

Her movement brought her husband to his senses and his motor reflexes took over. Before he could take his left hand from the wounded right arm and leap from the bed, the king cobra struck him once more as if purposefully inflicting one last humiliation. Grabbing the reptile around the neck, he hurled it toward the foot of the bed and jumped away, all in one movement.

"Jesus Christ, Jenny," he puffed. "Look out. Get up on the bed. Now! Get up on the bed." He followed his own advice, leaping onto the mattress and bouncing around a bit until he gained some sort of balance. His heart raced, his mind reeling. How could a snake as large as this one get into their home? As his wife joined him, he began feeling sick to his stomach, and when he tried to speak, the thick juices in his mouth all but gagged him. He spit some of it out, but before he could utter a word, his mouth filled again. He looked at his wife, trying to communicate with her, but nothing seemed to work properly. His vocal chords seemed paralyzed and when he looked at the foot of the bed, he tried to scream but merely burbled grotesquely.

The king cobra reared up until its head hovered six feet off the floor, almost even with his own face. It hissed horribly and then lowered itself to the floor. Turning to the doorway, it slithered noiselessly into the hall.

Then Jenny reacted. She looked at her husband as he heaved and a thick mucus-like spittle ran down his chin. He groped for the wall behind the headboard and, when he found it, slid to the mattress. The goddamn snake had bitten her husband. Leaping from the bed, she looked about for something that would make a suitable weapon, but finding nothing, she charged the reptile that was still half in the bedroom, half in the hallway. She raised one foot and brought it down with all her might onto the reptile's back, but before she could launch a second attack, the tail zipped through the open doorway and into the hall.

Slamming the door closed, she looked at her husband who was convulsing on the bed, gurgling in agony. She ran to his side, grabbing his arm and fumbling for a pulse. When she found it, she felt it leaping and receding, pumping fast one second and slowing down the next. She needed to get help. What could she do? What was the emergency number? Nine something. Nine one one. That was it. She groped for the phone next to her side of the bed, dialed the number, and in an instant a voice crackled in her ear.

She took a deep breath and tried to speak calmly. "I want you to listen carefully, young lady. My husband was just bitten by a huge snake. I don't know what kind it was but I believe my husband is dying. I need someone here to help him—Now! I live at—"

"Are you sure, ma'am?"

"Of course, you idiot. I know a huge snake when I see one."

"Where is the snake now?"

"How should I know where the snake is? It must be in the house someplace. It was just here in our bedroom. I've closed the door. I'm safe for now but I'm sure my husband is dying. Please hurry."

"Give me your address."

"1520 Moon Street, Northeast. Hurry."

"How will the paramedics get in if the snake is still in the house?"

"That's their bloody problem. I won't leave my husband. Break the door in. Good grief, what's the matter with you? Can't you hurry?"

"I'll dispatch a police car to assist. Thank you, ma'am."

To Jenny Lane it seemed to take forever to hear the far-off distant wailing of sirens, and when she did, she thought they would never find the house. But it seemed that the ambulance and police car arrived simultaneously and stopped directly in front of the house. She could hear the voices below her window talking about breaking in and the possibility of a vicious snake.

Her husband's gurgling brought her attention back to him. His eyes were rolled back in his head, their whites staring blankly at her. His mouth was open, tongue hanging askew, thick almost pasty saliva running down both sides of his face. What could she do for him?

Below, the first blow was struck against the heavy front door.

Her husband's body jerked spasmodically, his arms flailing about in smaller and smaller motions while his legs twitched.

Another blow from downstairs accompanied the sound of splintering wood.

Her husband gasped, trying but unable to draw in a breath. He tried again without results, and trying to exhale brought an expression of pain across his face. He gasped once more and then no longer moved.

The third and final blow brought the door crashing in, and she heard the excited voices of men in the foyer. She caught bits and pieces of what they were saying, cautioning each other to watch out. It seemed to take an eternity, but in time she heard footsteps in the hall outside her door.

"In here," she croaked and sat down on the bed, her shoulders falling forward when she held her head in both hands. Then she wept uncontrollably.

"The house is safe, Mrs. Lane," the uniformed policeman said quietly. "We found no trace of any snake, big or little, in the house. You'll be able to go downstairs now, if you wish. There's a detective on his way here to talk with you."

Jenny Lane stared out the window into the night. He husband was dead. The medical examiner was still hovering around his body on the bed, and she couldn't stand to watch. The doctor looked very professional as he went about his duties, working on the body of her husband who looked so much smaller in death than he ever did in life. As President of Middleton University, her husband had been in charge of every moment of his life. Although he was slight in build and short in stature, he dominated any situation into which he was thrust. Her husband had been a giant despite his size.

"Mrs. Lane?"

A strange voice from behind made her wince. It was neither the uniformed policeman nor the doctor. Almost afraid to turn around for fear she would have to look at her husband, she finally spun slowly to the side, keeping her back to the bed. "Yes?"

"I'm Detective Sergeant Tony Alexander, ma'am. I'd like to ask you a few questions. Why don't you let me take you downstairs. Perhaps I could make you a cup of coffee if you'd let me."

"Perhaps you know best."

Helping her down the stairway, Alexander said, "I'm very sorry for the death of your husband. Do you feel up to talking about what happened?"

She stopped, frozen in her tracks halfway down the steps. Grabbing his arm, she said, "It was gigantic, the biggest snake I've ever seen. It killed my husband. Why? Why did a large snake come into my home and kill my husband?" Her voice broke and the overdue tears cascaded down her cheeks.

Alexander caught her around the waist and continued down the steps for fear the woman would totally collapse on the stairway. He helped her into the living room and into an easy chair. She clung to his hand for several moments then slowly released her grip.

"He's dead, isn't he?" She searched his eyes for a contrary opinion.

"I'm afraid he is, ma'am. Can you talk? Would you like that cup of coffee?"

She nodded, crying softly to herself. Any-

thing to help her get over the trauma would be
welcome. She'd even try whiskey if he
suggested it, but she knew there wasn't a drop
in the house. Her husband would never have
permitted it—but he was dead. Now, if she
wanted to buy some liquor and get rip-roaring
drunk she could, but it wouldn't be fun without
him. They never had drunk anything stronger
than wine or usually tea and coffee. She
watched Alexander say something to the
uniformed policeman, who left the room, then
he turned back to her.

"How do you think that snake got in, Mrs.
Lane?"

She shrugged. "It was so big. Gigantic.
Never saw anything like it."

"How big would you say it was?"

She shrugged again.

"How long?"

Another shrug.

"Would you say it was ten feet long?"

She nodded. "Bigger. Much bigger."

"Twelve? Fifteen feet?"

She nodded again. "Bigger. Really. Much
bigger."

"Eighteen, twenty feet? You must have
some idea."

"At least thirty or forty feet long. Gigantic!"
Her eyes widened.

"How big around would you say it was?"

She held up her two hands, forming an "o"
with the index fingers and thumbs of each
hand. "Like this."

Alexander noted in his pad. "About three

inches in diameter. Victim's wife says the snake
was thirty to forty feet long. Probably an
exaggeration." He underlined the word
"exaggeration" and looked up.

"I kicked it. I did. Hard." Vigorously
nodding her head as if to support her statement, she grinned at Alexander. "I really did. I
kicked it so hard."

"You did? Where?"

"On its back. It was going through the door
into the hallway, and I was so mad at it that I
stomped on its back before it got all the way
through. Then I slammed the door. I did." She
sobbed, snuffling at the same time. Did the nice
looking young man believe her? All they had to
do was find this huge snake with a footprint on
its back and they'd have the murderer of her
husband. The snake had killed him right before
her eyes. She felt the saline flood renewing itself
and then the tears came again.

Alexander stood when he heard footsteps
on the stairs and left the living room to stand in
the foyer. The medical examiner stopped at the
bottom step and motioned for the detective to
be quiet. "I think we've got another one like the
Stewart case."

"I gathered that from what Mrs. Lane has
been telling me, assuming of course that she's
not just being hysterical."

"What'd she say?"

Alexander smiled grimly. "A thirty to forty
foot long snake that's about as big around as
this." He made an "o" with his fingers like the
woman had done.

The examiner shook his head. "Don't be too cynical. I did some research after Stewart's autopsy and learned a little about cobras. King cobras, that is. They're the most poisonous snake in the world because of the copious amounts of venom they can inject into a person. Although I doubt the length that she's giving you, the longest one on record for quite a while was eighteen feet and some inches. Now, there's been one reported at over nineteen feet. I'm sure if you woke up to see a snake say, sixteen or seventeen feet long in your bedroom, it would probably come across like the King Kong of snakedom. D'you know what I mean?"

"Yeah, I think so. Just where in hell did a snake like that come from, Doc?"

The examiner shrugged. "There you've got me. That's a mystery. At any rate I won't be certain that this one died from cobraism until I get the body to the lab. I've taken some blood and saliva samples to work on until it's delivered."

"Keep me posted, Doc." Alexander turned back to the living room but stopped when he saw the uniformed policeman coming from the kitchen carrying a cup of coffee. He took the cup and nodded when the police officer told him it was only instant because he couldn't find anything else.

Alexander walked into the living room. He'd have to glean as much from Mrs. Lane as possible and then put it all together for his investigation. Several things stood out in his mind now without having to probe too far. He wanted to find a connection between Doctor

Stewart and Charles Lane, who was President of Middleton University. Why would the newly elected chairman of the biology department and the president of the school wherein Doctor Stewart taught both die of cobra venom? Then, too, he wanted another visit with Archer Buchanan. Buchanan seemed to be the resident expert on cobras and was the only one in town to have access to that particular type of reptile. By all means, he had to talk with Buchanan. Buchanan would have a lot of explaining to do before Tony Alexander felt convinced that the biologist was in the clear on these deaths—or should he classify them as murders? He had come close to accusing Buchanan when he had called on him while investigating Richard Roman's death. At least that one was readily explained—no cobra venom there, just a fall off an 85 foot bluff.

It would be very interesting to see what Buchanan had to say this time.

Sergeant Alexander handed the cup of coffee to the sobbing woman. "Do you feel like answering a few more questions, Mrs. Lane?"

"Who's ugly?"

"That man. The man who keeps coming down close to my face now. I don't like him at all."

"What's he doing?"

"He's got something in his hand. He just cut a piece of my dress away. Now Mommy won't be able to sew it up unless he gives it back. Mommy will be so mad at me—and at him for doing that. Oh, now I see. He's got a dolly in his hand, a little brown doll. It looks like it's made of clay or something. Ouch!"

"What is it, Nita?"

"He pulled my hair. Darn him. That hurt!"

"What's he doing now?"

Nita's eyes widened for an instant. "Why, he's wrapped the piece of my dress that he cut off around the dolly, and he's sticking the hair that he pulled out of my head into the head of the dolly. Why do you suppose he's doing that? And he's dumping something oily on me. I wish he'd stop."

Bahadur waited for the next event to unfold, his eyes darting from side to side beneath their hooded lids. It wasn't possible. After all these years, how could it—

"He's yelling something at somebody and rolling the doll in his hands. I hope it's not me. I'm in enough trouble with Mommy and Daddy without him getting mad at me, too."

"Can you understand what it is he is saying?"

Nita shook her head. "It sounds like

monkeys chattering. No, wait. I can say one of the words. She-sha-by. Something like that. And there's another one. Ah-va-tar. I wonder what they mean."

Nita suddenly jumped as if startled by a loud noise.

"What is it, Nita? Why did you jump just then?"

"I heard a gun go off. Somebody shot a gun, and now everybody's real quiet. Wait. I can hear my Daddy. My Daddy's coming for me. Thank goodness. I don't like these people at all. Hurry, Daddy, hurry!"

Nita visibly relaxed from the tense upright position she had held since recounting her dream in detail.

"What is going on now, Nita?"

"My Daddy's here and everything is fine. There's another man with Daddy. He's got a uniform on and he's yelling at the man who tore my dress. It serves him right. It's a good thing my Mommy didn't come along. She'd really get him."

"Now where are you?"

"My Daddy's carrying me back through the jungle. I'm not afraid any more. Everything will be all right. I just hope my Mommy isn't mad at me. She might spank me."

Bahadur sat back on the desk. His shoulders slumped but he didn't ask any more questions. "You will rest for a moment, Nita. When you awaken, you will feel refreshed and your back will not hurt you. Rest now until I tell you to awaken."

How could any of this be? Had they had the child long enough to complete the rite? He had no idea based on what Nita had said in her childish voice. As a child, she wouldn't have been aware of everything that had occured. If they had gone far enough, had they been successful? Had it worked? Once in his life, he had fully believed in things of this sort.

Standing, he walked behind his desk. He'd have to call Archer and fill him in on what he had learned. As soon as he brought Nita out of the trance, he would call the biologist and talk with him.

"Can you hear me, Nita?"

She nodded.

"When I count to three, you will awaken and you will not remember anything you have told me. When you go to sleep, you will dream only of those things that will be helpful to you and beneficial to you. Do you understand me?"

Again, she nodded.

"One. Two. Three."

Vitality bubbled in Nita's eyes when the word three was spoken. Instantly looking about her and realizing that she had been hypnotized and was now out of it, she said, "What did you learn, Doctor Bahadur? What did I say?"

"Unfortunately, I did not record the session. Had I known you would be so interested, I would have recorded it and played it for you." He smiled.

Nita picked up on the man's discomfort. Was he tired? Or had she said something while under hypnosis that had upset him? What could

that have been? From the exterior, Lal Khan
Bahadur appeared most unflappable, most in
control of any person she had ever encountered. What then could have made him
come across as being uneasy? She caught him
staring at her, his eyes unblinking, the hooded
lids barely twitching. She turned away. He made
her feel ill-at-ease. If he felt the same way,
perhaps they had developed a mutual dislike
for each other. Or had he learned something
about her and her dream that had changed his
opinion of her? But what could that be?

"Can you explain the dream to me now,
Doctor?"

"As I said earlier, I can only lead you
through the labyrinth of your mind. You and
you alone will be responsible for solving any
dream that might bother you."

Nita winced. Any dream that might bother
her? What did he mean by that? Should she even
ask? For some reason, she felt as if the man
held her in some sort of different regard than
when she first entered his office. If anything,
the man seemed to be hedging on broaching
the subject of her dream and whatever she had
said while under the hypnotic spell.

"Can't you tell me anything, Doctor?"

He smiled but it wasn't the same confident,
cold smile he had displayed before. It seemed
unsure, almost nervous. Yes, that was the word.
If Nita had to hang a tag on Lal Khan Bahadur
right that instant, it would be nervous.

"Let me tell you this, Nita. I have learned

much and have much to ponder now that you
have told me your dream in its entirety. Right
now I feel it is complete. There might be more
detail that will come out if we have more
sessions together, but I should like to think it
over and see what logical conclusions I can
draw."

"But . . ." Nita fell silent for a moment. He
seemed to be contradicting himself, since he
had said earlier that only she could decipher
her dream. Now, he wanted time to think about
what she had told him. That didn't make sense.
At least it didn't make sense to her. And what
did he mean by "if" they had more sessions
together? Didn't he want to assume the respon-
sibility of her treatment? Perhaps she should
just let him alone for the time being and see
what developed. If the dream wasn't heavy
enough for him to consider treatment, then why
should she worry about it? In time it would go
away. Still, her curiosity had been aroused.

"I think, Doctor Bahadur, that you should
tell me what was said. I feel it is my right to
know."

"Of course it is your right, child. I didn't
mean to imply that you would never know. All I
want is some time to think about it, dissect the
dream down to its basic components, then put
them back together in such a way that you will
be able to better understand it. If I were to try
explaining things now, I'm afraid both of us
would become hopelessly confused."

She thought about his last few statements.

He seemed more in control now, but was that an act?

"Will you see me again, Nita?"

Nita felt her skin crawl when he smiled. He was back to his usual, oily self. For some reason, she felt she couldn't believe him even though he seemed sincere enough when he now mentioned seeing her again.

"I guess I'll have to if I'm ever to understand my dream." She stood and realized that her back felt normal, totally free of pain.

"How do you feel?" He stepped from behind the desk.

"I feel fantastic. My back doesn't hurt at all. What did you do?"

"I did nothing. That is merely the side effects of hypnosis. People usually feel as if they've had eight hours of undisturbed sleep when they wake up. In time, I'm sure your back will begin paining you again. But for now, enjoy."

She smiled. If nothing else, her trapezius muscle was not annoying her at the present and that was something for which she could be thankful.

"If it is all right with you, Nita," he said, opening the door for her, "I will call you when I feel I am familiar enough with your dream and its implications. At that time we can make an appointment. Is that acceptable to you?"

"Of course it is, Doctor." She extended her hand, grasping his in a tight, strong grip. When she pulled hers away, she noted once more that her hand was perfectly dry.

She turned, starting down the hallway, feeling Lal Khan Bahadur's eyes following her every move. When she turned the corner, she relaxed, smiling to herself when she heard his door close.

Bahadur hurried to the phone, quickly dialing a number.

Archer carefully held the rod with the small noose at one end away from his body. The young king cobra, almost 11 feet long, writhed in the grip of the rope holding it by the neck shortly behind the head. The phone jangled loudly, and Archer, despite reacting to it, did not change his course of action. He walked toward the cage at the back of the lab where sunshine poured through the windows, and, sliding open the cage door with his free hand, gingerly brought the king cobra toward the opening. After inserting the deadly reptile into its cage, he closed the door until only the width of the stick remained. Opening the noose from his end of the holder, he withdrew it, pushing the door closed.

"Hey, I'm coming already," he called out to the phone at the opposite end of the room. Walking hurriedly toward the incessant ringing, he picked up the receiver, thrusting his head down to pin it to his shoulder. "Hello? Archer Buchanan here."

"Ah, yes, Archer. It is Lal Khan Bahadur. I

must talk with you.''

"You sound strange, Doctor. What's wrong?'' Suddenly, he remembered that Nita and Bahadur had had an appointment that day. "Is everything all right with Nita?''

"Nita is fine.'' He hesitated. "I must talk with you, however. I have learned something that seems to defy description, much less belief. When can I speak with you?''

At best, Archer thought Bahadur sounded mysterious, even frightened, but decided he might be overreacting.

"I suppose just about any time you'd like to, Doctor. Do you want to come here?'' Archer turned around, freezing in position.

Facing him was the young king cobra, the brightly colored one he had just put into its cage, rearing off the floor at least five feet, its mouth open, its fangs glistening.

"Archer? Archer, are you there?'' Bahadur's voice rang in his ear.

The only sound Archer could concentrate on was the loud, growling hiss from the snake confronting him.

# PART IV

## CHILL OF DEATH

# 15

Archer's eyes widened. The youngest of the three king cobras reared up, confronting him not seven feet away. Its tongue, flicking in and out, had by this time detected the adrenalin pumping through Archer's body. After what seemed minutes but in reality had been no more than two or three beats of the man's racing heart, the snake hissed loudly again. Outside of the cage, the sound was even more terrifying, more unrestrained, more unconfined.

Archer froze. Clamping the phone tightly to his ear with his shoulder, he stared. How much venom could the snake have left? He had just taken a goodly amount from it. Still, that meant nothing other than the rapidity with which a victim could be dispatched. The more poison entering the system, the quicker the victim died. The less poison, the longer and the more likelihood of antivenom being introduced into the system and saving the life of the one bitten.

"Archer? Are you there?" Bahadur's voice sounded small, far away.

After an agonizing search for the strength to answer, Archer managed to whisper the one word, "Yes."

"What is it? What's wrong?"

For fear of upsetting the snake by making any sudden movement, Archer tried speaking without using his lips unless necessary, choosing his words carefully. "Snake out o' cage."

"Good heavens. Where?"

"Se-en 'eet away."

"Don't move."

"Right."

"Can you distract it?"

"How?"

"Anything in your hand that you can move that would take its attention away from your body?"

"Yes. Noose on rod."

"Good. Listen to me carefully. You must do what the snake charmers do. Keep its attention with the rod in your hand. Move it to one side very slowly. If the snake's head and attention follow it, you will have less to worry about."

"What i' it doesn't?"

"It *will* follow the rod you hold. Try it. Are you doing it?"

Archer moved the stick in his hand, toward the door at his left. The noose wiggled ever so little as his hand shook, transmitting his fear to the loop of rope at the end of the rod. The snake hissed, its hood expanding, and turned a fraction of an inch, riveting its attention on it.

"What's happening, Archer?" Bahadur's voice seemed to carry enough excitement and tension for both men.

"It's watching it."

"Good."

"Now what?"

Bahadur didn't answer and Archer suddenly realized why. With the snake watching the noose, the only thing in his possession that amounted to a weapon of defense, was being guarded more or less by the king cobra.

"Now what?" he asked again.

"I don't suppose you have another noose nearby?"

Archer tried to take in the desk with his peripheral vision but could not see everything from where he was standing. Picturing the desk top in his mind, he tried desperately to recall what had been there before he turned his back on it to find the snake confronting him. "I . . . I don't know. I can't see the desk from where I'm standing."

No answer from Bahadur.

"Do I dare turn -y head a -it without -ear of the snake striking?"

"You might try it, although I wouldn't if I were in your position."

"I got no other choice."

Archer turned his head some, no more than a hair's breadth.

The snake didn't divert its attention from the gently bobbing noose.

Archer turned his head a little more. The edge of the desk came into his field of vision. Another quarter of an inch and a bit more of the desk.

The snake held fast.

Another tiny move and a little more desk top.

The snake continued fixing its disconcerting stare on the piece of rope.

How long would it take before he would be able to appraise the items on the desk? At the rate he was going, he thought his beard would be quite long and the snake would have lost its youthful coloring.

The hair in his nose vibrated as if he might sneeze any minute. The last thing in the world he needed was something like a sneeze, over which he would have absolutely no control. Opening his mouth, he breathed through it, taking the passage of air away from his nostrils.

Feeling the pressure of the snake and the length of time it was taking him to turn toward the desk, Archer moved his head about half an inch at a time.

The snake hissed loudly but did not turn toward him.

Would the king cobra be able to strike at him without its head being squared toward him? He tried to remember everything he knew about the threatening reptile. Their strike was fast, lightning fast, but not always 100 percent accurate. In fact, he had read where the king cobra, despite its lofty ranking among poisonous snakes, was not considered the deadliest because of their inability to always strike their victim the first time. Another thought popped into his mind. They could not strike farther than their heads were raised above the ground, give or take several inches. From where he was positioned now, Archer could still see the cobra and calculated its head to be no more than five feet off the floor. And it was at least seven feet away from where he stood.

"Archer? Are you still there? Are you all right? What's the snake doing?"

As best he could Archer related the position of the snake, the height of its head and that he could see more of the desk. He risked irritating the snake and moved his head a full inch. The only reaction was another loud hiss, but the snake continued fixing its attention on the stick in Archer's left hand. Even though the cobra's head was not squared at him, Archer felt the reptile was watching every move, no matter how infintesimal it might be.

"What are you doing now, Archer?"

"I al-ost turned toward the desk. I can see-there's another rod on it. Al-ost in -y grasp." His neck muscles screamed from the tension of holding the phone to his head.

When Archer sounded the "p" in grasp, the snake hissed loudly and turned toward him but did not move. That little closing of his lips had been all it took to get the cobra's attention back to him. As long as it stayed where it was, Archer stood a good chance of picking up the other rod.

Projecting his arm outward, toward the desk, Archer moved it a millimeter at a time, barely able to discern his own progression. After what seemed an age unto itself, his hand hovered over the handle. Slowly, his fingers closed on it, and grasping it in his sweaty palm, he raised it from the desk.

For the first time he noticed his arms were wet. His forehead dripped sweat onto his cheeks, narrowly missing his eyes. If a drop or two got into his eyes, in effect he would be blinded for a second or so until the tears could wash out the saline liquid.

"What's happening?" Bahadur cried into his ear.

"I got another rod. I can distract it and loo-one end over his head."

"Be careful, Archer."

"Want to trade places?"

"No. Just remember to move in super slow motion."

"I know, I know."

"If I hang up, will you be all right?"

"Why?"

"I can call for help or I could hurry over there. I'm not that far away."

"You know a-out snakes. You come. Others might be hurt or cause snake to strike."

"I'll be there in minutes."

Bahadur hung up, and Archer heard the monotonous hum of the dial tone. He wished he could drop the phone, but that would only tend to provoke the snake and cause an attack. He'd have to manipulate the decoy stick in one hand, try to open the noose and drop it over the head of the cobra with the other, while holding the phone to his head with his shoulder.

With the control stick in his right hand, he manipulated the rope, opening the noose enough to drop it over the head of the snake. The one in his left hand, still extended out toward the reptile, wiggled from the tension in his fatigued muscles. The snake fixed its baleful glare on the closer object, which to it was the more threatening, and ignored Archer.

Once the loop was open far enough, Archer began bringing it around in a circle, a degree at a time, toward the side and rear of the cobra's head.

Lal Khan Bahadur, his white brocaded tunic tail flapping in the air, ran full tilt across the campus toward the John Thomas Science Building. Students and faculty alike stopped to watch the dignified Indian charge across the grass, leaping a row of bushes and taking the steps that led to the entrance of the science building two at a time. Without stopping his headlong flight, Bahadur raced up the steps, toward the third floor.

In order to drop the noose over the head of the snake, Archer would have to take one step toward him. Moving the stick in his left hand more than he had, Archer took the necessary move when the snake hissed extraordinarily loud and with one deft motion dropped the loop over the head just as the door opened and Bahadur stepped inside.

"What took you so long?" Archer asked as the phone hit the floor. He held the reptile, whose head was securely restrained by the loop, at arm's length. Although the snake weighed no more than ten or so pounds, the weight seemed more because of his exhausted muscles.

"Are you all right?"

"Yeah. Let's get this thing back where it belongs. That was quite an entrance you made." After depositing the snake in its cage, he quickly closed the door making certain it was securely fastened this time.

"I don't understand."

"The way you opened the door and walked in could have made the snake strike at you or me. Lucky thing I already had the noose on it."

"I did look through the window and realized that you were ready to catch it. That's why I didn't hesitate." Bahadur smiled. "You *are* all right, aren't you?"

"A little stiff from all the slow motion movement, but I'm fine." He moved back toward the front of the room and sat down heavily in the chair behind the desk. Taking several deep breaths, he watched the Indian come toward him and sit on the chair opposite him. "Before, when you called, you sounded a little different, Doctor. I asked you if everything was all right with Nita."

"Are *you* all right? Do you feel strong enough to talk?"

"Is it that serious, this thing you want to talk to me about?"

Bahadur nodded. "I was about to say, before you were interrupted by the cobra, that I had learned something that will defy description and will test you as a human being. It will also question your beliefs and convictions as a scientist."

"Well, you wanted to talk with me. Let's talk. First of all, Nita is all right, isn't she?"

"Nita is fine."

Again Archer felt the statement was incomplete. From the way he said it, Archer almost believed he was ready to add something like, "for the time being," but the man said nothing more. "Then, what is it, if it doesn't concern Nita?" Archer sat forward, anticipating the man's explanation.

"I'm certain you have heard the different expressions about the East and West never meeting on a common mental ground?"

Archer nodded.

"In many instances that is true. First, I want to say that Nita and I got along well. I hypnotized her and I believe I know the full content of the dream."

Archer frowned. He hadn't thought of the man using hypnosis on Nita. What if he had decided to take unfair advantage of her? He forced himself to nod in understanding while quelling the urge to shudder at the possible consequences of his idle thought. "What does it mean, Doctor?"

"For the benefit of clarity. I first should like

to tell you the dream as Nita explained it while in a hypnotic state."

Archer sat back, waiting.

Bahadur quickly recounted the hypnotic narration of the dream, and when he finished, Archer sat up straight.

"That's pretty darn near the way she told me. What does the dream mean?"

"That's just it. It is more of a recollection than a dream, of that I'm certain."

"How can you be certain? Have you told Nita?"

Bahadur shook his head. "I wanted to discuss it with you first."

"Is that ethical?"

"In this case, I believe so. It would have done Nita's frame of mind absolutely no good if I would have told her what I am about to tell you."

"All right. I'll go along with that—for now. Go ahead."

"By a recollection, I mean something that actually happened to her that she had buried in her subconscious for a number of years."

"You mean she actually was on an altar when she was a little girl? My God, that's unbelievable."

"I told you you would find it thus."

"Who had taken her?"

"From what I learned it was members of the Sheshaby cult."

Archer mouthed the strange word. "What sort of cult are they?"

"They worship Prajapati, the snake god."

"Go on."

"Prajapati has a snake for a phallus and is prayed to, much like Christians pray to Jesus and Buddhists pray to Buddha."

"That's silly."

"And that, my dear Archer, is why the East and West shall never meet on an intellectual or religious basis. Perhaps we find praying to a man who was allegedly crucified and for which there is absolutely no proof that he ever existed on earth a bit on the foolish side as well."

"Touche." Archer bowed his head. "I'm sorry, but on the surface it struck me as a bit . . . well, go ahead."

"In the East, in India, we worship different things in nature. It is not unlike your own American aborigines. To us, cattle are venerated. Snakes are worshipped. Those who deal in only the visible deities are formed into cults. I, myself, belonged to the cult that worshipped Prajapati."

Archer felt his mouth open. Why did he always think of everyone as being like himself? It was a fault that he had to overcome somehow. Maybe he could look on foreigners in a different way if he did. Not everyone could be a Christian nor believe everything Archer Buchanan believed.

"What was the purpose of the cult?" Archer found his own curiosity aroused, as much by the chance to learn something new as to help Nita solve her problem.

"We worshipped Prajapati. In the past, the people of India could not determine who the

one true God might be. For a time, Prajapati
enjoyed this honor. In time, other deities
supplanted Prajapati, but there were those who
hung onto the old ways. It is very complicated
to try to explain all of this to you, Archer. I may
skip large portions just to get the basic idea of
this particular cult across to you."

"Whatever," Archer said, holding both
palms upward.

"Vishnu, who came into being shortly after
Prajapati, eventually supplanted all others as
the supreme being or Preserver of Life. However
there were those who continued praying to Prajapati, and with the introduction of Shesha, the
many-headed serpent who supports the world
and with whom Vishnu sleeps during peaceful
times, our own particular cult was formed."

"Do you mean you belonged to the same
cult that apparently kidnapped Nita when she
was a young girl?"

"Not to that particular group but to that
cult, yes."

"That's unbelieveable. It really is."

"You have not even heard everything that
will stupefy you, Archer."

"What else is there?"

"The purpose of the rite as she described it.
This rite was a plea to Sheshaby, the changing
one, the offspring of Prajapati and Shesha
before the advent of Vishnu, to come to earth in
the form of a person."

"What?"

"The belief was—is—simply that by
providing the proper vehicle in which Sheshaby

can live, the avatar or the descent from heaven
will take place and the divine Sheshaby will live
with the cult for all time. Perhaps if you think of
the avatar as an incarnation, you will grasp the
fundamental belief."

"And you believe this?"

"I did believe it in my youth. Then, with an
education supplanted with some Western ideas,
my beliefs changed as I became more aware of
the printed word and the help I could give my
country and my people through its power."

"So what is the bottom line? The end result?
How does all of this hocus-pocus affect Nita?"

Bahadur stood, walking toward the back of
the room.

When he didn't answer, Archer stood,
flexing his muscles to find the stiffness leaving.
"Are you going to answer me?"

"How do you suppose the snake got out in
the first place, Archer?"

He shrugged. He didn't want to talk about
the cobra getting out of the cage. Still, now that
the Indian had mentioned it, his curiosity was
aroused. "I . . . I don't really know."

"The room is cool, so the snake should have
been sluggish. Still, it seemed rather active
when you had it in the noose. Perhaps the
warmth of the sun coming through the windows
activated it enough to seek freedom when it
found the door open a bit. I'm afraid my telephone call was ill-timed. I assume you had just
put it in the cage when I rang?"

Archer nodded. "Can we get back to Nita?"

"Of course. The rite Nita described to me

was the rite of changing. I—"

"You mentioned that already. What's that mean?"

"If the rite is successful and Sheshaby is attracted to the person or selected victim, Sheshaby enters the body of the person and will be able to assume its natural form as well as that of the person." Bahadur said nothing more, letting the information register on Archer's mind.

"That's utterly ridiculous. You realize that, don't you? You're an educated person. You're standing there telling me that you believe in this garbage? The next thing you'll tell me is the rite was successful and that Nita can turn into a snake." Archer's voice, rising in pitch as he talked, took on an almost hysterical edge.

Bahadur waited before speaking, giving Archer time to cool down.

"Nita was about six years old when the rite was held. She would have been ideal for Sheshaby to consider. I'm not saying it is true or that it works. I'm merely relating what she told me. She spoke in the voice of a child. I found it very difficult not to believe her."

"You mean you believe everything now?"

"I didn't say that. I said I found it difficult not to believe what she said. Her voice, the voice of a child, rang with sincerity and concern for everything that was, or I should say, did happen to her."

"You're a strange man, Lal Khan Bahadur. You're a psychologist. You're a sociologist who wants to help his country and his fellow

countrymen. And I think you want me to believe
in snake gods and people changing into
snakes."

"I didn't say you should believe, nor did I
say I believed in it. At one time, I did. I believed
with as much fervor as you believe in your Jesus
Christ. Today, if I am anything, I am nothing. To
be termed an agnostic would mean I belong to a
group. The same holds true for atheism. I
simply am nothing."

"So tell me, Doctor, as a psychologist,
about Nita. What is going to happen to her?"

"Right now, I feel she is psychologically
disturbed by the dream."

"That goes without saying, but what the
hell triggered it in the first place? Why is she
suddenly dreaming about an incident that
happened twenty-two years ago?"

"I'm afraid she said nothing that would give
me a clue there. Perhaps you know of something, Archer?"

Archer pursed his lips and walked back
toward the desk. What had happened out of the
ordinary? Of course. It had been a concern at
the time, but the doctors giving her a clean bill
of health and her winning the triathalon had
made the incident seem insignificant.

He turned to face the Indian. "Nita fainted
the first time she saw the cobras. Could something like that have anything to do with the
dream? It seems that it was shortly thereafter
that she said she started having it."

Bahadur came up behind him. "That might
very well be the reason. She has no history of

fainting? No history of being afraid of snakes?"

"Not of fainting. And I'm sure her fear of snakes is no more or less than that of anyone."

"It seems too coincidental not to have something to do with it. I hope you do not think ill of me for what I have told you, Archer."

"No. Why should I? I can't very well control what people believe. The only thing I'm concerned about is Nita and her welfare."

"Now that we know what the problem is, we can better attack it, don't you think?"

"I want you to tell me one thing, for my own peace of mind. Tell me that the rite you mentioned could not possibly be the same rite that Nita described."

"If I were to tell you that, I would be lying. She mentioned Sheshaby and the word avatar. She had no idea what they meant, but how else could she know them unless she had heard them used in the way she described?"

Archer looked past Bahadur, toward the snakes and through the window. It was crazy. Impossible. This was the twentieth century. Things like this didn't—couldn't happen. Not in a million years. "Tell me, Doctor, has the rite ever worked? Did anyone ever take on the form of Sheshaby?"

"I myself have never seen it happen. There were those who were older who said they had witnessed such things in the past. I don't know. If—"

"Take your education into consideration, then answer the question."

"Under that circumstance, I would have to

say it could never happen. Logically and biolo-
gically it is totally impossible."

"What was the purpose of such a foolish
venture?"

"If the rite worked, and Sheshaby did come
to earth to take over the body of the person
selected, that person would be venerated for
the rest of his or her life."

"What about now, twenty plus years after
the fact?"

"The cult members would have tried to stay
in contact with the person if nothing happened
immediately. After a while, another person or
victim, if you will, would be selected."

"Just what was supposed to happen?"
Archer didn't want to ask the questions he
found himself voicing, but some driving force
made him do it. And now that he had asked the
question, he didn't want to hear the answer.

"The selected one would turn into a
snake—a giant king cobra, the mightest of all
snakes."

Archer turned away. "Rubbish."

"It is foolish, in a way."

"It's stupid."

"I agree, but—"

"But what?"

"It may work. It was supposed to have done
so in times past. What if it worked in Nita's
case?"

"Oh, come on, Bahadur, who are you
kidding? You're a man of science and logic. Tell
me how the body of a woman Nita's size, one
hundred fifteen pounds maximum, is supposed

to compress itself into the body of a king cobra that wouldn't weigh over twenty pounds or so. It's physically impossible."

"I know. I agree."

"And still you can look me in the face and say that it can happen?"

"How can a few kernels of plastic puff up into a piece of styrofoam many times the size of the kernels?"

"But the weight factor isn't taken into consideration."

"The bumble bee is not supposed to fly, yet it does."

"I won't believe it about Nita. No way. The examples you're giving me are facts of nature, and I won't—"

"And what I have told you is a fact of nature, a nature you know very little about."

"Is Nita going to be all right?"

Bahadur shrugged. "She should be. We have no proof of anything that we have been discussing. No evidence at all."

"What if she continues to dream?"

"She shouldn't—at least not for a while. I gave her a post hypnotic suggestion that she would not dream of this in the future, that she should in time forget all about it."

"Is there anything else that can be done until she doesn't dream any more."

"I wouldn't have her come to the lab anymore, not while the cobras are still here. I'm sure that they would upset her and possibly trigger the dream."

"Are you sure she told you enough to let

you know that the rite actually took place?" Archer needed more than just the word of Bahadur. He wanted proof of some sort. But for now all he had going was the man's word and description of the rite Nita apparently took part in over 20 years ago.

"The only thing she didn't mention was the Shaman rolling the doll-like figure that represented her into a rope of clay. The rope would be fashioned into the likeness of a king cobra and prayed over. Of course that could have been done after the girl was taken away. Everything that was needed to be done where she was concerned had already taken place."

"This whole thing is crazy. I think I need my head examined for even entertaining the thought that what you've been saying is correct."

"Perhaps. But who is to say which belief is right and which is wrong, which is crazy and which is sane, when you are dealing with mysticism and the unknown?"

"Are you going to persist in the idea that Nita could turn into a snake?" Archer found the courage to laugh, and the sound seemed to break the spell he felt he had been under since Bahadur had arrived.

"For all practical purposes," Bahadur said, when Archer stopped laughing, "the rite was completed. If nothing has happened thus far in her life, it is more than likely the only trauma involved in her recollection of the dream. That can be taken care of with normal psychiatric techniques. All you must do is care for her until she is free from the burden of the dream. I merely wanted to tell you everything that was involved. Now that I have, we can approach the problem in a normal way. Do you not agree?"

Archer nodded. Finally, the man was beginning to make some logical sense. "I will, Doctor, and yes, I agree that we should approach the problem in a logical way. We have your telephone numbers. May we call on you at any time?"

"Of course." Bahadur bowed and turned, leaving the lab. The door no sooner closed, than the phone rang, breaking into Archer's thoughts.

"Hi, darling."

"Hi, yourself. Where are you?" He forced an air of calm into his voice.

"At the gym. I was going to stop by and see you but thought I should call first."

"I'm glad you did," he said softly, knowing he should keep her away from the lab at all costs. "I was just on my way out to get a cup of coffee. Why don't you meet me at the lounge. Save both of us some steps and time." He bit his tongue. Why had he said that? Maybe she wouldn't pick up on it.

"Fine by me. When?"

"I was just about to go out the door. See you in a few minutes." He hung up. At least she wouldn't be exposed to the cobras today, and he would certainly not tell her about the close call he had had with the snake getting out of its cage today. That had been too close.

"So how was your appointment with Bahadur," he asked, sipping his coffee.

"He hypnotized me. You'd be amazed how great I felt when I came out of it."

"Really."

"No fooling. I . . ." she said, hesitating while picking up her cup of coffee. Her fingers buckled and the cup dropped to the saucer, smashing it to pieces and showering both herself and Archer with hot coffee. "Oh, I'm sorry." She grabbed for a paper napkin and dabbed at the hot liquid.

"What happened?"

"I don't know. It was as if my hand and arm had no strength. My back suddenly jerked with a spasm and then I dropped the coffee."

"Come on, Nita, you're going to the doctor. Right now."

"This instant?"

"You got it," he said, grabbing her wrist and stopping before he injured her more.

"Now how did you get that?" the young doctor asked, lightly running his fingertips over the black bruise on Nita's back.

"I don't know. How bad is it?"

"Well, it's about the blackest bruise I've ever seen. No purple at all other than a twinge around the edge. Absolutely jet black."

"Good Lord."

"What's wrong?"

"Well, I first noticed it Saturday morning.

There was hardly any mark there at all according to Archer. Then yesterday morning he said it was purple. Now, you're saying it's black? Is that normal?"

The doctor shrugged. "Why don't you slip your top on and let's talk a little."

Nita pulled the blouse over her head and sat back on the examining table. "Can Archer come in? I'd like him to hear whatever it is you've got to say."

"I suppose it's all right." The doctor went to the door and motioned for Archer to come in. He had waited in the doctor's outer office while Nita had been examined.

"What's up?" He looked first to Nita and then to the doctor.

"Do you know how she might have gotten this bruise?"

Archer shook his head. "I've no idea. It just seemed to be there a couple of mornings ago."

"It's about the most ugly bruise I've ever seen. I'm amazed you can walk around as well as you do, Nita. Doesn't it hurt a good deal? The trapezius muscle can really bother a person if it's been strained."

"Of course it bothers me, but I have a pretty high threshold of pain. It won't keep me from competing, will it?"

"Competing?"

"I'm slated to compete in an Ironman Triathalon in California soon."

"No way," the doctor said quickly. "If you can be rid of every sign of the bruise by the time the week is up, you might be able to get the muscle in shape in a month or so. You have no idea how badly injured this is. The discoloration is centered in the trapezius muscle but extends completely to the shoulder and to the buttocks."

"What?" Nita and Archer chorused.

"You heard me. Why are you so startled?"

"Because, Doctor," Archer said, "the bruise was about as big as both my hands put together yesterday. I didn't see it this morning. Did you look at it, Nita?"

"Not this morning. I almost tried, but it hurt so, I thought I wouldn't overtax myself by trying to look in the mirror."

"There you are, and I rest my case."

"Doctor?" Nita looked at him, her eyebrows arching more than usual, her green eyes boring into him.

"If you can't stand the pain to turn and look in a mirror, you surely can't train for something as rigorous as a triathalon. Forget it. This event will just have to go on without you. I'll prescribe some pain pills and a series of exercises that will help alleviate the pain."

Nita's face fell, her worst fear realized. Standing, she offered her hand to Archer, who took it. They left the doctor's office after he had given them the prescription and instructions for treatment of the injured muscle. Neither spoke. Their dejection, each for a different reason, ate at them.

While walking toward the quadrangle, Archer took Nita's hand in his. "Are you certain you don't remember anything about hurting your back?''

"I don't remember a thing. A person would think something like that would be a vivid memory."

They continued walking. Now, Archer was more puzzled than ever.

# 16

Archer stared into his half-filled cup of coffee, catching an occasional glimpse of his reflection. He hadn't slept much the previous night. Even though he thought Nita might have been awake at different times, he had not tried talking to her. She had rolled and tossed, trying to find a comfortable position. Her back must have bothered her despite the pain killers the doctor had prescribed. She would take two of the pink and white capsules and be free of the pain for a while, only to have it renew itself when the narcotic had worn off.

When he got up that morning, she looked tired and haggard from the lack of sleep, and he felt he must look about the same—but for different reasons. His mind had not shut down during the night. Mental images constantly formed, lingering for a while and then dissipating, only to be replaced by others. And so the night had passed.

Nita showered and left to go to the gymnasium where she had an appointment with one of the trainers. She had called after they got home from the doctor's office in the afternoon and set up an early morning meeting. It was just like Nita to want to get on with the treatment as soon as possible. That way, she would be rid of the pain that much quicker.

She had not said much after they got home, and Archer knew she had been silently bemoaning the fact that she wouldn't be able to go to California and take part in the televised Ironman Competition. He knew she doted on competition, and that the televised part was merely superficial. She wanted to compete with others who were her peers and have the opportunity to compare her physical prowess with them.

But Archer found it difficult to think of Nita and mundane things such as an athletic competition. He was concerned—no, greatly worried—about Nita and her future. The dream had risen in their lives like a specter, and he had no idea where it would lead.

He emptied the remainder of his coffee in the sink and rinsed the cup out. Picking up his briefcase, he left the kitchen and started toward the campus. But cutting across the quadrangle, he could reach the science building within a few minutes, but once he reached his laboratory, would he be able to concentrate sufficiently on his work? Would his fatigue brought on by sleeplessness affect his routine? Would his mental anguish concerning Nita bother him to the point where he would be ineffectual?

The morning air, brisk, clean and hinting of the coming winter season, seemed to act as a tonic for him. His mind cleared and he began seeing the whole of the problem squarely placed before him. Nita and he would see the problem through to the end and find a solution that would allow them to continue their lives in the manner in which they had before the dream came along.

Archer thought of the dream and Bahadur's explanation. That was preposterous—pure, unadulterated bullshit. Somehow, in the light of early morning sunshine, clear air and birds singing in the trees, the whole theory that the Indian had thrown out to him seemed to take on an almost comic aura. Nita, the woman he loved, could never turn into a snake! He found himself grinning and half-laughing aloud. It really *was* funny, like something out of an old black and white horror movie from Hollywood in the 1930's.

Physically, he knew it was impossible. Nita weighed 115 pounds. A king cobra even 20 feet long could not weigh much over 20 or 21 pounds. Where did the other 95 pounds go? He chuckled to himself and quickly coughed when two students who were walking toward him looked at him in a strange way. He mumbled a greeting and hurried on.

The next thing Bahadur would try convincing him of would be that Nita was somehow responsible for Al Stewart's death and that of Charles Lane. Sure, they had both died of massive doses of cobra venom, but there had to be some rational explanation. And "rational" was the key word. A woman turning into a snake was hardly rational, hardly believable, hardly admissable as evidence in a court of law.

Nevertheless, the ugly head of coincidence raised itself, spitting facts out to Archer's mind. Al Stewart, Richard Roman and Charles Lane all had died after the fact had been established that they were either going to be the head of the biology department or opposed his own candidacy. But that had to be coincidence. It just had to be. What else could it be? After all, he didn't want the chairmanship—at least not now. He had too much to do with his experimental work and his own teaching load. He didn't want it, and Nita knew he didn't want it. But because of her competitive nature, she wanted him to want it. She wanted him to be the chairman. She had said that she wanted to be married to the chairman of the department.

The bell tolled half past the hour of seven when Archer reached the science building. He would take Bahadur's advice on one point. Hurrying into the basement, he fumbled with his key ring when he reached the locked door to the supply room. After opening it, he turned on the light and entered. Poking through the shelves he finally found what he was looking for and took a roll of muslin from its place. He turned off the light, locked the door and started up the steps toward the third floor.

Again, thoughts of Nita and her insistence on his being the chairman of the department rose to the surface of his mind. She had protested, when he explained he wanted to do his work and not be bothered with the extra duties of the chairmanship. But that had been after Al died. When it became obvious that Richard Roman would be elected, Richard had died as well, but he hadn't been bitten by a cobra. That was the one flaw in Bahadur's theory, not that the Indian had even hinted that Nita was responsible for the three deaths. But it was his crazy idea that Nita might be able to transform herself, somehow, into a snake because of the rite in which she had been forced to partake.

When Archer reached the door to his lab, he unlocked it and entered. There had been the spoor of a large snake on top of the bluff from which Richard had fallen to his death, but he wasn't completely certain and hadn't said anything to the police at the time. Since he was the only one aware of it, he would never divulge it to anyone—not even Nita.

After depositing his briefcase on the floor next to his desk, he took the roll of muslin to the back of the room. Laying out a length of material sufficient to cover the three plastic cages, he pulled out his pocket knife, cutting the cloth. He draped it half over the tops and down the back that faced the door to the lab. At least now, if Nita stopped in unannounced, she would not be met with the sight of three king cobras.

His thoughts remained on Nita. Bahadur
had said she had used words that would have
been totally unknown to her unless she had
been there. And he thought about her com-
plaints of feeling constantly chilled. Still, that
had to be purely coincidental. So she felt cold
once in a while. So what? If he thought about
her teeth long enough, he was sure he could
mentally picture them as being fanglike, too.

Then, with his mind's eyes, he suddenly saw
Nita lying in the middle of the living room,
nude, the way she had been the morning the
police arrived to inform him of Richard's death.
Why had she gone in there to sleep—and in the
buff, yet. Later, she had teased him about
having taken her gown and robe off at the same
time. His brow wrinkled. She had found it, she
said, stretched out full-length on the couch, the
gown inside the satin robe. What would that
have looked like? As if she had pulled it over her
head, both at the same time, without opening
the robe. Then, laying both garments, one
inside the other on the couch, it would have
looked as if she had *crawled out of her clothing*.

"Come on, Archer," he said aloud,
chastising himself. If he looked long enough for
ghosts he'd find something in every cupboard.
If he thought about Bahadur's idiotic theories,
he'd begin believing them sooner or later. He
had to stop. And stop now!

Covering his face with his hands, he shook
his head. There was one other bit of information, circumstantial evidence at best, that
he had avoided. Purposely ignoring it had not

made it go away. Now, he felt he had to confront
it squarely. The bruise on her back. Sergeant
Alexander had told him that Mrs. Lane had
kicked at the cobra—no, that wasn't the right
word. Hadn't he said stomped on it when the
snake was going through the door from the
bedroom to the hallway? Something like that.
The next morning, Nita had complained about a
sore back muscle. Then, the next day, Sunday,
it had become discolored around the bruise.
Monday, when they went to see the doctor at
the University Infirmary, the color had been
almost pitch black except for the purplish
border surrounding the mark, and Archer
learned from the doctor that the bruise had
grown considerably. At first, when it was
visible, it had covered most of one trapezius
muscle, the left and part of the right, but when
the doctor looked at it, he said it extended from
her shoulder to her buttocks. Bruises didn't
usually grow that much.

Archer stood. He was driving himself crazy
with his thoughts. Walking toward the back of
the room, he stopped, staring at the cobras.
They in turn fixed their gaze on him. He had to
do something. He had to talk with someone—but who? Not Nita. Not Bahadur. Who? Of
course. Father Brown. He was an up-tempo sort
of person, one Archer felt he could confide in
without appearing to be a raving lunatic.
Perhaps he should talk to the priest in the
confines of the confessional. That way he knew
he would be protected, that Brown would not be
able to tell anyone what they talked about. But

that was not really the intention of the
Sacrament of Penance. No, he'd have to take his
chances and talk to him face to face, lay everything out for the priest to examine, then he
could give Archer sage advice on how to handle
the notion that the woman he loved was in
reality a giant king cobra. Archer shuddered.

After returning to his desk, he picked up
the telephone and dialed Father Brown's
number.

"Father Brown here."

"Father? This is Archer Buchanan."

"Archer? How are you? What can I do for
you?"

"Got a minute or an hour?"

Brown laughed. "Of course. What's up?"

"Let me tell you. Then, you can tell me how
to handle it. All right?"

"Want to do it on the phone or would you
prefer coming here to my office?"

"Let's do it on the phone. I don't think I
could stand having you laugh in my face. I don't
want to see your grinning smile. Okay?"

"This doesn't involve confession, does it?"

"No, nothing like that. Let me tell you about
it." Archer launched into the account, carefully
choosing his words to avoid sounding paranoid
or hysterical. When he finished, he waited.

"For what it's worth, Archer, I wasn't
smiling in the least while you were talking.
That's some story. You won't mind if I cop out
by saying I'm highly doubtful of what it is you're
hinting at. In fact, you could say I'm highly
skeptical of the whole thing, that is until I

remember who's talking to me. Then, the skepticism leaves and the dubiety returns in force."

"So, can you help me, Father? I'm just about at my wit's end."

After several seconds, the priest said, "I'm not equipped to handle something this bizarre, Archer. Don't misunderstand me, I'm not trying to pass the buck. It's just that the story you've told me should probably be handled by a competent psychologist or psychiatrist."

"But I went to Bahadur, or rather Nita did. He's the one who got me thinking all these weird things."

"You overlooked the word 'competent' when I used it. What do you and Nita know of this man? Very little, I wager. Considering his origins, I'm willing to bet he would let a sacred cow walk over his own children and kill them, if such were the case, without lifting a finger to stop the animal."

Archer didn't speak. Bahadur had said something to the effect that East and West would never meet on an intellectual basis. Could the dark-skinned man be that right? Could there be things in the Eastern philosophy that the Western mind could never compre- hend? Perhaps not on an individual basis. Archer could embrace some if not all of Lal Khan Bahadur's beliefs and philosophies, but his telling them to someone such as Father Brown would lead nowhere. The individual might embrace, but the masses would never. That had to have been what Bahadur meant. Did

that mean that Archer Buchanan, biologist,
B.S., M.S. and soon to be candidate for a Ph.D.,
was about to throw away his own logic and
absorb that of an Eastern sociologist/psycholo-
gist/former snake cult member?

"You might be right, Father. Perhaps, we
were too hasty in going to Bahadur. I'm sure he
thinks differently than you or I."

"Why don't you talk with Doctor Morris. I'm
sure he could give you a good deal of insight on
the overall problem. I do wish Nita were more of
a churchgoing type. It would be easier for me to
speak with her. But until that time . . ." His
voice trailed off.

Archer wondered if he was supposed to feel
guilt for loving Nita the way he did without her
wanting to go to church. He could understand
her reluctance in that area. It had simply been a
matter of too much of a good thing. Well, he
wouldn't let Father Brown's inneundoes bother
him. One day, he and Nita would be married and
both would go to church.

"Well, thanks for listening, Father. If I need
you in this respect, I'll call you. All right?"

"That's fine, Archer. You do that."

Archer hung up just as the door to the lab
opened and Nita walked in. Before he said anything, he looked to the back of the room to
make certain the cages were covered on this
side. That bit of advice from Bahadur had been
worthwhile. If the snakes triggered the dream,
the additional sight of them might only serve to
prolong the nightmare.

"Hi, darling," she said, closing the door without a sound.

"Hi." He stood, moving toward her, his arms outstretched. Now that he saw her in person, he felt like a fool. His own thoughts were eating at him like a cancerous growth. In time, if he allowed it, the thoughts and theories would drive a wedge between Nita and himself that there would be no hope of their ever being together peacefully.

They hugged, her arms around his middle, his encompassing hers. She felt so good, so loveable. How could he have entertained, even for a split second, the stupid, mind-boggling thoughts he had had?

Tipping her face up to his, he kissed her lightly on the mouth. "Your face is cold."

"It's rather nippy out."

Without letting go of her, Archer reflected on her cool skin. Forget it. Drive it out now. Once and for all. Get rid of the idea.

She squeezed him tighter.

For the next several minutes, Archer held Nita and when they parted, he kissed her again on the mouth. Her lips were still cool. Surely, by now she should have warmed up.

"Once more?" he asked and felt guilty for wanting to feel her for the reason he had in mind.

"My, aren't you the romantic one this morning." She moved closer, encircling her arms around his neck.

"How was your treatment at the gym?"

"It feels much better."

Archer brought his mouth to hers. Their lips parted and when her tongue shot into his mouth, he fought to control his sense of revulsion. Her tongue was cold, too.

# 17

A breeze ruffled the curtains of the living room, adding an almost summery feeling to the apartment. November, which could be both warm and chilly on alternate days, had been unusually balmy, and Nita and Archer would have normally welcomed it. But a nervous atmosphere gripped the living room and the man and woman seated in it.

Despite picking up on Archer's high-strung mood, Nita felt it necessary to air her own grievances. She ran one hand through her hair, inhaling deeply.

"I wonder just how competent that doctor really is."

Archer, if he heard her, said nothing.

Because he ignored her, she said, "Archer, are you listening to me? I said I wonder just how competent that doctor really is."

"Huh? Oh, why do you say that?"

He looked at her, but she felt he wasn't seeing her. If he had brought home a problem from the lab, he was breaking one of his own rules—leave his work at work and forget all about it at home. It was a good rule, but she wanted to talk about her back pains and her apparent inability to compete in California. She wanted to discuss in depth those things that were irritating her the most. She wanted to argue with somebody, and the only somebody who was available wasn't cooperating.

"Because my back doesn't hurt me that much. What does he know?"

"He happens to be the school physician who happens to take care of the athletes' physical problems. He knows what he's doing, all right. How far do you think you'd get in the physical for the California triathalon, assuming they have one."

"I don't know if they do or don't. That's not the issue. He's keeping me from doing what I want to do."

"For your own good."

"Hah! My own good tells me I should not do what he says and go to California."

"I wish you wouldn't carry on like that, Nita. You'll only upset yourself. Why not accept the situation?"

"I can't. I'm already upset. I'm unhappy, Archer, and you don't seem to care."

Archer looked at her. Care? She had no idea how much he did care. The ideas zipping through his mind would have boggled hers, if

he told her of Bahadur's theories. What would
she say if he told her of his inability to totally
reject them? Not that he was accepting them,
but the fact that there seemed no rational
explanation to any of the angles he examined,
the same angles the police were investigating,
almost smothered him. Archer pictured a giant
king cobra, then he looked at Nita. Then the
king cobra replaced her. He shuddered and
turned away.

"Can't you handle my problem, Archer?"

Why didn't she keep quiet? He was thinking
of something so different from what she was
talking about that he was liable to blow up at
her any minute. And what good would that do?
They'd fight, then they'd make up, and what
would be solved? Nothing. Her back would still
be an issue, and he would still be wrestling with
the illogical arguments of Lal Khan Bahadur.

"It's not that I'm not handling your
problem, Nita. I'm trying to be a little more
objective about it. What good can possibly
come of your competing in California, possibly
injuring yourself more than you already are,
and then not being able to complete the work
on your Masters by the end of the semester? To
me, that's the goal that should be uppermost in
your mind, not some competition."

"That's where you and I differ. I love to
compete. It could very easily be my life, if I
choose it to be. You obviously don't understand
the competitive psyche. If you were competitive, you'd have been in the running for the
chairmanship of the biology department, but,

no, you have your work that must be completed first. Then, once you get your doctorate, you might think about wanting to be the head of the department. I can't stand that sort of wishy-washy attitude. Hell, go for it. What's the matter with you anyway, Archer?'' Her voice, carrying an hysterical edge, dripped with sarcasm.

"Hey, simmer down. That's not the issue. Let's assume you don't compete in California and that you do finish your Masters work on time, what—"

"Don't worry about me finishing. I always finish. I'm way ahead of my work, so don't even think that there's a chance that I won't be ready by the end of the semester."

Archer nodded. She was certainly in a feisty mood. He'd seen it once or twice before but never to such a finely honed degree. "Okay, have it your way. When you finish your Masters at the end of the semester, what happens then?"

"What do you mean?"

"Will you leave then? Will you stay here? What are your plans?"

She turned to look at him. "I hope you have something to ask me about that time, something that will affect both of our futures."

Archer fixed his attention on the blowing curtains beyond her. The words should have sent a chill of excitement through him, but the tone of her voice almost frightened him. She was really upset, and if she were being tender right at that moment, he failed to see it. And as far as both their futures were concerned, he wondered. Did they have a future together? Did Nita even have a future of any kind? An anxiety that he had never known gripped him, bombarding him with doubts for her safety and his own sanity.

"What's wrong with you tonight?" Nita's voice cracked.

She sounded concerned for the first time since they had sat down following their evening meal. Not much had been said after their embrace in the lab or on the way home. Once they had finished eating, they had been drawn, as if by a magnet, to the living room—something they usually didn't do, unless neither had work to prepare for the next day.

"Nothing." Archer continued staring at the billowing curtains. The air gushing in had slowly grown cooler as the evening wore on. By morning, there would be a definite bite to the air.

"Archer, I know you well enough to recognize the fact that something is really bothering you. What is it?"

"Nothing." He jumped to his feet, walking to the window. He lifted the curtains, peering outside.

"Archer, tell me."

"Damnit, Nita, there's nothing bothering me that talking about right now is going to fix."

"Oh, for heaven's sake! What's bothering you that you can't discuss with me? Come on, tell me. I can help you. Maybe it'll get my mind off my problems."

"No! I'm tired, and I'm going to bed."

Archer turned and stormed from the room, slamming the bedroom door behind him.

Nita stared at the closed door. What was eating him? Just something else to fuel the fire of her anger. Now Archer, the man she loved, was acting like a moody schoolboy whose girl friend had turned him away for someone else. He was acting childish, immature. What could be bothering him that he couldn't talk over with her?

Turning away from the door, she glared at the mute television set. She seldom relished her anger, but for some peculiar reason she found herself doing just that. She had so many different things bothering her that she found herself almost savoring the degree of upset she encountered with each problem.

As for Middleton University, she could actually hate an inhuman entity such as a school. The people in it, those responsible for her hatred, were singled out. Charles Lane, the late president of the school, had certainly paid for his indifference and had died horribly. It served him right for wanting to by-pass Archer for the chairmanship of the biology department. What did he know? He was dead. That was all that counted.

Images of Al Stewart and Richard Roman swam through her mind. They had had legitimate claims to the chairmanship, but then, Archer did, too. If he had only been a bit more aggressive, the race would have been an interesting one. Although Al was at least 15 years older than Archer and Richard but a year or so, Archer was by far and away the better teacher, biologist and researcher. The last, his ability as a researcher, had not gone unnoticed when the grant from the government had been awarded. She doubted very much if either Stewart or Roman would have been successful if their names had supplanted Archer's. No matter. They were dead, too.

She moved in her chair. Her back pained her terribly. Her new position brought the bedroom door into view. What was Archer doing? Was he really going to bed? It seemed rather silly. It was so early. Why had he stormed out like that? What could be bothering him? After glaring at the door for several long minutes, her back pain grew once again.

That stupid doctor! Sure it hurt, but that could be overcome. The triathalon wasn't tomorrow. She healed fast. She always had. She could be ready, and she just might consider going against his wishes. He really couldn't stop her.

She moved once more, pain telegraphing itself to her brain. Once again facing the television set, she could see the ruffling curtains. She had better close the window before she retired. Did she even want to retire for the night with Archer? He made her so angry. Not just angry. Furious was a better word. She felt furious with him for lying to her. He had to want the chairmanship. He simply had to. It was human nature to want to be in control. Of course, that was it. He really *did* want it but preferred for her and everyone else to think that he didn't. That way he wouldn't have to face the embarrassment of losing the election. But he had to realize now that he could have it, almost for the asking. She would have to say something to him tomorrow about that. Even though she felt she had the solution to the problem at hand, she still was angry over his attitude. It wasn't very nice of him to be like that and upset her. If he changed his mind and didn't want it, or the school wouldn't select him, she had no idea what she would do.

Nita leaped to her feet, stifling a scream of pain that involuntarily formed in her throat. Her back, her neck and her buttocks all burned with an intense pain the likes of which she had never before experienced. What was going on? That bruise was a mystery, too. How had she gotten it? Who was responsible for it? Someone or something had to be. One simply didn't get a bruise that huge without an injury of some sort, and an injury that could produce a mark that big would certainly remain fresh in the victim's mind.

Pacing up and down the living room, Nita stopped each time she reached the entrance to the hall, peering at the bedroom door. Why didn't Archer come back out? She wanted someone with whom she could talk. If she didn't talk she feared she'd blow her top. Her anger was getting the best of her reasoning.

When had the bruise shown up? Just last Sunday. No, that wasn't right. That was when Archer saw the bruise and she did by looking in the mirror, but her back had pained her

Saturday morning when she awoke. What had happened Friday night? Racking her brain, she failed to uncover any overlooked action or accident that might have caused the injury, but she recalled the elusive dream wherein a man and woman were running around screaming something.

Hadn't something happened Friday night? What? Charles Lane, the president of the university, had died. An evil grin crossed Nita's lips, curving into a malevolent scimitar. He deserved to die. When she thought about the man's death, the pain in her back intensified until she wept. How dare it hurt that bad. How dare he propose keeping Archer from the chairmanship. How dare . . . A woman's face manifested itself in her mind. Who was she? She couldn't recall ever before having seen her. Why would she suddenly imagine a woman's face? The woman's face grimaced, twisting almost into a snarl. No, it was fright. That's what it was, not anger. The woman's face disappeared, and then Nita's back exploded in renewed pain. That was it. The woman was responsible for her injury. And now she realized who the woman was!

She shivered. She felt cold. The window. The cold air coming in. She wanted to close the window. She wanted to feel comfortable and warm, but she couldn't, not with the window open and the cold night air gushing in. The curtains furled inward and she trembled.

Feeling an inability to move, she rubbed her arms to get the circulation going. She felt as if

she were freezing. What was wrong? Managing
to turn in a half circle, she caught a glimpse of
the chair in which she had been seated and the
closed bedroom door across the hall through
the living room door. Archer was there behind
that door. She should call him. For some inexplicable reason, Nita needed help, needed
Archer, needed someone to help her survive
whatever it was that was happening to her.

Her chest hurt, and she recalled the night
she thought she was having a heart attack. Her
arms hurt now, too. They had ached fiercely
that night as well, but she hadn't had a heart
attack. Then, what did happen that night? She
tried to recall. A void. Nothing.

Rubbing her arms even harder, she stopped
for an instant. They felt strange, peculiar,
rough, as if . . . She wrapped her arms around
her upper body. She had to get warm. She
should close the window, but she couldn't
move.

Her chest heaved outward then constricted
for an agonizing moment, pulling in until she
thought her heart would burst from the
pressure. The pain spread to her abdomen. A
mighty heave outward was followed by intense
constriction until she felt she would separate
into two segments. The aching sensation
spread throughout her body. She couldn't stand
it much longer.

Pirouetting in a circle, she spun around,
collapsing in the easy chair. Her breasts heaved
upward, when she tried breathing. What was
next? She had no idea. Death would be

welcome. Death would eradicate the awful pain tearing at her.

Nita could feel her life's essence being squeezed into nothingness. She could sense her own vitality, her very nature, being pressed into oblivion.

When her head began aching, she felt as if it were being crushed in a vise. The pain built on both sides and she sensed her skull being elongated, pressed with an indefinable force into a new shape. Her head stretched, lengthening into a tubular form; her eyes moved to the sides, her forehead and nose becoming as one, her mouth stretching into a wide, grinning slit.

Her body stretched, pulled by an unseen force and power, into a length almost four times her height. First, her legs moved out from the bottom of her slacks then pulled back in, her shoes dropping off onto the floor. When the legs disappeared, her body writhed, pulling back and up across the chair.

Then her arms pulled into her blouse sleeves, the skin rippling with small scales. She wanted to scream. What was happening?

She opened her mouth to scream and the last thing she heard before completely becoming deaf was the loud, growling hiss emitting from her mouth.

The change complete, the king cobra slithered up the chair back and down to the floor behind it. Nita's clothing remained where she had been seated. The shoes on the floor lay at angles to the empty slacks. Her panties were hidden within the slacks, while above, clinging to the material of the easy chair, her blouse, its arms stretched at right angles to the body of the pullover, gave the impression of an invisible person sitting in the chair.

After it fully dropped onto the floor, the snake reared, its head turning from side to side, its hood flared open. Fixing its stare on the bedroom entrance, it moved toward it. Outside the door, the cobra reared up higher, until its head was six feet above the floor. Pecking at the closed entrance, the reptile's nose bumped it, sending out a soft knock. The snake's inability to hear did not respond to the answer inside. "Yes?"

Then, as if realizing what it had done, the cobra turned, crossing its own body and raced back into the living room toward the open window. Its tongue, tasting the fresh air, deciphered the different scents. For one final time, it turned, staring at the bedroom door, as if longing to go there instead. Then the head plunged through the open space to the ground five feet below. After the tail disappeared between the billowing curtains, the snake slid into the dark night.

# 18

Archer jumped at the sound of the knock on the door. Nita—she wanted to make up. "Yes?" His voice sounded strange in the silent room. The tap at the door was the first noise he had heard since he came in, other than the cough or whatever Nita had done a few minutes before in the living room.

Why didn't she answer him now? Sitting up in bed, he stared at the door. She was probably standing on the other side, crying silently. Their first real argument. Their first real fight. He shook his head. Even the most solid of married couples at one time or another would disagree and have a dispute of some sort. They had been most compatible since they first met and had seldom if ever had so much as a slight disagreement, even as to what they should prepare for dinner or which TV show to watch.

Archer dropped his legs over the side and stood up. Stretching, he walked to the door, reaching out for the knob, then he stopped. "Nita?" No answer. Perhaps she had changed her mind and didn't want to talk now. Why push the issue? He didn't necessarily want to talk right then, either. He barely had had time to sift through his feelings. He found it distasteful to think about Bahadur's religious cult and its strange beliefs and practices when Nita was so close by. How could anyone in their right mind accept the idea that a person, a warm-blooded person who weighed over 100 pounds, could change into the shape and being of a cold-blooded reptile that weighed but 20 pounds or less? Absolutely ridiculous!

Archer turned away from the door and returned to bed. Lying down, he interlaced his fingers behind his head and stared at the ceiling. He wouldn't go out until he had completely eradicated the weird thoughts and images racing through his imagination. He loved Nita too much to run the risk of saying something foolish and losing her forever.

The king cobra moved through the cold wet grass. A heavy dampness hung in the air and fog clung to the trees' top branches, lending an eerie grayness to the already dark night.

The snake moved sluggishly because of the cool night air. Crawling slowly, almost lethargically, it came to the campus. Gliding through the grass where it was better camouflaged, the reptile made its way toward the quadrangle. It passed the Alan Ede Memorial Bell Tower, snaking its way toward the street on the opposite side. When it came to the street, it stopped momentarily, raising its head off the ground to check the open expanse in both directions. Assured that it was alone, safe and unthreatened, the king cobra lowered its upper body and torpidly undulated across the cold blacktop street.

"I know when my George passed on, I was almost completely crazy from the loss. He was such a strong man in mind and in body," Kay Emory said, looking from one person to the next until her gaze fell on Jenny Lane.

Jenny turned away. What an idiot! The way the woman talked, one would think her husband was the first person ever to have died. When she felt a cool hand on her own, she turned to find Melissa Stewart, reassuring her that things would somehow all work out. Melissa's Al had died the same way Charles had. She trembled violently when she recalled the awful night and the sight of the giant snake.

"There, there," Melissa cooed soothingly.

"I'm all right. I was just recalling the night."

"You poor thing, it must have been horrible. I was lucky in that respect, not having seen the thing, the . . . the king cobra."

"Well, I should be going," Kay Emory whined, standing.

"Yes, I should be going, too." Sandy Fitzgerald stood, smoothing imaginary wrinkles from his pants.

The rest of the faculty members who had attended the afternoon services and believed it their duty to stay with the widow stood as well. Each had in his own insecure way felt that he would become the center of conversation if he left too early. Accompanied by their wives or husbands, the members now lined up once more to offer their tired condolences and weary accolades to the dead man's wife.

Jenny stood near the door, holding it open, accepting each proffered hand one more time. After each passed through the doorway and into the cool night air, she breathed a sigh of relief. When only two or three remained, she walked with them toward the parked cars lining the curb, leaving the door stand open a few inches. A breath of fresh air was what she needed more than the cliches each was muttering.

"I suppose you'll be all right, but if you need anything, don't hesitate to call," Melissa said quietly when they reached the front walk.

The king cobra, once it had crossed the street and left the campus behind, knowingly made its way down the opposite side, keeping clear of the sidewalk where it could be most readily noticed. After passing one street, it turned into the next, making its way toward the house with several parked cars in front.

"You can bet on it, Melissa. Of all the people

who attended the services, I feel you're the only one who truly understood my loss." Jenny dabbed at one eye with her ever-present handkerchief.

"That's because, other than being a good friend, I can truly empathize with you. Now, so I have everything straight, the memorial service at the school is the day after tomorrow. Is that right?"

Jenny nodded. It had been her wish that Charles be interred with only a few people present. The idea of the entire college faculty and town dignitaries being present somehow didn't seem right. There would be a service held at the university's nondenominational chapel, and once that was over, the memory of her husband could wither and die to whatever degree of expediency each mourner desired. Death itself was a function of life, but death at the bite of a poisonous reptile was an irony Jenny thought she might never get over.

Both women jumped when a cat snarled loudly, the sound ending in a throaty growl.

"At least life goes on and there will be more cats in a few weeks," Melissa said, forcing an air of lightness to her voice.

Jenny laughed despite her inner pain. "I guess you're right."

"Remember, call if you need anything or just want to talk. In fact, I hope you won't mind if I call you for some of the same."

The cat realized something was coming, but it had difficulty in recognizing the scent.

What was that? The cat had once before smelled the same peculiar odor but had not encountered whatever it was.

The bushes where it hid provided adequate coverage for the feline. Nothing could come up from behind since it backed onto the foundation of a house. The bushes did more than conceal it. It could see the world but nothing could see it.

The cat's ears twitched at the minutest night sound and it turned its head. The something was coming closer, very close. Was it in danger? It wasn't a dog or a person. What was it?

Fixing its attention on the people standing by a car next door, the cat blinked its eyes, sifting the air with its nose at the same time. Then the something was right behind it, next to the foundation of the house. Snarling loudly, the cat leaped from the bushes, and the king cobra continued curling its way through the spreading yews, unseen by anyone or anything other than the cat, which had dashed across the lawn toward the far side of the street.

"I think it would be terrific if you did, Melissa."

The two women embraced as the Emory car pulled away from the curb.

"Why don't we get together for lunch—say, tomorrow?"

Jenny pursed her lips for a moment. "That would really be nice. We can talk, and I can have

a change of scenery. Right now, the prospect of
endless days in the house without Charles
coming home seems dreadful. Yes, let's."

"I'll call you first thing in the morning."

The snake fixed its gaze on the two women
standing on the front walk. Lowering its head, it
slowly stole across the grass toward the front
entrance of the Lane house. When it reached the
steps and small front porch, it passed under
and came up on the side of the open door.
Raising its head and upper body, its tongue
tasting the air every second or so, the cobra
stuck its head inside, through the doorway. The
warm air invigorated it, and working its ribs and
loose skin and belly scutes, it slipped into the
front hallway.

"About what time?"
"By nine. Will you be up by then?"
Jenny nodded. "If I can sleep, I'll be up by
seven. Talk to you then."
They embraced once more, and Jenny
watched Melissa get into her car and drive
away. When she was alone, she turned, walking
up the flagstone path toward the front of the
two story house. She stopped, admiring its
simple yet elegant lines. Maybe she should sell
it. Why be saddled with the expense and trouble
of keeping up a large, four bedroom house. She
certainly didn't need it for prestige, now that
Charles was gone. She felt a tear building in the
corner of one eye. Flicking it away with an index

finger, she bravely shook her head as if to dislodge her sorrow, and squaring her shoulders, she walked toward the front entrance.

Closing the door behind her, she yawned. That was a good sign. At least her body was sending signals that it was tired, exhausted, ready for sleep. She'd turn out the lights downstairs and go to her bedroom. She paused. Maybe it would be advantageous to sleep in one of the other bedrooms. Last night, she had rolled and tossed all night. What had George Burns said about sleeping alone once his wife had died? He had had trouble, too, but when he decided to lie on her side of the bed, he found that he thought of her as being with him and from then on slept on that side. Maybe she'd try that first. Why move to another room? That would be giving in to her sorrow and sense of loss.

Jenny walked toward the dining room. The table, its basket of flowers centered on it, dominated the large room. A breakfront displaying antique dishes stood against the far wall. Charles had always loved this room. She looked up at the beamed ceiling, then fumbling for the switch at her left, she turned off the lights without seeing the king cobra pressed along the baseboard of the wall to her right.

Turning, Jenny went to the living room. There, she would have to turn out the sconce lights and table lamps and pull the drapes. Little by little the room darkened as each lamp or light was extinguished.

The snake, its pupils enlarging to see better in the darkened dining room, moved to the doorway where the woman had just been standing. It watched her walk down the short hall and step into the living room. Without a sound, it moved after her.

Jenny turned out the first two small lamps on the table behind the couch. One more to go and she could start up the steps. She yawned again. She felt certain she would sleep well tonight, if for no other reason than that she hadn't slept well last night. Her body, exhausted as it was, would see to it that she slept, and that meant that her mind would also rest.

Moving around the couch, she reached out to turn the switch on the last lamp and caught a movement out of the corner of her eye. What was that?

She turned toward the double doorway to the hall. Then she saw it, the body curving its way into the living room. A tiny scream leaped from her throat and she stood rooted to the spot, fascinated by the sight.

Where had it come from? It had to have been in the house all along, but the police had searched everywhere—everywhere except where the snake had chosen to hide. Now it was back. Why? Why did it come back now? She stared at it, her eyes widening to the point that her eyeballs could have popped out.

She finally managed to scream but the

snake didn't respond. Instead it continued into the room and once its tail had entered, the reptile reared up, voicing its growling hiss.

Jenny felt a coat of perspiration forming over her body. Droplets formed on her forehead and in her armpits and between her breasts. Once they gained sufficient weight, they coursed downward, blinding her for a moment, tickling her sides until her bra straps absorbed them or until they stopped at the bottom of the cups.

Why couldn't she move? Her arms, her legs, her head all felt as if they were fused together. She was more of a statue than a living, breathing human being. Her attention fixed on the snake's head facing her. She could almost feel the coldness of its gaze.

Its mouth opened, the dim light reflecting off its fangs. The cobra hissed and moved toward her, stopping when it was ten feet away.

Jenny felt an overwhelming urge to urinate, and when she couldn't stand the tension any longer, her muscles gave away and her bladder emptied. The noise of the liquid striking the oriental rug built as a damp spot formed, the drops splashing with a tiny, almost surrealistic sound. Even though her tension seemed somewhat eased, Jenny still could not move, her body refusing any command from her befuddled brain.

The snake moved forward again, stopping eight feet from her.

Why didn't it simply do it? Why didn't it bite

her? Get it over so she could die quickly instead of piecemeal the way she was. Jenny's body ached from standing so rigidly. If she could only move, at least she could try running out of the room. Maybe she'd be lucky and the snake wouldn't attack if she did try. Estimating the distance between her and the double doorway, she wondered how fast the snake would react if she suddenly dashed toward the exit? She had to cover 12 feet while the snake had to cover eight. Could she beat the reptile? Just how fast could it move?

As if reading her mind, the cobra moved closer until it lay only five feet from her.

She could never try now. What would happen next? The damned thing seemed to be stalking her, enjoying the hunt as if there were an intelligence behind each move.

Jenny felt her heart would erupt with the effort of beating so fast. Her temples pounded, and in the half light of the single lamp, the snake seemed to be growing and receding in size. Was she about to faint? That might be the best thing that could happen. If she passed out the snake might think she was dead and leave. But where could it go? It would still be in the house—someplace.

She felt her head swimming, and the whole room seemed to be revolving now.

Then, the cobra swiftly struck. The jaws closed on her calf, pressing downward, shooting venom into her blood stream. After a long second, during which it chewed on her leg, to get as much venom into her as possible, the snake released its grip and slipped back, rearing up to strike again.

Shocked, Jenny stared. Had she been bitten? Her leg didn't hurt that much. Perhaps in the dark, the snake had misjudged and merely brushed by her leg. That had to be it. Her vitality suddenly restored, Jenny dashed for the doorway.

The snake already rearing to a height of almost six feet, lunged forward, burying its fangs into her arm. The jaws worked up and down, closing with a fury that pumped more venom into the woman.

As she ran, Jenny threw her bitten arm outward to dislodge the cobra, pulling one fang loose that remained in her tricep. The snake flew a few feet away and landed across a chair as Jenny fumbled with the front door lock.

She heard the growling hiss coming up from behind her and feverishly turned the last lock. Throwing open the door, she plunged headlong into the night finally bringing her vocal chords into play, screaming at the top of her voice.

"Help! Help me! Somebody help me! It's back. I've been bitten. Help me! Please!"

The door slammed back into the jamb with such force that it bounced open again without the latch working.

The king cobra stopped at the open door, peering into the darkness beyond and the figure of the woman running wildly away from the house. Then, it lowered its head, the hood contracting, and fled into the darkness itself.

Across the street, lights began going on as Jenny Lane's pleas for help filled the night.

# 19

Why hadn't Nita come in or knocked again? Archer stared at the ceiling. It was time to go out and apologize. He had acted like a juvenile. He felt badly about having been so short with his answers and stubborn about refusing to discuss what had been bothering him, even though it still gnawed at his mind. The whole thing was crazy—as crazy as his thoughts and interpretations of what Bahadur had told him. How could he, Archer Buchanan, a man of science and a man who believed in God, possibly entertain the idea that the woman he loved could change from a beautiful, loving person into a giant, deadly king cobra? What did they call something like that in the movies? Lycanthropy? Yes, that was it. The ability to change into a wolf. God, how could he still want to explore the theory?

Sitting up, Archer dropped his legs over the side of the bed and stood. He ran a hand through his silvery gray hair, shaking his head at the same time, as if to dislodge the irrelevant thoughts from his mind. He felt stupid, idiotic. If he ever told Nita, she would question his sanity. Maybe that was it. Perhaps he was going insane and should be confined. Anyone who ran around spouting off about women changing into snakes would not be allowed to run free for very long. It would take no time at all for the boys in the white coats to show up and truck him off to an institution for the mentally incompetent.

"Nita?" He called out, hoping she would hear him through the closed door and come in while he brushed his hair.

No answer.

"Nita?" He put the hair brush on the bureau and walked to the door. Turning the knob, he stepped into the hallway. "Nita? I'm sorry. Really I am. I was thinking about too many ideas and theories at once. My imagination got carried away, that's all. Forgive me?"

He glanced into the living room and, finding it empty, turned automatically toward the kitchen. When he found it empty as well, he concluded she was in the bathroom.

Knocking softly on the door to that room, he called out again. "Nita? Come on. I'm sorry for the silent treatment I gave you a few minutes ago. What are you doing? Paying me back?" He forced a laugh, even though he felt the situation was anything but laughable.

He knocked louder. Still no answer. Reaching out tentatively, he turned the knob and found it yielding. He opened the door. The light was out and the room deserted.

Where had she gone? Out? Without telling him? He went to the front door. The lock was in place as was the chain. If she had gone out, she hadn't used that door. Still, why should she? They normally used the kitchen door simply because they were a few steps closer to the campus by going that way.

Archer returned to the kitchen and found the door there locked and chained as well. Now where could she be? Certainly not hiding. That would be a bit on the childish side. He felt he had acted irresponsibly enough for the both of them for a lifetime.

"Come on, Nita, where are you?"

He hadn't really checked the living room. All he had done was quickly look in and then searched the rest of the apartment. Perhaps she had fallen asleep on the couch. Still, wouldn't she have awakened when he called her name?

Hurrying down the short hallway, he entered the living room and stopped short once he was able to take in the small room. Empty. A sense of panic began building in Archer.

"Ni—" His breath held when he saw the clothing on the easy chair. Her blouse and slacks and shoes, all lay in a position as if an invisible person were sitting in the chair. He ran to the easy chair and picked up the blouse. What had he hoped for? A diminutive Nita who would drop out when he shook it? "God. Nita, where are you?''

The question burning at the back of his mind grew then quickly receded as he pushed it as far back as possible, only to have it surge to the fore again. He couldn't—he wouldn't entertain, even for a second, the idea. How could he?

He picked up the slacks and froze when the waist fell open, revealing her bikini panties.

Dropping them, his shoulders slumped. ''Good God, it can't have happened. It can't. Nita? Where the hell are you?''

The logic of the situation hammered at him. The apartment was locked from the inside. He had searched each room and had found no sign of her. Her clothing, the same clothing she had been wearing when he had stormed out of the living room and into the bedroom, lay on the easy chair as if . . . as if . . . He couldn't allow himself to think of his Nita changing into a king cobra and sliding out of her clothing as the evidence seemed to indicate.

He whirled around in a circle, seeing the open window's curtains lifting in the cool November breeze. Running to it, he found it open almost four inches. If what he was thinking actually had taken place, then this was the way she had left the apartment.

He suddenly felt as if someone had pulled a plug, and all the strength and will power, all the education and understanding and intellect that he possessed, had rushed from him. What could he do? What should he do? How did one handle such a situation?

Perhaps he should call Bahadur. After all,
he seemed to be the resident expert on people
changing into snakes. Yet, for some reason, he
felt threatened by the man. What would
Bahadur do? Perhaps he'd want to take Nita
back to India and head up a snake cult. As
ridiculous as it seemed, he felt the idea could be
a valid and viable one where the enigmatic
Indian was concerned. He couldn't run the risk
of calling him and losing Nita for all time if
indeed the situation were as he feared it might
be.

Should he call the police? Hardly. They'd
simply lock him up in a nut house for the hopelessly insane and throw away the key. They
dealt in reality and crimes they could see and
understand. The police were out.

Then who? He needed someone's help. To
whom could he turn in this emergency? Who
would be able to understand such a
phenomenon? There had to be someone, but
who?

The square face of Tony Alexander formed
in his mind. No. The policeman would not be
sympathetic at all. He had suspected Archer at
one time. Why would he suddenly believe such a
cock and bull story now? Still, there was something about the man that came across as
compassionate. Would he understand? Could
he understand? Between Sergeant Tony
Alexander and Lal Khan Bahadur, he felt he
would stand a better chance of success with the
policeman. At least he would not offer exotic
solutions to the problem at hand the way

Bahadur undoubtedly would.

He had to call someone, and it might as well be Tony Alexander.

Archer picked up the telephone and dialed the police number displayed on the cover of the directory.

"Police headquarters."

"Sergeant Alexander?"

"He's out."

"How can I reach him? It's an emergency."

"Hang on. I'll patch you through to his car."

There were several clicks on the line before Archer heard the new voice.

"Sergeant Alexander."

"Sergeant? This is Archer Buchanan. From Middleton? Do you remember me?"

"Of course. What can I do for you?"

Whenever the detective spoke, Archer could hear the sounds of traffic and the car motor. Then when he spoke, the earpiece was quiet.

"The last thing in the world I want right now is derision from you. I have something pretty far out to tell you and all I ask is that you don't laugh and hear me out completely. Will you?"

"You got it. What's it about?"

"The deaths caused by cobra venom. I think I know how they were carried out."

"Yeah? That's good news, Mr. Buchanan. Go ahead. Tell me."

Archer launched into as brief account as he could without repeating himself. He felt Nita was in danger and the more time he took the greater the threat to her. When he finished, he waited.

After what seemed hours, the sound of the traffic buzzed in his ear but Alexander didn't speak immediately. Then, "That's some story, Buchanan. You expect me to believe it?"

"Of course. The evidence is overwhelming. I'm not any more thrilled about saying the woman I love is responsible than you are in believing the idea. Will you help me?"

"I don't know, Buchanan. How will it look on my duty report when I turn it in? 'Investigated a possible snake woman who was suspected of killing people.' You gotta admit that the duty officer is not only going to question me but my ability to understand police procedure and what to look for in a crime like this. I don't think I can help you."

"If another person dies, Sergeant, it'll be on your head. I'll raise such a stink that you'll never work as a police officer again. I'm not kidding."

"Are you threatening me, Buchanan?"

"You bet your sweet ass I am. I'll do any-thing to save Nita from whatever it is that's happening to her. Your neck and your career mean nothing to me. Understand? If Nita goes down, you go down with her."

There followed a long pause before Archer heard the crackle of traffic and the purr of the car motor again. "Where are you, Buchanan?"

"I'm at my home right now, but to save time, I'll meet you on Papin Street where it parallels the campus next to the quadrangle. Do you know it?"

"Yes. We're on the other side of town. I'll be

a few minutes. Get going. Will you be in a car?"

"No, I'll be walking. It'll take me a few minutes to get there on foot. If we're lucky, we should arrive about the same time. See you then." Archer hung up and hurried to the kitchen door.

Jenny stumbled down the sidewalk, her vision already blurring, her coordination such that she found it difficult to move quickly. Her legs wanted to do one thing while she thought they should be doing something else. Her heart beat wildly, sending the doses of venom through her system, affecting the nerves controlling her life's functions. The saliva in her mouth built, and when she found it almost impossible to swallow, she yielded to the temptation to spit it from her mouth. Instantly, her mouth refilled.

Moon Street lay deserted other than the few lights that had turned on in upstairs windows and the outlines of people standing in back-lighted doorways, investigating the calls disturbing the quiet night.

Jenny tried calling out again. Her saliva-filled mouth bubbled, gurgling with unintelligible sounds as she tried desperately to make her vocal chords work. Ahead, she could see the intersection where Moon Street emptied into Papin. There should be more traffic on that street. If she could make it, she might flag down a motorist.

The king cobra, weaving through the grass,

paralleled the sidewalk on which the woman
lunged forward in her flight. Despite the cold
air, the snake was able to stay abreast of her.
She stumbled with every other step. The snake
darted closer to her, lashing out to strike the
hapless woman once more. Then it did so for the
last time. The venom shot through its one good
fang into the woman's system for a second
before her momentum shook the cobra loose.
The snake fell to the ground, slinking off into
the night toward Papin Street, in the same
direction that the woman ran.

Jenny tried valiantly to scream again after
the snake struck again but incomprehensible
gurgles were the only sound coming from her
mucus-filled mouth.

Jenny Lane was dying. She knew she was
dying. She had seen her husband die from the
same sort of thing—snake bite. It seemed as if
she found herself in a mad nightmare. It
couldn't be real life. Lights from the houses she
ran past blurred to the point of indistinguish-
able blobs. In the distance, she thought she
heard voices calling.

"What's the matter out there?"

"Who's there?"

"What's going on?"

"Did someone call for help?"

"Hello? Who's there?"

The words all ran together in her panic.
Couldn't the fools see she was in desperate
trouble? Couldn't they see the snake? Where
was the snake now? Was it still stalking her?

Was it going to strike her anymore? How many
times had she been bitten? At least twice in the
house, and since she started running away from
her home, the damned thing had gotten her one
more time. Where was it? Was it going to bite
her again?

Archer walked briskly toward the quadrangle. He wanted to run but knew he would
only have to wait for Alexander to show up if he
did. He much preferred the policeman having to
wait for him. He had enough on his mind
without having to pace up and down on a sidewalk waiting for Alexander to arrive.

Archer stopped, freezing in his steps. What
was that? What was that call? Somebody had
just called out. No, it was more of a scream. Had
someone yelled for help? Then he heard it
again. It was coming from beyond the quadrangle. Maybe someone had accidentally found
the snake. Or should he say . . . Nita?

Archer broke into a trot, jumping off the
sidewalk to run on the grass where he wouldn't
make as much noise. The cry came again, but
this time it didn't sound like the word, "help."
Instead, it seemed to be more of a scream, and
he ran toward it.

The king cobra had left the woman
stumbling along the sidewalk and hurried as
best it could toward the lights of Papin Street.
When it reached the broad expanse of blacktop,
it hesitated for an instant before sensing that
the street was deserted. Crossing the cold

blacktop, the snake moved slowly now, barely able to make a decent rate of speed. It had to return to the place it had come from earlier. There it would be safe and warm. If it were warm, it could operate at full capacity. The way it felt now, it could barely move. The cold night air was rapidly getting to the king cobra.

When it finally reached the far side of the street and had gained the sidewalk, it moved onto the grass of the quadrangle. Ahead, a clump of bushes loomed out of the darkness. Perhaps it could find warmth there. Slicing through the grass, it came to the growth and coiled on the far side away from the street. It could go no farther.

Jenny stood, clinging to the small tree. Her head pounded, her heart beating furiously and her sense of balance leaving. The thick, soupy mucus ran down her chin, and when she tried to wipe it away, she found her arms and hands dancing in wild gyrations. Her whole body shook as she teetered on the edge of the curb. Spiraling around, she fell headlong into the gutter and died.

"Hey, Sarge, you think Buchanan is a little whacky?"

"He sounded serious. He hasn't struck me as the type who might be superstitious or go off half-cocked on an idea."

"Well, anybody who believes that his girl friend turned into a snake gotta have a few splinters in the windmill of his mind." Paul

Adams guffawed at his own joke.

"Just drive the car, Paul. There's a couple of things going for Buchanan. First, we got two deaths from cobra venom when there shouldn't have been cobra venom around. Secondly, let's assume there was a snake big enough to produce as much poison as the M.E. said there was in the two bodies. According to Buchanan, who's some sort of expert on the damned things, it would have to be pretty big to produce that much. So, assuming there is such a snake, where the hell has it been between times? Where's it go? How—?"

The radio crackled to life. "Car twenty two. Calling car twenty two."

"Alexander here."

"We just got a report that a woman is running down the fifteen hundred block of Moon Street screaming for help. Sounds like a drunk and disorderly. You want to check it out?"

"We're heading in that general direction. Yeah, we'll check it out."

"Ten-four."

The radio went silent.

"Which one you want to check first? The guy with a snake for a girl friend or the drunk?"

"Let's check the drunk first, Paul. Buchanan will hold that long."

Adams hit the siren, but Alexander reached over, turning it off. "Get your jollys off some other way. I've got a headache."

Smiling grimly, Adams pressed the accelerator to the floor, sending the car forward, much faster than the 38 miles per hour it had been going.

"I also want to finish the shift without going to the hospital. Slow down. We aren't in that big of a hurry."

Adams obeyed, letting the car slow down before turning onto Papin Street.

Fog shrouded the upper reaches of the Alan Ede Memorial Bell Tower when Archer reached it. He continued half-running, half-walking on the grass. He hadn't heard anything for the last few minutes and wondered who the person might have been calling out like that. The silence pressed in on him. When the bell in the tower sounded the three-quarter hour, he jumped. What time was it? He had no idea. He had lain down quite early but he felt he had been in the bedroom for at least two hours. That would make it past 11 probably. Could it be 11:45? What difference? He had to meet the cops. They had to find Nita before she killed someone again.

"You're crazy, Buchanan," he cried aloud. "You really believe that you're going to find a giant king cobra instead of Nita."

Archer shuddered, slowing his pace to the brisk walk he had used when first entering the quadrangle. Since the cries for help had stopped, he had no idea from which direction they had come in the first place. He felt he had been moving toward the cries, but now there was no sound at all other than his own footsteps.

If he cut across the last expanse of grass and skirted the clump of bushes to his right, he would get to the street much quicker than following the sidewalk.

He wondered where the police were. Why couldn't he hear the siren? Surely, they believed him and would hurry here, wouldn't they? Wouldn't they consider his call an emergency? Then why couldn't he hear the siren?

Approaching the bushes, he stopped when he saw movement ahead of him. Someone or something was lying beneath the overhang. Peering into the inky darkness of the shadow, he tried to focus his eyes but found the street-light from directly behind the bush was lighting it in such a way as to obscure his vision.

Then the king cobra reared up, its hood flaring open. Archer leaped back when the head soared over his own before lowering to a level even with his own eyes.

Great God! He had never seen anything so magnificent or huge. It exceeded his expectations. Then, he shivered when he realized that he was probably looking at Nita.

He called her name softly. "Nita?"

There was no response, no movement, nothing. Of course. How could the snake hear his soft whisper or even a loud yell? Archer stood perfectly still. If it were Nita, did she recognize him? Or did she lose her memory as a human being when assuming the shape and form of the snake? He shook all over, hoping the reptile didn't catch the movement. Jets of warm air shot from Archer's nose, and for the

first time since leaving the apartment, he
became aware of the temperature. It was more
than chilly. It was downright cold. The snake
had to be feeling the effects of the temperature
on its metabolism. It would be sluggish in the
cold air. Perhaps, just maybe, the snake could
be taken without harming it. Then, the whole
procedure that made Nita change might be
reversed. Perhaps Bahadur would know how.
Now he cursed himself for not having called the
Indian.

But what if Archer were wrong? What if the
snake was perfectly all right and could strike or
do anything it normally would? Archer could
not run the risk of moving for fear the snake
would strike him. How then did he propose to
capture the snake? Who knew where he was?
The cops might stop farther up Papin away from
the bushes where he stood. He could see the
street from where he stood, his head and
shoulders well above the top of the greenery.
Then, too, the snake could also be seen from the
street. Maybe Alexander would see them if they
came this way. God, he hoped that would be the
case. If the police stopped back a ways, and he
didn't show up, they might leave, and Archer
would be stuck confronting the giant reptile in
front of him for the rest of the night. Which of
the two would weaken first?

Now that the snake had reared up, Archer
could see it better. Studying it, he shivered
when the cobra's eyes and his locked in the
light from the street lamp. Baleful, malevolent,
almost disconcerting, the eyes didn't waver in

their fixed stare. Without lids, the snake's eyes would never blink or seem to move from whatever it set its gaze on.

Archer looked more closely. Could those eyes be seeing him with Nita's intellect behind them? How could he possibly contact her if it truly were Nita?

"God help me," he murmured.

The snake opened its mouth, displaying the single fang, and hissed loudly.

"Do you know where on Moon Street the woman's supposed to be, Sarge?"

"The dispatcher didn't say, other than it was the fifteen hundred block. Situations like this, the people who call in are usually only too eager to help. Somebody will be around to point out the direction she took."

"Weren't we supposed to meet this Buchanan guy on Papin by the quadrangle?"

"Uh-huh."

"We'll be going right by there to get to Moon. What if he sees us?"

"Then he'll see us. What about it?"

Adams shrugged. "I don't know. Just wonder . . . Is that him?" He pointed through the windshield, slowing the car at the same time.

"Where? He might not recognize the car without the light or siren."

"Over there by the bushes. What the hell is he doin'? Takin' a leak? Want to bust him?"

"Stop the car!" Alexander yelled, reaching for the door handle. He jumped out before the automobile came to a complete stop. Come on!'' Alexander pulled his snub nose revolver from its holster and approached Archer. Paul Adams got out of the car and followed his partner.

Archer heard the car coming. Could it be the police? It had to be, but why weren't they using the siren? What if it weren't the police? Then what?

''Buchanan?''

The call came from his left-hand side. It sounded like Sergeant Alexander.

''Yeah.''

''Christ, it's big, ain't it?''

''We're too late. She's changed. I don't know what'll happen next.''

''You can't be serious. You think that's your woman?'' Alexander scoffed, failing to smother the sarcastic laugh.

The snake hissed loudly, expanding its hood to its extreme.

''Just stand perfectly still, Buchanan. Don't move.''

''Don't worry, I'm not. Hey, what are you going to . . . No! Goddamnit! Don't shoot!''

Alexander sighted along the short barrel, steadying the pistol with both hands. He squeezed the trigger, gently at first, then exerted more pressure when he realized he had to hurry. Buchanan might move into the line of fire to protect that goddamned reptile.

The shot roared through the quiet night, and in a time frame too small to measure with the human eye, the king cobra's throat at the base of the hood exploded as the lead missle smashed through. The body of the snake coiled to the ground in slow motion.

Unable to move, Archer stared at the dead beast, tears filling his eyes. What if it were Nita? Good God, they had killed Nita!

Alexander and Adams approached, their guns at the ready, pointing toward the unmoving reptile.

Breaking from his moment of immobility, Archer raced ahead, pushing the police out of the way.

"Great God, you've killed her! You've killed her!" He sobbed the words, dropping to his knees.

When the police saw the snake was unmoving, they holstered their weapons and, one on each side, they picked Archer up, standing him on his feet.

"Mr. Buchanan, it was a snake, a goddamn snake. That's all. It wasn't any wom—"

"Jesus Christ! Sarge! Look!"

Alexander turned to follow his partner's outstretched arm and pointing finger. The snake was expanding in size. Freeing Buchanan's arms, both men reached for their weapons again, but before they could free them, Archer dropped to his knees again.

It *was* Nita. She was changing back. The body of the reptile shortened, growing stocky, assuming the proportions of a woman's figure. Nita's breasts puffed out, the gray scales disappearing. Her arms extended from the sides of the body while the tail split in two, forming her legs.

"Hey, what's going on?"

The voice came from across Papin Street as a curious neighbor approached the two officers standing on the far side of the bush. Soon, more people arrived, asking questions. Alexander, unable to tear his eyes from the transformation taking place in front of him, said, "Adams, keep 'em back, then radio in for help. This is un-believable."

The reptilian head rounded out, expanding until it assumed the outline and features of Nita, blood oozing from the gaping wound in her neck. Her head lolled to one side and Archer bent down to gently kiss her on the lips.

The voices of the prurient onlookers filtered through the quiet night, accompanying Archer's sobs as he held the naked body of Nita Galforth in his arms.

Behind him, the Alan Ede Memorial Bell Tower tolled midnight.

# *DARE TO ENTER THE DEMONIC WORLD OF JOHN TIGGES*

# MORE BLOOD-CHILLERS FROM LEISURE BOOKS

# ELECTRIFYING HORROR AND OCCULT

# Make the Most of Your Leisure Time
## with
# LEISURE BOOKS

Please send me the following titles:

| Quantity | Book Number | Price |
|---|---|---|
| _____ | _____ | _____ |
| _____ | _____ | _____ |
| _____ | _____ | _____ |
| _____ | _____ | _____ |
| _____ | _____ | _____ |

If out of stock on any of the above titles, please send me the alternate title(s) listed below:

| | | |
|---|---|---|
| _____ | _____ | _____ |
| _____ | _____ | _____ |
| _____ | _____ | _____ |
| _____ | _____ | _____ |

Postage & Handling _____

Total Enclosed     $ _____

☐ Please send me a free catalog.

NAME _____
_(please print)_

ADDRESS _____

CITY _____ STATE _____ ZIP_____

Please include $1.00 shipping and handling for the first book ordered and 25¢ for each book thereafter in the same order. All orders are shipped within approximately 4 weeks via postal service book rate. PAYMENT MUST ACCOMPANY ALL ORDERS.*

*Canadian orders must be paid in US dollars payable through a New York banking facility.

Mail coupon to: **Dorchester Publishing Co., Inc.**
**6 East 39 Street, Suite 900**
**New York, NY 10016**
**Att: ORDER DEPT.**